when you were everything

BOOKS BY ASHLEY WOODFOLK

The Beauty That Remains

When You Were Everything

when you were everything

ASHLEY WOODFOLK

DELACORTE PRESS

Visit us on the Web! GetUnderlined.com

Educators and librarians, for a variety of teaching tools, visit us at RHTeachersLibrarians.com

Library of Congress Cataloging-in-Publication Data
Names: Woodfolk, Ashley, author.
Title: When you were everything / Ashley Woodfolk.
Description: First edition. | New York : Delacorte Press, [2019] | Summary: In this story set in New York City and told in alternate timelines, teenaged best friends Cleo and Layla fall apart.
Identifiers: LCCN 2018060503 (print) | LCCN 2019000095 (ebook) | ISBN 978-1-5247-1592-2 (el) | ISBN 978-1-5-247-1591-5 (hc) | ISBN 978-1-5247-1593-9 (glb)
Subjects: | CYAC: Best friends—Fiction. | Friendship—Fiction. | New York (N.Y.)—Fiction.
Classification: LCC PZ7.1.W657 (ebook) | LCC PZ7.1.W657 Wh 2019 (print) | DDC [Fic]—dc23

The text of this book is set in 11-point Plantin.
Interior design by Ken Crossland

Printed in the United States of America
10 9 8 7 6 5 4 3 2 1
First Edition

To all the girls who broke my heart.

Losing you wounded me. Probably more than you know.
If I hurt you just as deeply, I'm sorry.

And I want you to know our friendship meant something to me.

It always will.

And to all the girls who feel left behind, forgotten,
forsaken by a friendship that wasn't supposed to be so tenuous,
by a person who wasn't supposed to be impermanent.

The hurt will always be there. But it gets better.

I promise.

The band that seems to tie their friendship together
will be the very strangler of their amity.

> —William Shakespeare,
> *Antony and Cleopatra:* act 2, scene 6

What's done cannot be undone.

> —William Shakespeare,
> *Macbeth:* act 5, scene 1

now

WHAT'S PAST IS PROLOGUE

Everything feels like a memory in a city when it snows.

It goes all blurry around its edges, like even as it's happening it's already an old photograph. The whole world seems softer, gentler, quieter. And when New York is the city where it's snowing, it's more like the version that's suspended in my snow globe collection, where everything about it appears to be small and clean and pretty, and where anything feels possible.

I climb the sixty-six slippery stairs that lead to the Manhattan-bound platform at the subway station closest to my family's Brooklyn apartment, looking down at my floral combat boots and humming along with the Nina Simone song swimming through my headphones. And for a moment I feel happy.

But the snowy morning is making me nostalgic for something I can't name; for a place or a moment that doesn't really exist. I think of the past but also of new beginnings bright with possibility. I can't help but think of Shakespeare, my favorite writer, whose stories are old but somehow still so right. My mind keeps spinning to friendship.

I haven't spoken to my best friend, Layla, in twenty-seven days, but the snow is making everything feel a little less real—even that. As I look out at the blurry city, I embrace the illusion that everything is fine because *it's snowing*. And in the snow, I can pretend that the sad things in my life are just dreams I've mis-remembered.

Maybe it's the weather; maybe the song. But I hear Gigi's voice in my head. My grandmother's been gone for four years now, but memories of her still hit me in waves. *Today is the day your life changes, Little Bird,* I hear her say. *Today things can be different and new and maybe even better.*

But then my wintry, soundtracked, semiperfect bubble bursts when I slip on the platform. And as I slam into the ground, the harsh truth of my own reality lands heavily, right on top of me.

"Damn, girl! You aight?"

"Oh my God!"

"Is she okay?"

"Everybody, back the fuck up!"

"Give them some room!"

"Pull her up, pull her up!"

About eight arms reach for me all at once. My left earbud has fallen out, but my right one is still tucked into the curve of my ear so that I hear the screech of trains entering and exiting the station and everyone's concern on one side and, now that the Nina song is over, Louis Armstrong singing "What a Wonderful World" on the other.

A little kid hands me my glasses, scuffed but unbroken, and a woman wearing a hijab, hipster glasses, and bright red lipstick digs through her backpack and offers me a Band-Aid without taking out her own earbuds.

"Thanks," I say to the kid and all the other strangers, because

4

it's times like these when I really don't get why New Yorkers have such a bad rep. When shit goes down, they're there for you.

Once I'm upright, I tuck the other earbud back into my ear so I'm drowning in sound again, just the way I like it, and take stock of my unfortunate situation. The leggings I'm wearing under my uniform skirt are ripped and one of my knees is scraped and bleeding a little, and worse, I see that my shoe is untied. I don't know if the rogue lace is the reason for my fall, but with my luck, it probably is.

Totally-Avoidable-and-All-My-Fault is kind of my brand.

People are still staring at me and I feel my chin wobble, an embarrassed rage-cry in the making. But then a garbled announcement that no one understands peals through the station.

"What?" a dude with a handlebar mustache says to no one in particular. "What the hell did it say?" There's some kind of delay and everyone groans. A dozen hands pull out a dozen phones. And just like that, no one cares about me anymore. This is why I both love and hate New York. In a city like this one it's easy to fade into the background. But it's also inevitable that at some point, by someone, you'll be overlooked. Or completely forgotten.

And that's when it hits me the way it always does: the fact that I'm alone; the fact that Layla is really lost to me. The unshakable certainty that we are never going to be friends again.

It's just like it was—just like it still *is*—with Gigi. I can forget about her for hours or even whole days, and then the truth rushes back like a brush fire, burning me from the inside out.

That person you loved? They're *gone*.

Gigi taught me to *pay attention when the world is trying to tell you something*. So for a second I allow myself to look and listen, to notice the world around me. But inevitably, that leads to noticing my utter aloneness, and to thinking of every ugly thing I've done that has led to this moment.

I limp over to the closest bench. I pull out my water bottle and squirt a little of its contents over my bleeding knee. And instead of taking in the world, the way I know Gigi would have wanted, I sulk.

There's a line in *The Tempest* about the past being prologue to everything that comes after, and I can't help but remember it as memories of Layla fill my head. The thing I didn't realize about having a best friend while I still had one is just how wrapped up she is in everything I do. Every outfit I wear or song I listen to. Every place I go. Losing someone can leave you haunted.

I look up, through the lens of still-falling snow, feeling the familiar burn of tears forcing their way to the surface. The Louis Armstrong song that reminds me too much of the day I met her is still pouring into my ears. I swallow hard and yank out my earbuds. I push the tears back down.

I'm sick of crying every time I see or hear or *feel* something that reminds me of her. But before I can move on, I have to shake off the weight of my past. Of *our* past. I need to rewrite our prologue before it destroys me.

So that's exactly what I'm going to do.

A THEORY & A SNOWMAN

When the train finally shows up, it's so crowded that I end up smashed into a corner between a stroller and the doors, and the guy in front of me is wearing a backpack he refuses to take off. One of the buckles is pressing against my boob.

I want to growl at this guy to put his bag on the floor, for everyone to give me some *goddamn space*, but I don't, because I don't do stuff like that. If Layla were here, she'd tell the dude off.

But she isn't! I shout inside my own head. *For fuck's sake, stop torturing yourself.*

So I imagine a clean sheet of paper. Mentally, I start making the list I need to rid myself of thoughts like these. The steps I need to take to rid myself of Layla . . . for good. The systematic way I'm going to unhaunt my whole life.

I get off a few stops later when we reach Layla's station—the one where she'd hop on the train every morning and find me. I'd always sit in the first car so she'd know to walk to the front of the platform to wait. When the train pulled in, I'd look for the smear of her black hair, or the blur of her hand as she waved at me. We met and rode to school every day that way.

I follow the flow of bodies toward the stairwell, push my way through the turnstile, and step out onto the sidewalk. I slip my earbuds back in, put on Ella Fitzgerald, and look left and right, making sure no one who knows me is around. The coast looks clear, so I turn my music up, cross my fingers, and keep moving. Something about skipping school makes me feel like I'm actually in control of my life.

I walk down Layla's block, taking in all the familiarities of the street. The way the door to the bodega on the corner doesn't close all the way. The ragged rainbow flag hanging from the fire escape of the building beside hers. The same yellowed flyer's been taped in the window of the deli advertising their "new" kosher salami since I was twelve.

We always got Popsicles at that bodega in the summer. We challenged each other to jump and touch the hanging threads of that flag whenever we walked past it. We never tried the salami, but we'd get sandwiches and ninety-nine-cent Arizona iced teas at the deli almost every time I slept over. If it was warm out, we'd eat on Layla's stoop.

I keep walking, past Layla's building and into the park where we first met. Its lawn is wide and a little green even though it's February. The grass is dusted with snow and it's still falling fast. I go to the exact spot where I was sitting the day I met Layla—the exact spot where she saw me crying about Gigi and where she started singing to make me feel better—and I text my dad.

Daddio, I send. You're off today, right?

His response comes almost instantly. Yep.

Can you meet me?
Cleo . . .
Daddy . . .

You better be on your way to school.

Not exactly.

SIGH.

I start typing another response, but then my phone starts to vibrate with a call.

"I . . . fell on the subway platform," I say to him instead of hello. It's a low blow, but I'll say whatever I need to get him here. "The trains were delayed and my leggings are ripped and it's snowing, and you know how the snow reminds me of Gigi. I just had an awful morning, okay? Please don't give me a hard time about this, Daddy. Not today."

He sighs, long and low. "Cleo, this seriously has to be the last time. If it isn't, I'll have to talk to your mother."

I gasp. *"Et tu, Brute?"* My dad knows almost everything about Layla, and that I've been skipping school to avoid her. But as long as my grades don't slip, he lets me get away with pretty much whatever I want. My mom's another story.

"This is the *last* time, Cleo."

I'm pretty sure it's an empty threat, so I grin.

"It will be. I promise. Now, can you meet me?"

"Where are you?" he asks.

—

He arrives about twenty minutes later. I grabbed a cup of coffee for him, and a tea for me, from the café across the street while I waited, so as soon as I spot him, I run over and push the steaming cup into his gloved hands.

9

"Oh, honey," he says as soon as he sees my leggings. He straightens his glasses and pulls me to him. He plants a kiss on my forehead and his bristly goatee tickles my eyebrow. "Why did you want me to meet you here? You should have just come over."

"I want to build a snowman," I say, hating that I sound like a five-year-old. "Correction: I *need* to."

He makes his Librarian Face—an expression of both confusion and intrigue. He makes this face when he's cautiously interested in or fascinated by a book, an idea, or a person. I've seen him use it with patrons at the library where he works when he's asked a particularly strange question, and as he reads articles on his tablet in the mornings. Since he moved out a few months ago I've seen this face (and him) a lot less, but it's still so recognizable that I grin at his eggshell-brown skin and dark freckles; his wide, scrunched-up nose. "A snowman," he says, and it's a statement and a question all at once.

"Yes," I say. "I have a theory."

He purses his lips to stop himself from smiling, and I know what this expression means too: he has no idea what I'm about to say next. "Okay," he says. He puts his heavy arm over my shoulders. "Tell me."

We start to walk, strolling past people walking dogs in coats and nannies pushing strollers. Snow is still falling and everything around us feels a little magical and unreal. I inherited my dad's freckled face, his poor eyesight, and his dreaminess too. He never rushes me to speak because he knows what it's like to be easily distracted—what it's like to get lost inside your own head. "I think," I say, "that I need to make some new memories. I think that if I make enough new ones in the right places, not being friends with Layla anymore will hurt a little bit less."

My dad sips his coffee. I look across the park at the tall trees and beyond them to where Layla's walk-up sits beside the bodega, deli, and fire escape, and my breath catches. If I could erase this whole block from the city, I would.

"And these new memories," Daddy says. "They start with a snowman in this park?"

I nod. "This is where I met her, remember? At that cookout right after Gigi died? But if we do something else in this exact spot, like build a snowman, maybe *that* will be the first thing I think of when I come here, instead of her."

"Ah," he says, something like sadness passing over his features. "I understand."

—

We build a snowman. When we're half done, I throw a few snowballs at my dad and he laughs and dodges them, making his own between searching for stones and sticks to put finishing touches on our creation. As we roll and pat and press the snow into new shapes, I pray that my memories are just as malleable as the snow in my hands. Hopefully my past is as rewritable as I'm pretending it can be.

READY FOR BATTLE

"So you wanna *skip school*, huh?" my mother says that night, the second she gets home.

I'm brushing my teeth, planning my next new-memory-making trip, when she squeezes into our tiny bathroom behind me.

I'm in pajamas, a satin scarf already wrapped around my head for bed, but she's still in the tight pencil skirt she wore to the office this morning, her blazer slung over her arm. Her high heels are hanging off the tips of her fingers (she'd never leave her shoes by the door) and there's barely any space between us at all.

"Oh crap," I mutter, pressing my thighs closer to the sink. Toothpaste droplets land on the mirror. I don't know how she found out, but then I remember my father's threat.

I spit and rinse my mouth out, getting more pissed with him by the second. Some things, like secrets between a father and daughter about said daughter skipping school, are supposed to be sacred. I take my time settling my toothbrush into the cup by the faucet. Not so long ago, it used to have three toothbrushes in it. Now it just has two.

"Did Daddy at least tell you why I skipped?" I ask, slowly turning around.

"No?" Her stormy face turns even stormier. "Your father *knew* about this?"

"Double crap," I mumble. "No?" I try.

She rolls her eyes and sits down on the edge of our tub. Her knees bump hard into my shins.

"Jesus, Cleo. I can't even look at you. And your father . . ."

For a split second, she seems . . . hurt. Like we've ganged up on her. Like our life together is a fight and she's all on her own. But then she's right back to looking like she's ready for battle.

"Give me your phone," she says, holding out a manicured hand. I snatch it from the counter, where it's innocently playing "Blue in Green" by Miles Davis, and clutch it to my heart.

I slip out of the bathroom and head down the hall, negotiating. "Mom, no! Please? Anything but my phone," I whine.

"I don't want to hear it, Cleo." She follows me to my room, where I reluctantly hand it over. She pockets it and storms out, slamming my door so hard the row of snow globes on my shelves rattle. I flop down on top of my blankets, knowing I'm probably grounded on top of losing the phone. When she yells back to me, "Your father's picking you up first thing tomorrow. You'll get the phone back on Monday," I bolt upright.

"MONDAY?!"

then:
July

EVIL GENIUS

"What are you wearing t-t-t-tonight?" Layla asked me.

I stretched out on her pale blue sheets. The window was open and the humidity was punishing. Even the creases behind my knees were sweaty.

"It's so hot," I said. "What can I wear to be as close to completely naked as possible?" Layla laughed as she pulled on a long, thin-fabricked dress, its pale pink color delicate and pretty against her sun-kissed brown skin. She lifted her dark wavy hair from where it was tucked against her back, then shimmied her little "new dress" shimmy. Her reflection winked at me in her full-length mirror. "I'm sure mmmost of the guys, and a few of the girls, w-would freaking *love* that," she said, raising her thick eyebrows.

I rolled my eyes, because dating was the last thing on my mind. I was mostly just nervous to be going to my first big high school party. As rising sophomores, Layla and I had been invited to a grand total of two, and I'd skipped the first one earlier that summer because my dad had gotten us tickets to Shakespeare in the Park. I was only going to this one because Layla was making me, and because Valeria's building had rooftop access that would provide an excellent view of the fireworks.

"You have a dress like this, right?" she asked a few minutes later, holding out a thin black thing in my direction. I took the wisp of clothing in my hands, rubbing the smooth fabric between my fingers.

"You own something in black?" I asked, teasing her because black was *my* signature color, and the majority of her clothes were as light as the walls of her bedroom—lavender and seafoam, shades of powdery pink, pale yellows, and sky blues.

"Shut up," she said. "D-don't you?" I nodded, though the dress that hung in my closet wasn't nearly as delicate.

"So you should wear it tonight. . . ." Her mouth was still open, so I knew the sentence wasn't finished. Sometimes, Layla's stutter caused her to get blocked so badly that words got stuck in her throat and no sound came out at all. I waited.

She closed her mouth, cleared her throat, walked over to her dresser, and tried again. "W-with these." She pulled out a pair of shiny gold hoop earrings. "And you should p-put in your c-c-contacts. Oh! And let me do eyeliner. You have great eyes, C-Cleo." I always hated that my name began with one of the hardest consonants for her to pronounce.

I stepped up to her mirror, holding the dress in front of me. I took my glasses off and stepped even closer to my reflection so I could see my face more clearly. *Will anyone even notice my "great eyes" with all these freckles? What does having "great eyes" even mean?* But Layla knew about this stuff in a way I didn't. She'd cared deeply about aesthetics for as long as I'd known her, and she's been wearing at least a little makeup since the first time her older sister showed her how to use a mascara wand when we were still in middle school.

I pulled Layla's dress on and it was way too tight. I had curves in every place she didn't, but she refused to acknowledge that we were completely different sizes.

"I like, don't know how to party," I said, immediately taking the dress off. "Do you think people will be drinking?"

Layla pulled off the pink dress she was wearing and slipped into a yellow one before wrapping me in a hug. Her voice was soft and raspy and her hair and skin smelled like sandalwood. She pulled back and looked at me.

"Cleo. Obviously there will b-b-be drinking. That d-doesn't mean *you* have to drink. I'm not g-going to. And if some d-douche tries to make me or you, I'll k-k-kick him in the balls."

I laughed. It made sense that she smelled like a forest and sounded like the beginning of a wildfire. She had a temper, and once it was lit, the girl could burn.

To take my mind off the party, off the way Layla wanted me to look and who all might be there *drinking,* I said, "So I got this email from Novak today."

Layla looked at me and cringed. "Why is a *t-teacher* emailing you in the summer?"

I grinned and flopped back down on her bed. "She's spending part of the summer at the Globe Theatre in London," I said a little dreamily. I'd been obsessed with everything about London since I was twelve—the tea, the culture, the landmarks—and Layla knew this. My London snow globe was the most prized one in my collection.

I noticed a blankness on Layla's face, so I added, "The, like,

Elizabethan theater originally built by the Lord Chamberlain's Men." Layla blinked. "Shakespeare's freaking playing company, Layla! *Shakespeare's freaking Globe!* Are you kidding me right now? I thought we were *friends.*"

Her eyes cleared a little. "Oh *that* thing, right." Her mouth opened, and closed, and opened again. "Okay so, um, wh-wh-wh-what'd she say that c-couldn't wait till school started?" I groaned and lay back on the bed staring at the ceiling again.

"Well. She sent me a bunch of pictures of London and the theater. She said that it's incredible, which, duh. But she also said that there's this Young Scholars Summer School there. I think most of the people who go are older, like about to attend *university,* that's how Novak said it." I sat up and laughed a little and so did Layla. "But you only have to be sixteen to apply, and I guess she told the professor who heads up the program about me. That I'm—"

"A Shakespearean expert?" Layla finished for me. She lifted her hand and stared at it like she was holding Yorick's skull, and theatrically recited, *"To be or not to be,"* in a bad British accent.

"Shut *up*," I said, throwing the dress I'd slipped out of a minute earlier at her head. She dodged it and I didn't point out that that's not even the scene where Hamlet holds the skull. *"Anyways.* You have to apply and be accepted and everything, and they only take a handful of kids a year. But she said you get to see tons of productions, and like, hang out with the actors, and go to lectures *at the theater* and the whole point of it is to discuss how Shakespeare shaped the rest of English literature."

Layla picked up the dress I'd thrown and walked over to me,

laying it across my lap. She said, "So like, b-basically your Shake-spearean w-w-w-wet dream?"

"Gross," I laughed. "But yeah, kind of. It sounds freaking amazing. But I can't apply until September. Novak said she'd write me a recommendation and help me with everything, but she wanted me to start thinking about it now. And I mean, if I get in, this time next year I could be in *London*."

"Your dream c-c-come true," Layla said. "Oh! I c-c-c-could come visit you and mmaybe we could spend a w-weekend in Paris with my aunt Khadija!"

"Yes!" I shouted. I pulled a different dress from Layla's closet, stood up, and stuck my head through the hole made from the straps and the hanger so that the thin fabric fell in front of my body like I was wearing it. Layla danced over to her laptop and put on "La Vie en Rose" by Louis Armstrong just for me, and we proceeded to twirl around her bedroom for the next three minutes as Layla's smooth voice mixed with Louis's gruff one. When Layla sings, she doesn't stutter at all.

I was back in front of the mirror with the dress still hanging over my head, and Layla and I were debating whether I should keep my braids up or wear them down, when Layla's mom pushed the bedroom door open.

"Mama! You're sup-p-p-posed to knock!" Layla whined. I ripped the dress from over my head and let it fall to the floor.

"Hey, Mrs. Hassan," I said.

"Hi, Pinky," she said, rubbing her hand over my hair. "Ma-muni, what are you two doing?" She bent to kiss Layla's forehead.

Mrs. Hassan gave me a Bengali nickname basically the second she met me. I don't know why I'm Pinky to her, or why

21

Layla's Mamuni, but I love the way it makes me feel warm and wanted. I smile up at her.

"I t-t-told you, Mama. We have that p-p-party tonight? At Valeria's?"

"That's right," Mrs. Hassan said. She glanced over at me. "Naomi know about this party?"

I nodded. Mrs. Hassan and my mother had spoken on the phone almost daily since Layla and I met the summer before middle school, so we rarely tried to put anything over on them. "Good. And there will be parents at this party, yes? I want to call and speak to them."

Layla said, "Of course, Mama." She pulled out her phone, dialed a number, and handed it over. I had no idea who was on the other end of the line, because I was pretty sure there *wouldn't* be parents at this party, but Layla was inexplicably brilliant sometimes.

I watched as Mrs. Hassan spoke to . . . someone. She asked about alcohol. She asked about curfew. She asked if boys would be there. And whoever was on the phone gave all the right answers. Mrs. Hassan smiled and nodded and by the time she handed Layla's phone back to her, she seemed completely confident that we'd be attending a chaperoned, boy-free, alcohol-less party.

Layla was an evil genius.

"So, are we deciding what to wear?" Mrs. Hassan said as she picked up the dress I'd dropped, and her eyes widened the tiniest bit beneath the sheath of her deep purple hijab. "I hope neither of you is planning to wear this . . . undergarment?" Layla burst into a fit of giggles and I was grateful to be as brown as I am; my skin hid most of my blush.

"It's a slip dress, Mama. And it's *perfect*. C-C-C-Cleo would look great in it. But what d-do you think? Should she wear her hair up or, or, or d-down?"

Mrs. Hassan looked like she was considering, and I was dying of embarrassment right there in front of the mirror. "I think," Mrs. Hassan started, looking at the dress. Then her dark eyes found mine. "I think that you, Pinky, are an intelligent, talented, beautiful young woman. And a dress, however thin or short or *perfect*, won't ever matter as much as your brain."

I smiled. "Thanks, Mrs. Hassan."

"I think hair up," Layla said, sticking her fingers into my braids like she hadn't heard her mother at all.

YOU OVER EVERYONE

In the end, I decided to wear a strappy black tank top, a very short pair of jean shorts, and Layla's earrings—a bit of a compromise that satisfied Layla but that felt a lot more *me*. I piled my hair and wore it up, and though I let Layla put a little eyeliner and mascara on my eyes, I still wore my glasses.

In the mirrored elevator of Valeria's building, Layla was fixing her makeup. I was still nervous. I knew there would be drinking at this party, and I'd never drunk anything stronger than Coke. I knew Layla would want to talk to everyone, while I'd only want to talk to her. But when I turned to tell her that I was freaking out, she looked as nervous as I felt.

I poked her arm. "Are you worried Valeria won't like your lip gloss or something?" I teased.

"Shut up," Layla said, but her normal playfulness was missing from her eyes. I touched her arm and when she looked at me she seemed genuinely hurt. "Wait. Are you?" I asked more seriously. Layla sighed.

"Not my *lip gloss*. B-but, like, maybe me? She's in ch-ch-chorus and I really want to audition this year. So I k-k-kinda want the chorus g-g-girls to like me. It's stupid."

In the same way I dreamed of London, Layla had always dreamed of being onstage.

"No, it's not." I bit my lip, feeling bad that I'd teased her. "But I mean, you know you're a shoo-in for chorus. And how could they not like *you*?" Layla didn't answer, but I knew she was thinking more about the way she spoke than the way she sang. I stepped in front of her so she had to look at me.

"Lay. Everyone loves you. And if they don't, screw them," I said. Then I texted her Y.O.E.

It was a code we'd had since middle school that we'd say to each other all the time. *You Over Everyone.* It was the answer to almost every question we could come up with to test our loyalty to one another.

Who would you want next to you in a jail cell?

Who would you want to take down zombies with during the apocalypse?

Who would you save in a fire?

You over everyone.

She grinned, grabbed my hand, and said, "Though she be b-b-b-but little, my b-b-bestie is fierce," stealing a phrase from *A Midsummer Night's Dream* that I've always wanted to embody. I grinned and pretended to dust off my shoulder.

And then the elevator doors opened.

—

Valeria's apartment was packed. There were a ton of kids I recognized right away from our school, but there were lots of people we didn't know pressed against the walls and bouncing to music in her kitchen. It was clear right away that most of them were rising juniors and seniors, and that we were some of the youngest people there. I got a panicky feeling in the pit of my stomach almost immediately. Sensing it, Layla looped her arm through mine and pulled me farther inside.

The girls in chorus were sitting on couches around a coffee table in the living room—prime real estate at a party like this one. But before I could point them out to Layla, a song we both loved started to play. We started singing out loud from our quiet corner of the party, like we were back in Layla's bedroom, worries about the party and impressing the chorus girls nearly forgotten. We were laughing and shouting right in each other's faces when a tall white girl who I'd never seen before walked up to us. I stopped, but Layla's eyes were closed so she was still belting out lyrics at the top of her lungs in her clear, effortlessly pretty voice.

"You *need* to join chorus!" the girl sort of shouted when Layla paused for a breath. Layla's eyes popped open and she looked at me, and then at the girl, clearly a little embarrassed.

"What?" she asked.

The girl had long red hair that was pinned back on one side, revealing an earlobe pierced by two tiny gold hoops. There was another hoop through her right nostril. Her eyes were the green of hard pears, her cheeks the mottled pink of soft peaches. She had just a dusting of freckles (while I had a little over a million), and she was wearing a short denim dress that I instantly wanted.

"You really think I'm g-g-g-good enough?" Layla asked.

The girl smiled wide, showing her braces. "Are you kidding? Your voice is kind of unbelievable." She seemed completely un-

26

fazed by Layla's stutter, which made me love her for a second. She didn't even blink.

Layla looked over at me again, and I smiled and nodded, because I'd been telling her the same thing for forever. I pushed my glasses further up my nose.

"I'm Layla Hassan," Layla said to the girl. "And, this is C-C-Cl-Cleo B-B-Baker." Layla normally hated saying my name because it's so difficult for her (she was always more fluent with soft sounds than the hard ones).

I grinned. "Hey," I said quietly.

"I'm Sloane Sorenson," the girl said. "Valeria's cousin. I just moved in here, with her, my aunt, and uncle. I'm gonna be starting at Chisholm in the fall."

"That's awesome!" Layla replied a little too enthusiastically. Her mouth hung open for a second before she was able to continue. "And you're g-gonna b-b-be in chorus?"

"That's the plan," Sloane replied. "You know Valeria and everyone else, right?"

"I kinda know Valeria, b-b-but *nobody* else," Layla said, and before I could react, Sloane was pulling her away.

I stood there awkwardly for a second, wanting to follow but feeling a bit like I wasn't invited. Then Layla looked back at me. *Come on,* she mouthed. I grinned and followed her.

THE CHORUS GIRLS

In the living room, the chorus girls were laughing.

Sloane introduced Layla to everyone, and then Layla introduced me. Sloane sat in the center and pulled Layla down beside her.

Valeria smiled at me, but the other girls just kept talking. I stood there for a second until Layla said, "You-y-you mind scooting over for C-Cleo?" They did, a bit begrudgingly, and I squeezed in. But my hips aren't small, so it wasn't the most comfortable seating arrangement. And I was right on the edge, barely a part of them at all.

Though the chorus was much larger than these five girls, I learned over the next twenty minutes that they were the most popular. They were the five you wanted to impress if you were going to successfully infiltrate the theater kids clique, and they were the queens of the Shirley Chisholm Charter Girls Chorus.

Dark-haired twins, Cadence and Melody York, were sitting dead center telling a story about some new boy they'd just met. "He's gorgeous," one was saying. "He just moved here from Atlanta," said the other. They were pale and petite and pretty, sopranos who never did solos, only duets, and the biggest gossips in school. They knew everything and they told everyone, and the only thing they cared about more than the latest rumors was music.

Sage Robertson had skin the color of gingerbread and long, relaxed hair. She was a mezzo-soprano, though she bragged that she could go lower. "I have range," she assured us (though I had no clue what mezzo-soprano meant), and then she started talking about a concert she'd seen by a band I'd never heard of. Layla knew them, though. Sage was poised and measured in everything she said, maybe seeming more so as she sat next to the twins, who bounced and squealed and tossed their hair when they talked about anything. I could imagine her in Paris smoking a cigarette, or at a gallery talking about art with college students. I felt like a little kid as I sat next to her.

Valeria was a contralto (didn't know what that was either), and had the prettiest voice, according to them all. A cloud of auburn curls surrounded her light brown face: based on the pictures all over the apartment, a perfect blend of features from her white dad and Puerto Rican mom. There was nothing about her personality that screamed Queen Bee, but she'd gotten into a prestigious summer program at Juilliard, so the girls just kind of made her the one everyone else listened to. That was, until her cousin Sloane arrived.

When Sloane started to talk, everyone listened even though she was the new girl in town. And Sloane talked to Layla like she was the most interesting person at the party.

"You're cool," she said to Layla, after Layla told them about getting one of her sister's college friends to pretend to be Valeria's mom so she could come to this party. Sloane said it with a small smile, like she was pleasantly surprised.

"Not really," Layla said. "I stole the idea from a TV show." But when Sloane laughed, I could tell Layla was proud of herself.

I just sat there, not completely left out, thanks to Valeria, who asked me a few questions, and Layla, who sort of gestured at me to agree with her about certain things, but definitely on the outside. And that was what I'd been afraid of—Layla spreading her wings and leaving me grounded.

I was happy for her, I really was. But I felt a little like I was disappearing.

—

The stars were out when I pushed my way onto the roof, and the sky was as dark as it could get in a city as full of light as ours. I wrapped my arms around my torso, though it wasn't cold at all.

I'd gone up alone to see the fireworks, which soared from Coney Island every Friday in summer. I made an excuse about having to call my mom and then headed up the back stairwell on my own. I *did* have two missed calls from my mother, but I had no intention of calling her back. It was just nice to be out in the fresh air; to be alone instead of lonely; to be physically above it all.

I was taking a picture of the skyline when a text notification slid onto my screen.

Daddio: Having lotsa SOBER fun?

I smiled a little and sent him a quick one back.

Not really? I'll tell you about it later.

Not really SOBER??
No. No. Jeez. Relax. I haven't had a sip of alcohol. Not
really having fun.
PHEW. I mean, I'm sorry the party sucks I guess. But
Jesus, Baby Girl. Don't give your father a heart attack.

I rolled my eyes, and because I felt a little guilty texting *him*
and not returning *her* calls, I shot a text to my mom.

I'll be home by 11.
Why didn't you pick up when I called?
It's loud.
Call me.

"Ughhhhh," I said aloud. I started typing another text to my
mom, *Aren't you with Daddy? He knows where I am AND what I'm
doing*, when I realized she probably wasn't. She'd been working
late a lot lately, and they'd been barely speaking even when they
both were at home. I was trying my best not to think about it.

Before I could hit send, though, I got a message from Layla.

Where'd you go?
Roof. You coming up?

Just then, someone bumped into my arm and my phone
slipped out of my hand.

"No! Shit!" I shouted, fumbling for the phone. A large brown
hand snatched it up, when it was, I swear, *centimeters* from the
ground.

"Holy . . . ," I said, staring at the magically quick hands.

"You're welcome," said a voice that was, without a doubt, baritone—maybe even bass (the one vocal range I *did* know). It made me think of thunder, and all the Shakespeare plays that start, ominously, with storms.

When I took my phone and looked up, I saw that the voice belonged to a beautiful black boy in a spotless white T-shirt. There was a small bronze key hanging around his neck from a navy blue shoestring, and because my brain is the worst, it was at that exact moment that I remembered how Layla said some people would love me coming to the party as close to naked as possible.

I blushed. Hard. Then, to try and recover, I cleared my throat and shot back, "I didn't say thank you."

The beautiful boy smirked. His teeth were as white as his shirt; as white and shining in his dark face as the stars were in the night sky.

He crossed his arms. "Guess I'm sorry, then? For saving your phone from what was sure to be a screen-shattering fall."

I lifted an eyebrow. "Um. *You* bumped into *me*. If anything, you *should* have saved my phone."

He laughed then, and I grinned and looked away from him.

"My bad then, Shorty. Glad I could be of service." He reached out his hand. "I'm Dom," he said.

"Not a shorty," I replied.

"Damn, sis, can you give me a break?"

Then *I* laughed. "Yeah, sorry." I grasped his hand. "Just not having the best night."

"You *are* mad short, though," he said, grinning again while our hands were still touching. I pulled away and swatted at him.

He took a step back and I just ended up grazing the soft fabric of his shirt, dangerously close to his collarbone. (I've always had a thing for collarbones.)

A voice I'd recognize anywhere interrupted us. "Cleo Imani Baker!"

"Jase!" I shouted, turning to hug him. Jase Lin and I had dated most of ninth grade. We ended it on mostly good terms on the last day of school, but I hadn't seen him all summer.

His thick bangs were hanging over his narrow brown eyes and he was wearing the tiniest bit of eyeliner. The neck of his black T-shirt was stretched out, so I could see how golden the skin of his chest was from playing soccer, presumably shirtless, since June. I was very well acquainted with *his* collarbone.

"I see you've met my dude, Dom," he said, clapping Dom on the shoulder. "He went to soccer camp with me and Mason."

Mason, Jase's best friend, stepped out onto the roof next, with roughly half of the kids who'd been in Valeria's apartment. It was suddenly very crowded and very loud

"Yeah, she and I are old friends," Dom said. He turned to look at Jase and Mason, and I noticed a swirling design cut into the close-cropped hair on the back of his head. "I saved Shorty's— I mean *Cleo's*—phone from near-certain demise."

"Oh God," I muttered.

"So by now you know," Mason said, "that Cleo used to be Jase's girl."

"Really?" Dom said, sounding more interested than I thought he should.

I made a pukey noise. "Um, excuse me. I'm a lot more than that, Mase."

"Right, right, right," Mason said, thinking. He threw his arm around my shoulder. "Dom, this is Cleo Baker. Old-ass books and music lover; horrendous soccer player and all-around unathletic human; the shortest person I know." He paused like he was searching for some positive thing to say about me and was having a hard time coming up with anything. I slapped his arm, and as he flinched, he added, "Oh, *and* English-tutor-extraordinaire!" probably because I was the only reason Mason was still on the soccer team. Before I had the chance to say *you're welcome*, he turned to Dom and said, "And, you know. She used to be Jase's girl."

Both Jase and Dom cracked up, and I punched Mason so hard in the shoulder he genuinely winced. "I hope you find cooler people than these losers to hang out with, Dom," I said.

"Well," Dom said. "I did just meet *you*."

I blinked. I bit my lip to hide an inexplicable smile.

Layla came out a few minutes before the first fireworks exploded above our heads, and joined our little circle. I moved aside to let her in and tried not to dwell on the way she'd excluded me on the couch.

"Where'd you g-g-go?" she whispered to me. "Why'd you leave me?"

"Because . . . I didn't know who the bands were you guys were talking about. I can't sing, so I don't know what mezzo-alto means or whatever. And no one was talking to me," I whispered back.

"Mezzo-alto isn't a thing," Layla said. She sighed and pulled out her phone, like *she* was mad at *me*.

"Have you met Dom?" I asked her, to try to melt whatever was making her so icy, and when she shook her head and waved, I introduced them. Mason flicked Layla's collar and made a funny face at her, but she just stayed quiet.

I took out my phone to text her, though she was right beside me. We did that sometimes.

> You good? I sent.

She sent back a shrugging emoji.

> Were those girls bitchy after I left? Do you want to leave?
> No, they were nice.
> So what's wrong?

Layla typed. I watched the fireworks while I waited for her to text back.

> Sometimes I just wish I didn't stutter.
> I just wish this wasn't a thing I had to think about all the time.
> Like I'm at a party, having fun, and I don't want to have to think about this.
> Did someone say something? It usually doesn't bother you this much.
> It's just, a lot of new people, you know?
> I guess?

Usually I was the one nervous around new people, not Layla.

> You don't get it.

I looked over at her. She was staring up at the fireworks, and the bursts of color were reflected almost perfectly in her wide, dark eyes.

We suck at parties, I sent, and Layla smiled at the message a little.

When I turned around, Dom was watching us.

He stepped a little closer and said, "You wanna see a magic trick?" I kind of frowned at him. But then Layla nodded and started watching his hands. We all did.

Dom pulled a coin out of his pocket and held it up in one of his hands for us to see. "I'm gonna make this disappear," he said. Mason crossed his arms like he'd seen this a million times, but the rest of us were riveted. Then Dom rubbed his arms, I guess to point out to us that he didn't have any sleeves, and when he opened the hand that was holding the coin, it was gone. He held up both hands next, and the coin wasn't in either. I gasped and clapped.

Layla said, "How d-d-did you do that?" even though she'd been mostly quiet since she came out onto the roof.

Dom's eyes got big like he was offended. "C'mon, girl. A magician *never* reveals his secrets," he said.

"Magic?" I asked, after everyone else had gone back to watching the sky. But what I really meant was *Thank you for making my friend less sad.* Dom shrugged, like what he'd done wasn't a big deal.

"You seemed to enjoy it," he said. "Cleo of the 'old-ass books and music.'" He paused and angled his body more toward mine. "Exactly how old is this old-ass music?"

I shook my head. "Mason's an idiot. But he's talking about

36

the jazz-age stuff I listen to. Ella Fitzgerald, Billie Holiday, Louis Armstrong—stuff like that. My grandmother used to play it all the time so it's kind of comforting to me, I guess."

Dom nodded and said, "My pop likes Nina Simone. You listen to her?" I nodded too, and he smiled his thousand-watt smile. I could see the design cut into his hair more clearly now that he was up close. It looked like the swirling blues in Van Gogh's *The Starry Night*. As he stood there set against the real night sky, talking to me about music, something about him felt heavy with inevitability.

"Where'd you come from anyway?" I said, because I was almost certain he didn't go to my school.

"I just moved here from Atlanta," he said. "So I came from Georgia, I guess." He must be the new guy Cadence and Melody were gossiping about earlier.

His eyes were full of something, but I didn't know him well enough to say what. The night was young, and so were we, and everything else felt bright in the dark all around us. So I just smiled at him. This party had kind of sucked, but I felt happy to be under the same sky with Layla, watching fireworks on a warm summer night. I looped my arm through hers, holding her close. And as the night ended, it felt more like something new, just beginning.

now

EXITS AND ENTRANCES

I spend most of the weekend after the snowstorm in Daddy's warm apartment. Since the divorce, I'm officially supposed to spend every other weekend with him, and I squeeze in a little more time whenever I can. We mostly sit around in our pajamas when I'm over, drinking hot beverages, talking about the books we've read recently, and listening to music. But this weekend is a little different.

On Saturday, I spend most of my waking hours planning new-memory-making strategies. When Daddy sees me making a long list of all the places that remind me of Layla, he says: "You can't approach your whole life like it's a homework assignment, Baby Girl."

This is such a Daddy thing to say that I have no trouble ignoring it completely. "But I can, though," I say, before turning back to his laptop, where I'm reading articles about friendship dissolution and typing out my list and watching videos about how to get over a breakup. "As a librarian," I tell him without looking away from the screen, "you should value research as much as I do." He just shakes his head and pours me more tea.

By Sunday afternoon, I feel poised and ready to overwrite

some memories. I decide to head to Dolly's—Layla's and my favorite diner. We'd meet there every weekend, usually on Sundays, to finish up last-minute homework, so it seems like a fitting place to start. Sundays are always a little sad because I have school the next day, and for Daddy and me, because we both know we probably won't see each other all week. Now that I don't end my weekends with Layla at Dolly's, they're extra depressing.

"Wanna come with me?" I ask, but he doesn't seem into the idea. "I don't want to think about her every time I walk past that restaurant," I tell him as I slip my arms into my coat.

"I'm just not sure this is the best way to go about things, Cleo. I understand that you're sad, but new memories don't just make old ones go away. You were friends with Layla for a long time, and now you just aren't anymore."

"Harsh, Daddy."

"I guess what I mean is . . . It's not so easy to rewrite history."

I shrug, like *I don't want to talk about this anymore,* but once my dad's on a roll it's hard to stop him.

"All the world's a stage, right?" Daddy continues, starting to quote one of his favorite Shakespeare passages. *"And all the men and women merely players; They have their exits and their entrances."* I want to roll my eyes, but begrudgingly, I nod. "I think it was just Layla's time to exit, honey. And that's okay. Why don't you just stay and have dinner here, with me?"

I want to tell him about my fall and the song that was playing; about hearing Gigi in my head that morning on the platform; about signs and how she always told me to pay attention to the universe. But I don't want him to know how my chest tightens at the sight of the most random things because of how intertwined my and Layla's lives had become; how much I now hated her and how much I miss what we used to have.

I look at his coppery eyes, so like mine. I reach up and straighten my glasses because they're perpetually crooked.

"What should I do instead, then?" I ask, crossing my arms.

"It will just take time," he insists.

"No offense, Daddy," I say, standing up, "but I have to try something."

I kiss his cheek and head to Dolly's on my own.

DOLLY'S

When I emerge from the subway station, a few blocks from Dolly's, the icy layer that covered the city for the last few days is starting to melt, making the streets glisten like they're covered in a million flecks of glitter. Scaffolding and tree branches are dripping all over pedestrians and parked cars, and a few people even have umbrellas open like it's raining.

The diner where Layla and I used to spend so much time is old and completely adorable. I still love the pale blue awning, and the script DOLLY'S that's painted on the widest front window. I'm obsessed with the food. And I adore the familiar way the door jingles, announcing my arrival as I push it open.

There are a few cushy booths, a bar with stools, and mismatched café tables near the windows. There used to be a hostess, but no one comes forward as I step inside. I seat myself at one of the smaller tables, under a portrait of Langston Hughes.

Since the beginning of the winter, the art featured on the walls has been a collection of famous black creatives in the style of classic Italian Renaissance paintings. Zora Neale Hurston rendered in the same pose as the *Mona Lisa* is over the table next to mine, and James Baldwin is in a gilded frame right beside her lounging like *Venus of Urbino,* but in a suit and tie. There are two girls sitting in a booth in the corner under Louis Armstrong, who's leaning against a table like Raphael's *Portrait of a Young Man.*

The girls in the booth are splitting a pair of earbuds, connected to one phone, listening to the same song. Layla and I used to do the same thing, and I miss the half sounds of sharing music with her.

I feel her absence like it's something physical in moments like these—like a part of me is actually missing; actually gone. It's all kinds of devastating.

I swallow hard and force myself to focus. I need to figure out what new memory I can make here all alone.

I'm drinking my second glass of water, rereading a battered copy of *Othello* I always keep with me, and I've already ordered dinner when I hear a familiar voice say my name.

"Cleo?"

When I look up, Dominic Grey is standing at my table, wearing a pale blue apron that reads DOTTY'S across the chest, and the muscles in his arms flutter under his skin as he sets plates and glasses on the table. The small brass key strung around his neck bounces off his chest as he tucks the serving tray under his arm.

"Hey," I say. I look behind him like someone might be playing a trick on me. "You . . . work here?"

He looks down at himself like he's forgotten what he's wearing. Or like he doesn't know that his abundance of hotness is spilling all over the place.

"Not exactly," he says. "This is my grandparents' joint. I usually stay in the kitchen." He pauses and scratches his neck. "I like to cook."

"Oh," I say, and I didn't think I could be more undone by him being in such an unexpected place at such an unexpected time, but then he said *that*. I've seen him around school but I haven't *talked to him*, talked to him since before winter break . . . for a number of reasons. I try to think of something else to ask him but all I can come up with is, "How's it goin'?"

He tilts his head. "You're being mad weird, Shorty."

"Weird?" I ask, even though I know exactly what he means. After everything happened with Layla, I kind of dropped out of my whole life. I look at his eyes for a second, but with the sun slanting through the window, they're the crystal clear brown of iced tea in a glass pitcher—too golden and pretty for me to hold his gaze for long.

"*Mad* weird," he repeats. He lowers himself onto the edge of the chair across from me and frowns.

"I mean, you've been MIA as hell for weeks. Then you skip school on Friday, show up at my grandparents' diner, and ask me how it's going, like I'm a stranger?"

He's the last person I would have expected to notice my absence. It gives me a little thrill, and it's almost enough for me to forget about my problems for a minute. I lean forward, my elbows on the table.

"Aww, did you miss me?" I ask.

Dom smirks and ducks his head a little. "Maybe," he says.

"No one to copy from in AP lit, huh?" I ask.

He rubs one of his big hands over his short, intricately cut black hair. "Exactly," he says.

Another voice forces its way into our conversation as someone new approaches our table. "Where were you on Friday?"

It's Sydney Cox, fashion club president and a girl I tutored last semester. She failed her English midterm and needed to do some extra credit, which she aced with my help. She looks at me and tosses her wildly curly hair off her shoulders, revealing bright gold earrings that look like shooting stars. She seems to notice Dom later than she should.

"Oh, hey," she says. "I didn't know you worked here."

"Why in the world are there so many Chisholm kids here today? And, I kind of don't?" he says.

"You guys short-staffed today or something?" I ask him.

A pained expression crosses Dom's face, but he catches himself and smooths out his features quickly.

"Yeah, something like that."

Sydney barely waits for him to finish. "Whatever. Listen. Cleo. I was looking for you on Friday. I was wondering if you could read my paper and like, give me some feedback on it." When I look at her blankly, she adds, "The one for Novak's class? I tried texting you, but you didn't text back."

"Oh. Yeah, sorry. My mom confiscated my phone after I skipped on Friday. But, like, how did you know I'd be at Dolly's? You don't even live around here."

"Stalkerrrrr," Dom whispers. I kind of laugh, but Sydney gives him a look that could melt ice.

"It was a shot in the dark. You don't remember bringing me here when you tutored me last semester?" she asks. I shake my head. "You totally did. And you said that you and Layla came here every Sunday. So I took a chance, and here you are!"

Even hearing Layla's name makes something inside my chest

fracture, and I take a deep breath, trying to shake it off. Sydney must think it's a sigh of annoyance or something.

She leans closer. "You gotta help me," she whispers. "Please. I'm desperate."

"Oh, shit," Dom says, and we both look at him. "Shit," he says again, and then he says it a third time. "Are you talking about that *Macbeth* paper?"

"Yep," I say. "It's due Tuesday."

"You didn't forget about it, did you?" Sydney says next. "It's worth like, half our grade."

"Shit," Dom says one last time, and at the same time I turn to Sydney.

"I don't think he'd be cursing to himself if he'd already sent a perfect draft to Novak."

I don't know why I say what I say next. Maybe because Sydney is already taking out her phone to email me her draft. Maybe because Dom looks terrified and a little pathetic when he was so confident a minute ago.

It doesn't hurt that he's hot.

"You need help, too?" I offer, and Dom's deeply brown eyes grow wide.

"You'd do that?" he asks. "Even right before it's due?" I shrug, and nod.

"Can you come by here after school tomorrow?" Dom asks, his whole face brightening.

"Not until she helps me," Sydney interjects.

I put a hand on each of their arms. "Look. I'll help Sydney today, and you tomorrow, Dom."

"That's right. Me first," Sydney teases, and her pale blue eyes dart from Dom to me until I promise to send her notes on her paper the second I get home.

—

Between Sydney asking for my help and Dom coming back and forth to my table all night, my mind is perfectly preoccupied with homework and Shakespeare, with Sydney's dumb jokes and Dom's adorable grin.

As I leave, I smile to myself. This new-memory thing might actually work.

A WARNING

Mom hands me my phone without a word Monday morning as we walk down the hallway of our apartment building. It isn't until we're outside, standing on the sidewalk where we usually part ways, that she turns to me.

"I got a call from Layla's mother on Friday. *She's* who told me about you skipping." She pulls out her phone. "Just so we're clear, you're definitely grounded, but I'm working late again tonight," she says. "And I need to be able to get in touch with you." I'm all giddy for about five seconds, but when she starts walking in the same direction as me, I realize she's *escorting* me to school and I pause on the sidewalk, poised to negotiate.

"If you keep my phone, do you still have to come with me to school?" I ask, holding it out to her even though I can see a ton of missed texts and calls.

She doesn't think the question is funny.

"I never had to worry about you skipping when you and Layla were taking the train together every day," she says under her breath but loudly enough that I can hear her. "When is that before-school program of hers going to end, again?" She's asking about the lie I told her to explain why I don't meet up with Layla in the morning anymore.

"Dunno," I say, lying more, keeping my eyes on my phone so she won't be able to tell. My mother thinks Layla is the most perfect kid alive, so she'd be devastated if she knew I didn't have such an "excellent influence" in my life anymore permanently.

I take mental note of the fact that Mom doesn't mention the most obvious reason I never used to skip school: that Daddy used to be the school librarian at Chisholm before he started working in the main branch of the New York Public Library, so he'd notice right away if I was absent. She smooths a strand of her thick black hair and tucks it behind her diamond-studded ear. Then she reaches out and does the same to one of my braids.

Her hair is relaxed and cut into a neat, even bob, while mine is natural—my braids fuzzy and draped all over my shoulders. She's stopped making me straighten it, but I know she'd still prefer if I did. As soon as she lowers her hand, I shake my head to get a dozen more of the braids in my face again.

She sighs deeply, like in the last ten minutes she's gotten her fill of Cleo time for the month. The feeling is mutual.

Mom and I have never exactly gotten along. Gigi used to be our referee, but since we lost her, we've been drifting further and further apart. It probably doesn't help that the year Gigi died was the same year I got my period, acne, and my first crush; the same year Mom's PR business really took off. While I cried constantly, losing it over just about everything, Mom threw herself into work. We fractured. And Mom making Daddy move out in December was the final straw. We've been a different kind of broken ever since.

"Can I at least trust you to go into the building, or do I need to get off the train and walk you inside?" she says as we push through the turnstile and onto the platform. I pocket my Metro-Card and roll my eyes so hard I see stars. Just as I'm about to respond, her phone rings, probably saving us both from saying something we'd regret. She fishes it out of her bag and says, "Naomi Bell," in a singsong voice. She was only ever *Naomi Baker* on her marriage license and her passport.

"No," she says into the phone in her "white-lady voice," as I used to call it. She sounds just a touch more proper whenever she's on a business call—her gerunds regaining their *g*'s and her Brooklyn accent ceasing to exist. "*No.* That is completely and absolutely *unacceptable.*"

I take out my own phone and catch up on what I missed. I see Sydney's desperate messages first.

Cleo. I need you.
How do I Shakespeare?
Where are you even?
HEEELLLPPP.

They make me laugh. Next, I see one from Dom. Got your phone back yet, Shorty?

Right below his message I see a name I haven't seen in months—a name I thought I'd never see on my phone again. Layla.

I need to talk to you.

Something about the message makes me instantly angry. My temperature rises. Just as I'm well on my way to forgetting that she exists, she reinserts herself into my life with a dumb, vague text. I'm tempted to send her something awful back, something like *Well, I never want to talk to YOU again,* but that's when my mom's voice chirps loudly right next to me, her call having ended as abruptly as it started.

"So, as I was saying. I really need you to take a more active role in your education, Cleo. You're a sophomore, and you'll be going off to college soon, but as a young black woman everything is going to be more challenging for you. People will expect less of you just because of the way you look. So if you need me to physically walk you into that building, I will, just so you understand the gravity of the situation. As a matter of fact, I'd like to know why *they* didn't call me about your absences. But I'm running late and—"

"I don't think I'll get lost between the station and the four blocks it takes to get to school," I say darkly, thinking more about Layla than anything else. The school *has* been calling our landline, but I've been deleting the messages before Mom gets home. Her blood-red nails, which have been tapping away at the screen of her cellphone, freeze, and she takes a step closer to me. When I look up, her eyes are shining like the raindrop-shaped black diamonds in her earlobes. Her voice comes out low and fast.

"Watch your mouth, *Cleo Imani.* My concern is not unfounded."

I want to roll my eyes again, but I'd risk an even more embarrassing public scolding. I look left and right, but the other people on the platform aren't paying us any attention. Sometimes it feels like my whole life is playing out for whoever is close enough to see it.

"I *know*," I whisper in her direction, hoping my tone is even enough that it won't earn me a quick, stinging pop across the lips. Naomi *Bell* brings the same ferocity to everything she does—she is not opposed to making her point by any means necessary, as a publicist *or* a mother.

"Okay, then," she says.

I straighten my glasses and stand beside her, wishing she were more like Gigi; wishing I could make everything about us better and nicer and easier; wishing that either I were still friends with Layla or I could somehow make every trace of her disappear from my life forever.

The platform rumbles, and we both take a step back. The train is coming, and it feels like a sign.

Or a warning.

then:
August

THE FIRST DAY

When school started, things were weird almost instantly.

For one thing, Jase was acting like we were all best friends.

"Lay!" he said, throwing his arms wide, calling Layla by *my* nickname for her. Since he and I no longer kissed, he was not allowed to use that, but I didn't know how to take the term of endearment away from him. Besides, what's in a name and all that, right?

I mean, his name means "healer," but we broke up.

"Cleo Imani Baker," he sang next, and though we were cool and everything post-breakup, we weren't hang-out-in-the-hall-before-class cool. Layla nudged me in the ribs and widened her eyes in Mason's direction. He was a few feet away from us, and she clearly wanted to go talk to him. I realized then that Jase didn't really want to talk to me—he was just wingmanning it for Mason. I sighed and slipped my arm out of hers to let her go.

"Hey, Jase," I said flatly. "I'm gonna be late."

This wasn't exactly true and Jase knew it, so he was at best undeterred and at worst encouraged. He took a few steps closer to me, and I could smell the sweetness of the product he used in his hair. It made me remember what his collarbone felt like against my lips. It made me want to hide.

I kept my distance, but Jase didn't, and when he lifted one of my long braids, I swatted it out of his hand.

"Jesus, chill, Cleo. I was just going to say, I like this." He gestured at my hair.

My braids were fresh; my edges, laid. I was wearing a loosely knitted black sweater over my uniform shirt, and my favorite floral combat boots. It was the first day of school, so of course I looked good.

"Oh," I said. I tossed a handful of the braids over my shoulder with a flourish. "Thanks."

I tried to get Layla's attention, but she was still talking to Mason, who was touching the collar of her shirt.

"I'll meet you in Mr. Yoon's class?" I said to Layla, hoping she'd take the hint and come with me, but she nodded kind of absently, not getting it. So I just straightened my glasses and headed to the stairwell alone.

"I'll walk with you," Jase said. And before I could tell him, *No, thank you,* he was on the stairs above me hopping up them backward like an overgrown five-year-old.

"How was the rest of your summer?" he asked me.

"It was okay. I hung out at that new coffee shop by my building. Layla dragged me to some concerts. So, normal, I guess. How was yours?"

Jase grinned, and his dimples were just as cute as I remembered.

"Pretty okay," he said. "My parents are riding me about

balancing soccer and grades and keep threatening to make me quit the team."

I frowned. I knew how much Jase loved soccer. He shook his head. "Don't look so concerned. It's just typical Asian parent shit." Then a little wrinkle creased his forehead. "But I guess I've . . . missed you?" he said. "Am I allowed to say that?"

I paused on the stairs. I didn't miss him, not like *that*.

"Not like *that*," he said quickly, reading my face again. "Not like *let's get back together*."

"Good," I said. "We broke up for the right reasons. And look, I know you're only stuck with me right now because Mason is trying to hook up with Layla. I get it. You don't have to lie or pretend you really want to hang out."

I started walking again, wishing Layla were there, wondering what it would be like when she started dating Mason for real (because it felt pretty inevitable). Would Jase and I have to have these awkward interactions all the time?

"God, I suck at this," Jase said. He reached for my hand and gently turned me around. We stepped to the side to let a herd of other students pass, and I was standing on a higher step than him, so we were eye to eye. "I'm not 'pretending,' Cleo. I'm just trying to say, you're the kind of person who is obviously not there anymore when they're *not there*, if that makes any sense. We used to talk every day, and it sucks that we don't anymore. Is that so hard to believe?"

I crossed my arms. "Kinda," I said.

"What I should have said is I want to be friends—real

friends—because I liked you as a person long before you were my girl. Still do."

I smiled a little. "Really?" I asked.

He nodded.

"I guess I miss your big head, too," I admitted. *"Sometimes."*

"Right, so. Can we really try to be friends? It's gonna be a long three years if we don't talk to each other at all. And from the looks of those two"—he gestured in the direction of where we'd left our friends behind—"we're going to be spending a lot of time together."

I sighed. "Fine."

He grinned and I opened my arms. "Bring it in," I said, and when he hugged me, he lifted me off my feet.

—

After that, things got even weirder.

I made it to homeroom a few minutes before Layla, and I was slipping off my backpack when she walked in. I was shocked beyond words to see Sloane Sorenson step into class right behind her.

I'd saved a seat for Layla, right next to me. The only other empty desks were a few rows away, closer to the back, and for a second Layla actually looked a little torn, like she was considering sitting with Sloane instead of with me. But after Sloane shrugged and walked past me to find an empty seat, Layla came to take the chair next to mine.

"I was hoping Sloane w-w-would b-be in our homeroom!" Layla said as soon as she sat down.

"I didn't even know she was a sophomore," I said.

Layla nodded. "Oh. I thought I t-t-told you. When she told me a c-couple of weeks ago, I was really ssssurprised too."

"A couple of weeks ago?" I asked, and Layla nodded more. "We t-text sometimes," she said.

I glanced over my shoulder at Sloane as Mr. Yoon started taking attendance and going through the morning announcements. Though they both have reddish hair, Sloane's lighter-skinned than Valeria; taller too. But now that we were in a brightly lit classroom instead of in Valeria's dimly lit living room, or on her rooftop in the dark, I could see it a bit around the lips, and in the slope of her forehead—a family resemblance. She turned toward me and kind of frowned, probably because I was staring at her like a freak.

Just then the door of the class opened again. A boy with rich mahogany skin and a zigzag design buzzed into his short hair stepped inside. I instantly remembered Dom, but it was strange to see someone I thought I'd never see again in a place that guaranteed I'd be seeing him daily.

"Sorry I'm late," he said, and I'd forgotten that his voice was so low and heavy, like every word he said was a well-kept secret. "I'm a transfer and I went to like three other classrooms before I figured out this was the right one."

A few people giggled.

"No problem," Mr. Yoon said. He went over to the laptop on his desk. "What's your name?"

"Dominic Grey," he said. "But I go by Dom."

I wonder how I didn't notice that Dom was a sexy-ass name when we first met.

I nudged Layla. "Do you remember him?" She was texting

under her desk, and she had a half smile on her face. She looked up.

"I d-don't think so," she whispered.

"He was at Valeria's party, in the summer. He did that magic trick when we were on the roof?" I whispered back.

"Oh yeahhhh," she said. "I w-w-wonder what he's doing here."

"Transfer," I said. "Didn't you hear his heavenly voice?" Layla laughed.

I watched Dom's Jordan-clad feet as he walked down my aisle, and I was surprised when he paused right by my desk.

"Cleo, right? Jase's girl?"

"You're hilarious," I said.

"I know." He smirked, and I scoffed. "I like your shoes," he whispered before continuing past me. I looked down at my boots, then up again at the back of Dom's long body. He was lifting the shoulder strap of his bag over his head, taking the seat right next to Sloane.

From where I was sitting, I could see every detail of the design cut into his hair. It was different from that night on the roof, when it reminded me of Van Gogh's starry sky. Today it looked like a hedge maze, one I wouldn't have minded getting lost in.

"I'm new here, too," I heard Sloane say to him. I couldn't hear what he said back, but Sloane laughed, then reached over and folded down the collar of his shirt, exposing the smooth, brown skin that stretched over the knobs of his collarbone. I bit my lip and turned back to Layla.

"Who are you texting?" I asked her, because she normally would have been giving me crap by now about the way I was ogling the new boy. Plus, she usually only broke our school's screenless policy to text *me*, and my phone had been silent all period.

"I'm t-t-texting Sloane," she said. She glanced up at me and wrinkled her nose. "She's so funny."

I looked around the class, unsure of what planet I was on, where Jase wanted to be friends, Layla was texting someone who wasn't me, Sloane was in our grade, and Dom was right here, sitting behind me in homeroom. I was relieved when Mr. Yoon started roll call. At least my name and my presence were things I could control—things I knew would always stay the same—even if everything around me was moving in directions that made no sense at all.

THE STACKS, PART I

Layla and I compared our schedules after homeroom and quickly realized that was the only class we had together.

"This sucks," she said, pouting.

She actually had a little tantrum in the middle of the hall, throwing her backpack and semishouting about the world being unfair until a teacher came out of a classroom and said, "Miss Hassan, what seems to be the problem?"

When we parted ways, we hugged like we'd never see each other again, and I won't lie, I felt a little weepy.

Before she walked away I said, "Let's meet in the school library after last period to do our homework." She nodded and mouthed *you over everyone* before she walked away.

On the other hand, in addition to homeroom, I had three classes with Dom: chemistry, geometry, and AP lit with Ms. Novak. When I stepped into English, Dom was already there, sitting in the front row, a book open on his desk.

"Hey," he said when I walked in, like we were old friends or something.

"Hi," I muttered, still a little annoyed about how different my and Layla's schedules were.

"What are you reading?" he asked me. I'd grabbed a seat in the row behind him, diagonal from his desk which was front and center, so that he had to twist almost all the way around to see me.

"*Othello,*" I told him. "It's one of my favorites."

He pressed his lips together. "So you like betrayal, huh?" he whispered.

"No. What I like is the language." I recited a few of my favorite lines. "*What wound did ever heal but by degrees? She gave me for my pain a world of kisses. Men should be what they seem.*"

Dom poked out his bottom lip like he was impressed.

"But I won't lie," I continue. "The jealousy, betrayal, and revenge are pretty entertaining."

Dom let out a breathy laugh.

"Okay, okay," Ms. Novak said, calling class to order. "Welcome to AP English Literature and Composition. This year we'll explore novels, poetry, and plays from several different time periods in order to prepare you for the AP exam at the end of the year. Keep in mind, this is a college preparatory course, so this isn't easy stuff. But all of you are in *this* class because I believe my regular literature class wouldn't be challenging enough for your reading and writing levels."

Ms. Novak winked at me and I grinned.

I wouldn't say I was a teacher's pet, or that I was Novak's favorite, but she definitely liked me. She and my dad were really good friends, and after I aced her class last year, I knew I wanted to take her every year I was at Chisholm Charter.

She passed around a syllabus and I read the list of required reading to myself. I was really excited to see *Hamlet* as one of the first plays we'd be diving into.

"We'll spend most of the year learning to interpret the meanings behind the language in the works on the list in front of you, and learning to write about those interpretations. In other words, welcome to the art of coming up with convincing bullcrap, people."

The class laughed.

"In all seriousness, though, it's gonna be hard, but it's gonna be fun. I promise."

—

The rest of the day made me forget about the morning's weirdness, so when I stepped into the library after school to meet Layla, I wasn't thinking about homeroom or Sloane. But when I saw Layla sitting on the floor right by the door texting, I couldn't help but wonder who was on the receiving end. Luckily, Ms. Novak was there too, and she was leaning over the circulation desk talking to my dad.

". . . the application is pretty straightforward," I heard her say.

"Is she telling you about London?" I asked, skipping over to his desk. The application for the Young Scholars Program at Shakespeare's Globe was up on his computer. I gleefully clapped my hands. "It sounds friggin' perfect, doesn't it?" I asked him.

Ms. Novak pulled up some pictures next—all the photos she took while she was there over the summer. The three of us—me, Daddy, and Layla—crowded around the computer to see. Daddy shook his head and straightened his glasses. "It sounds perfect for *you*, Baby Girl."

"*Daddy*," I said, looking around. I hated when he called me Baby Girl at school. I glanced at Layla and we both cringed.

"Oh, right. *Cleo*," he said, correcting himself. I reached out and tugged his tie.

"I was explaining that you have to write a short statement of interest, and that the deadline is anytime between now and the end of October. I think you'll find out if you're accepted in December," Ms. Novak said to me.

"You'll read it, right? My statement of interest when I'm done?" I asked her. "I want to make sure it's perfect."

"Duh," she said, and I giggled.

"Stacks?" Layla asked after we'd gone through about a hundred of Ms. Novak's photos and I was in a full-on London-induced trance. I tore myself away.

"See ya later, Novak," I said. "Daddy, come grab me when you're heading home."

We walked back to our favorite corner of the library, and I started spreading out my books and papers and pens.

"How was the rest of your day?" I asked Layla. She had started taking her stuff out of her bag, but once everything was unpacked, she didn't open any of her notebooks. She was back on her phone, texting again.

"Eh, okay, I g-g-guess." She put her phone down and turned to me, dipping her head and sweeping all her messy waves up into a bun. "AP c-calc is going to be c-c-crazy hard. And I weirdly have a b-b-bunch of classes with Sloane."

All the kids at Chisholm are brainy, but Layla and I are brainy in different ways. She's great with numbers. I'm better with words. But I didn't think this would divide us in any real way until college. I wonder if Sloane is on the same track as Layla because she's into math and science too.

"Sounds like a nightmare," I said. I meant the math class, but it sounded like I was talking about Sloane.

Layla forced out a rush of air before she was able to speak the words, "Harsh, C."

"I meant calc!"

"Suuuure you did."

Her phone buzzed again and when she picked it up she grinned. Her fingers tapped across the screen. She paused. She laughed. "Sorry," she said, glancing at me. But she kept texting.

"I have a bunch of classes with Dom," I said. That got her attention, and she put the phone facedown on the floor.

"Were you staring at him as much in those c-c-classes as you were in homeroom?"

"Hahaha. You're so funny," I said. Layla nudged my arm.

"I'm just fucking with you. He's c-c-cute. You interested?"

"Not sure yet," I said. "I'm more concerned with not screwing up in Novak's class and getting into this Shakespeare program at the moment."

Layla nodded. "Well, you're bloody brilliant. You're quite a shoo-in, Cleo Baker, if you ask me. They should pick you over everyone, love. Always and forever." She said it all theatrically, in a much better British accent than she'd been using during the summer.

"Whoa!" I said, staring at her. "You didn't stutter at all just now!"

Layla smirked. "Yeah, me and my s-s-speech therapist have

been trying a b-bunch of new things out, including accents, and this thing c-c-called smooth speech? Since I d-don't stutter when I ssssing, she thinks I can trick my brain into thinking it's sssing- ing by speaking in an accent or in a sort of sing-y voice?"

"That's so cool!" I said. "But it's weird that you don't sound like you. Not the stuttering, just you know, your normal voice."

Layla shrugged, her mouth flopping open and closed— a block. She pointed to her own mouth, and rolled her eyes, frus- trated. Eventually she said, "I'm g-g-going to k-keep trying it out and we'll see. I d-don't think I'll talk like that all the time, or use accents or whatever. B-but it could be useful for stuff in class. P-p-presentations or reading or stuff like that, you know?"

"Totally. Okay, we should get some work done." I already had easily four or five hours of reading even though it was the first day. I pulled my earbuds out of my bag. "Wanna listen?"

Layla nodded and tucked one of the earbuds into her ear, and we leaned back against the closest bookshelf. I put on Billie Holi- day. With the first novel I had to read for Novak's class in hand, I watched Layla open her calculus book and grab a pencil.

We'd only been working for about twenty minutes when her phone buzzed again. She picked it up and started giggling, but I just tried to focus hard on the words on the pages in front of me.

"How much longer d-do you think we'll b-b-b-be in here?" Layla asked.

"Does there need to be a time limit? I thought we'd do what we normally do and stay till my dad left."

Layla bit her lip. "I might head out sssooner than that," she said.

"Okay . . . ," I replied.

"It's just that . . ." She put her phone down and looked at me. Her dark eyes seemed excited. "Sloane and Valeria are g-g-g-going to this record store that just opened, and I thought it c-could be fun."

"Oh," I said.

"But I mean, I won't g-g-go if you d-don't want me to."

I didn't want her to. But what I wanted more was for *her* not to want to.

I picked up my phone and changed the music just so I didn't have to look at her while I lied. "No, it's cool," I said.

Layla grinned. And the fact that she grinned made the pit of my belly ache dully, distantly. She wasn't paying enough attention to me to read between the lines. She wanted to go so badly that she didn't even notice I wasn't telling the truth.

She retied her Chuck Taylors and pulled out my earbud just as Ella Fitzgerald's rendition of "Over the Rainbow" started to play. I didn't realize she'd be leaving right away, but she started packing her stuff into her bag a second later.

"Oh," I said again, so low she didn't hear me. Ella's voice and Layla moving away from me made me think of Gigi, and other precious things I'd let slip through my fingers. I swallowed hard and sat up straighter.

"Thanks, C," she said, and then she was gone.

now

YOU ACTUALLY CARE?

As soon as I step into homeroom, I see Layla. I notice Dom too, but I'm so laser-focused on what might happen next with her, so nervous about what she might say, that I can't even acknowledge him when he smiles at me.

Layla abruptly walks over and my belly feels like it's full of heavy stones. She looks pissed, her brow furrowed, her eyes spitting fire. "Hi?" I say slowly.

"Did you get my t-t-t-text?" she asks. I nod and try to ignore how strange it is to hear her raspy voice. I've already forgotten the scratchy quality of it.

"Well, why d-d-didn't you text me b-back?" she asks next, and it sounds like an accusation. I shrug instead of telling her the truth—that I only got my phone back this morning.

Mr. Yoon asks everyone to take their seats so he can take attendance. Layla sighs and pulls her phone out of her pocket and mimes tapping her thumbs against the screen—she's going to text me. I nod and sit down in the middle row. She goes back to the rear of the class, where she's sitting next to Sloane. My stomach clenches, but I try to breathe deeply.

As Mr. Yoon calls out name after name, the texts from Layla

start to roll in. I can feel them vibrate against my thighs, but even after three pulses, I'm too tense to look down. I glance back at Layla, and she widens her big, dark eyes in my direction. I could have guessed the expression she would make before she made it, and I wonder if knowing someone's face as well as I know Layla's matters at all once you've done the kinds of things we've done.

I swallow, look at my lap, and start to read.

> My mom called your mom, right?
> What happened?
> Are you in trouble?
> **She called. I'm definitely in trouble.**
> Shit.
> **It's fine.**
> I didn't mean for that to happen.
> **You actually care?**

I ask this because it seems like she does. The possibility gives me a strange surge of faith in her that I wish I didn't feel. A long while passes before Layla's next message, and in the space between my words and hers, I think about what I'll say next if she doesn't hate me—and how I'll kill the stubborn hope blooming in my belly if she does.

> I'm having a really hard time with that paper for Novak.

I wait for Layla to say more, but when she doesn't, I send, **Okay . . . ?**

> So I went to Novak yesterday to beg for an extension.
> She said no unless I had like a family emergency or
> something. Which I didn't. Then she said she'd assign
> me a tutor.

There's a break before she sends the next message. A tiny pause where the bubbles that show she's typing make my stomach drop.

> You.

I swallow hard and look up as Mr. Yoon calls my name. "I'm right here," I say, even though I'm miles away from this classroom in my head. I don't want to tutor her. I'm not even signed up to *be* a tutor anymore. The hope I felt a moment earlier dissolves, and instantly Novak's on my shit list too.

> What does me being your tutor have to do with your
> mom calling mine?
> I was freaking out.
> I obviously don't want you to tutor me.

Ouch.

> Feeling's mutual, I send.

> So after school I was kind of losing it a little bit in my
> room and when my mom got home she heard me.

75

> She came in and asked me what was wrong and I kind
> of told her everything.
> **Everything?**
> Everything.

My face heats up. Tears sting the corners of my eyes. I never wanted *anyone* to know all of what happened between us—especially not Mrs. Hassan. While my mom thinks Layla's perfect, that's what Mrs. Hassan thought about me. Layla and I used to joke that we should switch mothers; that they'd both be happier if they had the other's kid.

I don't want Mrs. Hassan to know all I've said and done to Layla because I don't think I can handle her hating me too. Will she still call me Pinky when she sees me? My dad doesn't even know the whole story.

> I told her not to tell your mom about any of it.
> But when I was upset I kind of also blurted out that
> you'd been missing a lot of school and she got really
> concerned.
> You know how my mom is.
> I think she was just calling Ms. Naomi to make sure you
> were okay.

I feel a little solace from this bit of information. That even after Mrs. Hassan knew the very worst things about me, she was still worried. But I still text Layla again, just to be sure.

> **You really told her everything?**

She doesn't text back right away, and though she's less than ten feet from me, I can't bring myself to look back at her.

> Yeah.
> I told her.
> Now she knows you're a bitch and not the innocent little good girl you pretend to be.

These are the kinds of things Layla would say to other people *before*. But these are the things she says to me all the time in this after version of us. It still catches me off-guard.

I throw my phone into my bag and onto the floor just to put some distance between my heart and Layla's words. Mr. Yoon looks over at me, and so does about half the class. Layla and Sloane are probably smirking, but I don't turn around to see.

"You okay over there, Miss Baker?" he says.

I want to cover my face and shout *NO* because I am so angry. But I just stare at my desk, clench my teeth, and nod.

THE HOT SEAT, PART I

"Seriously, Novak?" I say as I step into my AP lit class. I toss my *Macbeth* paper onto her desk, a day early, and it slides into place next to a pile of other collected assignments.

"Um, hi?" she says. Ms. Novak sucks in her upper lip and clasps her small hands together before tucking them under her chin, and my brown eyes land on her gray ones with a challenge. Her willowy frame is always draped in long, flowy things, and today she's wearing a dress the color of chimney smoke that brings out the lightest parts of her eyes. I want to strangle her with the scarf she's wearing.

"What's up with you assigning me to tutor someone when I'm not even a part of the tutoring program anymore?"

She nods and pats the butterfly chair beside her desk— Novak's Hot Seat, we all call it, though we are rarely in trouble if she invites us to sit with her.

"Come. Sit," she says calmly.

I yank out the single earbud still tucked into the curve of my ear, and the Etta James song that accompanied me to class fades to silence just as more students begin filing in. "I got a pretty crappy message from the attendance office on Friday," she says once I'm seated.

I deflate, all my bravado gone at the mention of *the attendance office*. I see where this is going. I tilt my head skyward, resting my neck against the back of the chair, and look up at the ceiling. I sigh, but I don't say a word.

Dom walks in. He reaches out and tugs one of my dangling braids as he passes me, and his hand smells like almond soap and something else, something smoky and rich. When he takes his seat in the front row, I turn my head to look at him. He winks and my face feels as hot as it did in homeroom but for a completely different reason. So I look down at my lap, avoiding his eyes and Ms. Novak's, and trace the lines of my palm with the fingertips of my other hand.

"So it's true," Novak says. She puffs up her cheeks, blows the air out, and the papers on her desk flutter like butterfly wings. It isn't a question, but I finally lift my head to look at her and nod. She sighs again at my confirmation.

"Damn. Well, to answer your question, I assigned you to tutor Layla to make up for all the work you missed on the days you've been *skipping*, Cleo." She says the word "skipping" like it's a word she's never uttered before, especially not in a sentence so close to my name. Then it's my turn to be bewildered. I sit up a little straighter.

"But I kept up with everything, didn't I?" I ask.

"Not exactly. You always did your homework. And that was pretty boss, if I'm honest. But there were in-class responsibilities that I let slide when I thought you were out sick."

I nod, not wanting to put up a fight, especially after the way I stormed into her classroom. So embarrassing. I just want out of this chair as quickly as possible. "Okay," I say.

The class is getting rowdy, the way classes sometimes do before the teacher makes herself known. But when I glance at Dom where he's sitting in the front row, he's silently reading a book like the perfect human he is.

I turn back to Ms. Novak, an idea blooming. "What if I tutor someone else, though? What about Dom?" And just as I speak his name, the class goes suddenly still and quiet. Those weird silences always seem to happen at the most inopportune times, but the timing of this one is exceptionally bad. Everyone is looking at me. Dom is, too.

"Girl, Dom doesn't need a tutor," Ms. Novak says in a hushed tone. She looks from me to him and back again. She tucks a bit of her curly Afro behind her ear. "He's second in the class, right after you."

I'm too embarrassed to inquire about this further, to try to figure out why Dom would ask for my help on his *Macbeth* paper if he didn't really need it. And before I can say anything else anyway, Ms. Novak says that if I have any other questions I can talk to her about it after school.

"But keep in mind, this is kind of a punishment, Cleo. You did a crappy thing. You don't get to pick how this goes down when you're making up for something that shouldn't have happened in the first place."

Just before I head back to my seat, my eyes lock with Dom's. He smirks, his heavy eyebrows lifting, his white teeth shining, and I die.

then:
September

MILKSHAKES

The first few weeks of school passed in a blur of reading, tutoring, and homework. And while Layla sang almost constantly to get ready for chorus auditions, I wrote and rewrote my statement of interest for the Shakespeare program in London. I asked Layla to read it, and Layla's mom to read it, and my own parents to read it, while Layla demanded that all the same people listen to the three songs she couldn't decide between for her audition, and then, once she'd narrowed it down to one, we had to help her pick which rendition would showcase her voice best. She also asked Sloane, and she took her advice over everyone else's, but it didn't bother me. We were both so close to getting everything we'd ever wanted. Whatever gave Layla the best chance at making chorus was what I thought she should do, even if that meant listening to Sloane Sorenson.

Before I knew it, Ms. Novak was standing behind me as I hit send on my application, and then I was rushing off to the auditorium to see Layla perform. After weeks of preparation, auditions for chorus were happening that afternoon, and I felt almost as prepared as I knew Layla was.

But Layla still looked nervous as she stepped out onto the

stage. Her uniform shirt was a little wrinkled along the bottom from being tucked into her pants all day, which was how I knew she was really undone by this audition. Layla was normally meticulous about the way she looked because she had so little control, she told me once, over the way she sounded. She cleared her throat.

"Mmmmmy nnnname is Layla Hhhhhhhassssssan."

Her speech stuttered and stuck much more than it usually did. I stood up and moved a few rows closer to the stage from where I had slipped into the back, hopeful that if Layla saw me, she'd feel a little less scared and maybe her speech would even out a bit. I wished I had thought to text her about using one of her accents, or practicing her smooth speech in this real-life situation, but it hadn't even occurred to me.

"I know your name, Layla," Mrs. Steele said with what sounded like a smile in her voice. "There's no need to be nervous, hun. Can you match my pitch?" She sang out a note that was high and clear, and Layla took an audibly deep breath and followed suit. Her voice eclipsed Mrs. Steele's instantly.

"Excellent," Mrs. Steele said even as Layla held the note. I felt my chest swell with pride, as if I had anything at all to do with her talent. Sometimes it felt like everything about my friends belonged to me.

"Cadence, Sage," Mrs. Steele said, and the girls stood and walked up the stairs to the stage. "Let's try some harmonies."

They did a few different scales with Layla, testing her range. She sailed through each one effortlessly, and though she stuttered as she introduced her solo song, once she sang the first line, it was impossible to look away.

Kids from the hallway poked their heads into the auditorium, and a few other students who were there for friends gave Layla their rapt attention. She sang with her eyes closed and her head lifted, and her voice was undeniably special. Her shiny black waves fanned around her head and looked like a halo backed by the stage lights. By the time she was done, everyone was murmuring about her being the kind of powerhouse soloist the chorus needed, and I had to hold myself back from standing up and clapping like it was a real performance.

"Great, great work, Layla. Really," Mrs. Steele said after Layla's big finish.

I waited for her in the hall next to the stage exit door. When it opened, I applauded, but it wasn't just Layla who spilled into the hallway. Sloane was there, and the rest of the Chorus Girls were too (they had become a proper noun in my head). Plus a bunch of other girls who had just tried out.

"Cleo!" Layla said as soon as she saw me. She flung her arms around my neck and almost took me down. "That was t-t-terrifying. D-d-did you hear how mmmuch I stuttered on my own name?"

I laughed a little. "Yeah, but you did such an awesome job with the singing part of it! Should we go and get milkshakes to celebrate?"

Layla nodded and hooked her arm through mine. "Sloane invited me to hang out with them. Wanna c-c-c-come?"

"Sure, I guess," I said. I kind of wished it could be just Layla and me, but it was her celebration, and she'd probably be spending lots of time with these girls if she was picked to be in chorus, which I knew she would be. "I just need to ask my dad first. Come to the library with me real quick? I bet he hasn't left yet."

"Sure," Layla said. She glanced back at Sloane. "You g-g-g-guys mind waiting?"

Sloane was too busy laughing at something Sage had said to answer, but Valeria nodded. "There's no rush. We'll wait for you."

But by the time we asked my dad, went to our lockers, and made it back to the bit of hallway right outside the auditorium, everyone was gone.

"They said they'd wait, and then they didn't?" I said to Layla. I rolled my eyes a little. "Well, that speaks *volumes.*"

"Shut up," Layla said. She jogged a little farther up the hall to peer around the corner. "You shhhouldn't have taken so long, C-C-Cleo." I gave her a look, but she didn't notice. She hurried to pull out her phone.

"Don't blame *me* for this. They're the ones who said they would wait."

Layla sighed and started down the long, empty hallway toward the front doors. "You d-d-d-didn't really want to hang out with them, C-Cleo. I could t-tell. So you just took your time sssso we'd take t-t-too long and they'd g-g-g-give up on us and leave."

"I swear I didn't," I said. "But shouldn't you be a little more upset with them for leaving?"

Layla sighed. "You d-d-don't get it, Cleo. It's always b-been just me and you. When you're like Sloane and you have a lot of friends, it's harder to k-k-k-keep everyone happy."

She was texting as she said this, so she wasn't looking at me. I studied her face—the way she was saying this so matter-of-factly. It sounded rehearsed, not like she was speaking for herself.

"So like, if everyone w-w-was ready to go except us," she continued, "I g-get why they'd leave."

I guessed I *didn't* get it.

She pocketed her phone and looked up at the door as we got closer to the end of the hall. "Sloane thinks that in addition to ch-ch-chorus, I should go out for the w-w-w-winter musical."

"Really?" I asked.

Layla nodded. "She mentioned it right when I c-c-came off stage after my audition."

I didn't know how I felt about it—Layla with a speaking role—after what had just happened when all she had to say was her name. It unnerved me, which was probably ableist BS since I wasn't a stutterer, but I couldn't help it.

"I don't know, though," Layla said.

"I think you can do anything," I told her, which was mostly true. I just didn't *want* her to do everything, but it wasn't my call.

She smiled. "Thanks, C. I guess we might as well get those mmmilkshakes?"

We went to our favorite place and ordered the most ridiculous one on the menu to share. It was topped with an actual slice of birthday cake and covered in rainbow sprinkles.

"So good," we muttered to each other between bites. We were about halfway through the milkshake, and Layla'd just challenged me to see how much I could drink before I got brain freeze, when her phone buzzed.

"Oh, yay!" she said. "It's Sloane. They're at Washington Square P-P-Park."

"Cool," I said, massaging my temples. "Let's just finish this first. Slowly. How long are they going to be there?"

Layla threw an amused look in my direction and tossed some of her wavy hair over her shoulder. "Cleo, we're obviously g-g-g-going to the p-park now, duh." She waved down the waitress without another word, and I sort of paused, surprised at her. I wasn't used to our friendship being a . . . dictatorship. Usually we talked about what we were doing and decided together. As I sucked down what I could of the shake and put a few bucks on the table to pay for something I couldn't even finish, I was glad she had charged out of the restaurant ahead of me. At least she couldn't see the stank face I was making.

THE PARK

Needless to say, when we got to the park, I wasn't in the best mood.

"Oh my God, Layla, where have you been all my life?" Sage asked, as if *they* hadn't left *us*.

Valeria, Cadence, Melody, and Sloane all turned at the sound of our approach, and I bit my bottom lip hard to stop myself from rolling my eyes.

"Hey," Layla said coolly. She hugged them each, like she hadn't just seen them an hour earlier. "You g-g-guys remember my friend, right?"

Layla looped her arm through mine, which was a bit of a relief. It made me feel a little less invisible. At least Layla cared I was there, even if no one else did.

"Yeah. Your phone went off during my audition," Sloane said, like that was the only interaction we'd ever had. Layla looked scandalized.

It happened right after I texted Layla to tell her how well she'd done, and it was Layla's response to me that caused the sound to echo through the auditorium just as Sloane was about to start her solo. "Sorry about that," I said, scratching my neck, which I could feel heating up.

"It's cool," Sloane said. But it didn't sound like it was.

"Chloe, right?" Sage said, tilting her head so her layered black hair fell to one side. She was wearing a thin silver headband, and I knew if my mother could have her way, this was how she'd want me to look: contacts instead of glasses; pink nails instead of unpolished ones; relaxed hair instead of braids. Sage pulled some ChapStick out of her pocket and put it on while she waited for me to answer, and the metal headband glinted in the sun.

"*Cleo,*" I said back. I could hear how unfriendly my voice sounded. To be honest, the *Chloe* mistake was a common one. But I couldn't hide how little I wanted to be there, how much I didn't care to talk to these girls whom my friend seemed desperate to impress.

"Right," Sage said, smacking her lips. She didn't apologize for getting it wrong.

We clustered together right there near the fountain, talking about music and feminism; how much we hated the president and boys. Sage said she liked my braids, and Cadence asked me where I'd found my "crazy-cool" boots, and Valeria asked how I'd gotten so into jazz-age music. Layla was in the middle of it all, cracking jokes and being cynical and as the girls laughed and touched her shoulders, I felt happy for her.

They seemed to *get* her. They liked her in the exact way she wanted them to, without being a different version of herself. I smiled at how they all seemed to be welcoming her into their fold, and after a while I was laughing and enjoying myself too. I didn't feel as out of place as I expected, and I surprisingly felt a little guilty about not wanting to come out in the first place.

Even though it was September, the weather was still sunny

and warm. There was a guy with a huge bucket of soapy water blowing giant, wobbly bubbles that little kids and dogs chased and popped. There were people tossing coins into the fountain water—closing their eyes and making wish after wish. Tourists were everywhere. I slipped out of my denim jacket and stepped closer to the Chorus Girls. Maybe my "problem" with them was all in my head.

Just then, Sloane pivoted toward me and said, "So how did you and Layla, like, become friends?" She tilted her head and smiled, and up close I could see that her red hair made her cheeks seem rosier than they really were. She still looked innocent and sweet, her braces shiny and bright when she smiled, but then she added, "I mean, you two are just *so* different."

There was nothing inherently mean in the question itself, but it landed hard and heavy on my shoulders. I could tell this was a test. It was her way of asking me to prove something—though what, I wasn't sure.

"We met at a barbecue right before we started middle school," I said. "I was sad, and Layla hung out with me the whole afternoon. She made me feel better." I looked up at her. "She's good at that. And after that summer we were kinda inseparable. We had each other's backs no matter what."

Layla grinned and looked down at me. "Yep. And we're really not that d-different, Sloane. You just d-d-don't know C-C-C-Cleo like I do."

Sloane seemed unimpressed. "Huh," she said, and it sounded like, *That's it?* Or maybe, *That's nothing.* But it was everything to me. My skin suddenly felt too tight and I didn't want to be standing so close to her. I took a step back.

It might sound dramatic, but sometimes it felt like my friendship with Layla was a miracle. Sloane was right about one thing: we *were* different. But Layla saved me when I was the saddest I've ever been. I'll never forget that.

When my phone buzzed, I took it as an opportunity to move away from Sloane's dismissal. It was a text from my mom that said, Tell your father I'll be working late tonight.

Why don't you text him?

I did. I haven't heard back from him, so if you're still at school can you let him know?

I hated when they got into these moods where they didn't want to talk to each other and they used me as a messenger. Daddy clearly hadn't told her I was hanging out with friends after school either.

Fine, I sent, and then I forwarded Mom's message to him.

What else is new? he sent back pretty much immediately. I kind of grinned. He was right. She was late almost every night these days. My phone buzzed again with another message from my dad.

DADDY-DAUGHTER PIZZA PARTY?

I sent him a dozen pizza emojis as a yes.

Instead of walking back over, I sent a message to Layla:

I'm kinda bored. Can we leave soon?

When she didn't text back right away, I went looking for a bathroom. I normally would have never gone to the public restroom at a park, but after chugging that milkshake, desperate times called for desperate measures.

I pushed my way into the bathroom and it wasn't as awful as I expected. The floor was inexplicably wet, but it didn't smell too bad and most of the toilets were functional. As soon as I was done, still hovering over the seat and being extra careful not to touch anything, I heard the door creak open.

"Cady, this place is gross." It really wasn't. "You're not actually going to *go* in here, are you?"

"Ew, no. I just had to ask you something."

I breathed a sigh of relief, followed closely by the thought: *Crap.* It was Cadence and Melody. I didn't want them to know I'd just taken a pee in the bathroom they'd deemed unfit for human use, so I froze where I was, toilet-tissue wad in hand.

"What do you think of Layla? Like, honestly."

"Honestly? She's cute and cool. And her voice is amazeballs. But her friend is kinda a hanger-on."

"Oh my God, right? That's what I thought too! Stalker-vibes, almost."

"Totally," Melody said. "Like, why's she even still here? It's obviously not her scene."

"Sloane's not into the friend either," Cadence confirmed.

I have a damn name was what I wanted to shout. *I'm not some throwaway person.* But I stayed hidden; I stayed quiet. I couldn't react to their words because if I did, it would be all over school in a nanosecond. I knew Melody's reputation for not being able to keep her mouth shut—and if Cadence knew anything, you could assume Melody would within the hour, which was basically like buying a billboard or shouting the information from a rooftop. So I waited, and once they were gone I cleaned myself up, washed my hands, and headed back toward the fountain.

When I found Layla, I leaned in close. "How long do you want to hang out?" I whispered. I didn't mention what Cadence and Melody had said, because they were all standing so close.

"I d-d-don't know," she whispered back. She was still huddled between Sloane and Valeria. "I think everyone's g-g-g-going to go g-g-get food in a little bit."

"Oh," I said, trying to hide the instant disappointment I felt. "Well . . . can I tell you something?"

"Layla," Sloane said, like she didn't see me talking to her. "Have you ever thought about straightening your hair?"

"Oh yeah," Layla said. "I straighten it sssometimes, but it t-takes forever."

Sloane fingered a strand of Layla's fat waves. I wanted to slap her hand away. "Oh," she said, but I'd never heard an *Oh* that said as much as that one did.

For a tiny second, Layla looked a little unsure of herself, maybe even hurt, but she recovered quickly. "I mean, it d-d-doesn't take *that* long," she said. Sloane shrugged, and I tugged at Layla's arm.

"Bathroom," I whispered, and she finally peeled away from them to go with me.

"Where does Sloane get off telling you how to do your own hair?" I said once we were back inside the restroom. Layla was standing in front of the sink and mirrors.

"I don't know," she said softly. Layla was tugging at a few strands of her hair where they fell to loosely frame her face. She pulled two wide tendrils straight, let them bounce back into place, then pulled them straight again.

"You two are sooo different," I said nasally. "What was *that* about?"

Layla shrugged. A second later she said, "Do you think it looks b-b-better straight?" On any other occasion I would have given her my honest opinion: that it looks good either way. That I like it best when she braids it into cool crowns and stuff because I don't know how to do complicated styles. But because of Sloane's comment, I said, "It looks perfect just the way it is, Lay."

Her reflection smiled at me in the mirror, but she didn't turn around. I stepped up to the sink, careful not to touch it.

"I heard Melody and Cadence saying they don't like me," I told her.

Layla frowned. "Really?"

"Yeah. So can we just go?"

Layla had been watching my eyes in the mirror, looking at me without really looking at me. But after I finished speaking she turned to face me. She tugged at a few tufts of her hair again.

"I'm sure they d-d-didn't mean it, C-Cleo. I mean, they asked us to c-c-c-come meet them, right?" Layla looked back at the mirror version of me. "That has to count for something."

But they didn't invite me, and maybe that was what Layla was forgetting. They invited *her*. I felt it in my ribs, the pain of her refusal to immediately write off someone who was hurting me, to protect me the way she always had in the past. It fractured something inside me—her choice to be loyal to them instead.

I didn't know what to say next, so I pushed open the bathroom door. When we got a little closer to the fountain she looked down at me, then over at everyone else. For a second she went all breathless, her stutter catching the words in her throat before they could creep past her lips, and it felt like a sign; a warning that I wouldn't like what she said next.

"You mmmind if I stay here a little longer?" she asked.

"I guess I don't," I said, lying to myself and to her. "Maybe I'll see you later?"

I said it like a question, but Layla didn't answer. She just smiled. And as I walked away alone, past the other girls, I waved goodbye, but my heart wasn't in it.

"Bye, Chloe!" Sage said enthusiastically. And someone else said, "OMG, Sage. It's *Cleo*," but I didn't look back to see who.

"I didn't even invite her," I heard one of them say when they thought I was too far away to hear. I didn't turn my head for that either. I knew in my bones it was Sloane. A second later, I got a text from Layla.

Y.O.E.

For the first time, I wasn't sure I believed her.

now

LOLLY & POP

I still go to meet Dom at Dolly's after school, even though Ms. Novak told me he doesn't need me. Some part of me wants to find out why he asked for my help with the paper in the first place, but mostly I'm just happy that he did. I want to pretend that he's who I'm assigned to tutor instead of Layla, if only for a little while. Plus, if Sunday is any indication, Dom has the uncanny ability to make me feel better just by being himself.

The street is quiet save for the occasional jogger and small surges of noisy, busy people exiting the subway station on the corner. I ignore them all and look up at the sky, wondering what it might be like to live in a place with less light pollution—where I might be able to see dozens of constellations—stars worth defying, as Shakespeare wrote.

When Dom comes out of the restaurant, he's wearing a dark peacoat and he's wrapping a thick black scarf around his neck. He smiles at me and I can't help but return the grin.

"So, where to?" I ask, taking a small step away from him. Dom takes a beanie out of his pocket and pulls it down over his ears.

"Jesus, it's freezing," he says. He looks over at me and then reaches out and tucks the tail of my scarf against the only bit of my neck that's still visible. His hands smell sweet, like the soap from the diner bathroom, and they're warm against my skin. But I still shiver at the contact.

"My place is just a few blocks away," Dom says. "I live with my Lolly and Pop."

I grin and quirk one of my eyebrows. We start walking, and I look at him out of the corner of my eye. "Your who and what?" I ask.

He coughs out a laugh and lifts his backpack higher onto his shoulders with his thumbs. Steam from our warm mouths fills the cold air between us, and I imagine it forming the shapes of his words. "I meant, I live with my *grandparents*." He looks at me, and if his skin weren't the rich brown of molasses cookies, I think I'd be able to see Dom blushing. "But, uh, yeah. Lolly and Pop. That's what I call them."

"Oh my God, Dom. That might be the cutest thing I've ever heard in my life. Please," I say. I press my hands together like I'm about to pray. "Please explain to me how this immeasurable cuteness came to be."

It feels nice to be out of my own head. To be distracted by a beautiful boy on a beautiful night. Dom reaches into his pocket again, and this time he pulls out gloves. He nudges me with his elbow, and the streetlights make his face glow.

"Well, the short version of the story is that Lolly is what I call my grandmother. Her first name is Dolores, Dolly for short, and when I was a kid I couldn't really say her name right."

I nod and grin a little more while keeping my eyes on the ground, watching the steps we take in tandem. "Dolly of Dolly's Diner fame," I say. I hear a smile in his voice when he answers.

"Right. And I called my granddad Pop-Pop when I was little, and as I got older it shortened itself to just Pop or, you know, Pops." He pauses. "You ever notice how language changes over time like that?"

It sounds like a rhetorical question, so I don't say anything. But when Dom doesn't continue, I glance away from the sidewalk and up at him. He's looking at me like he's waiting for me to speak up. So I nod.

"Yeah," I say, because I think about language all the time. "Like, with my Granny Georgina. I always called her Gigi, which was her nickname for her whole life because it was short for Georgina. But it was also, ironically, the initials of my name for her: G.G. Words are kind of incredible that way. They have a mind of their own. But I guess the coolest thing about it is that by changing your language, you can change the way you experience the world. If that makes any sense."

When I look over again, Dom's still watching me. "It makes perfect sense, Shorty," he says.

I hesitate, then continue before I overthink what to say. "Calling my grandmother Gigi made me feel more grown-up than I was, you know? And hearing you call your grandparents Lolly and Pop changed the way I saw you right away."

"Wait," he says. He touches my arm and stops walking. For the moment, there's no one else on this part of the street. The whole block feels like it belongs to us. "How'd you see me before you knew about the Lolly-and-Pop thing?"

"You mean how did I see you literally five minutes ago?" I joke. He nods and he looks so serious. "Oh, I don't know," I say.

"You do!" he says, and then, softly: "Can you please tell me?"

The dark feels darker with the sound of Dom's voice filling the space between us, making me crave more quiet evenings and cold nights like this one. The darkness makes me love living in a place where taking a short walk with a boy after a day full of stress and sadness can feel like magic.

"You're Dominic Grey," I say. "You're . . . I don't know. This new boy who was instantly popular. You're a smartass and girls like you and you're on the soccer team already. You have these *haircuts* and all the coolest shoes. And though I've seen you do magic, which I guess *is* pretty nerdy"—he laughs at this—"I never would have guessed you'd be so into cooking that you'd work for free in a diner kitchen or call your grandparents such cute things. I thought you'd be into, like, cars and rap music or something."

He bites his lip. Then he nods. When he blinks, I can't help but notice how curly his eyelashes are—they nearly double back to touch his eyelids. He says, "Romanticizing people is dangerous, Cleopatra."

I squint at him. "Now I'm Cleopatra?" I ask. "Why can't you just call me by my actual name?"

He shrugs. "Change your language to change how you experience the world, right? I'm gonna call you Cleopatra, if that's cool with you. I wanna challenge you to experience the world a little differently. Maybe if I call you Cleopatra, instead of Shorty"—he grins, and I groan—"you'll start to think a little *bigger*."

I frown even though I kinda want to smile. "You're weird, you know that?" I say, and I start walking again even though I don't know where we're going.

"No weirder than you," he says as he follows me. "But you were right. I do like cars and rap music."

I laugh.

"Where's your Gigi now?" he asks a second later.

"She died a couple of years ago."

"Oh. My bad."

"It's okay."

We're quiet for the next few minutes. It's not exactly uncomfortable, but it's strange to walk and only hear the sounds of the city. Barking dogs and distant sirens; car horns and wind-rustled leaves. Plastic bags and crumpled paper blow along the sidewalks like tumbleweed does in old westerns; two kids run past us squealing. I haven't taken a walk with anyone since Layla and I stopped speaking, and between that and talking about Gigi, I feel the sadness descending again. But when I glance over at Dom, he has a look on his face that isn't quite a frown but may be the beginnings of one.

"So should I call them Mr. and Mrs. Grey?" I ask to lighten the mood again. "Or do I get to go with the endearing 'Lolly and Pop' too?"

"Oh, Lolly and Pop, without a doubt," Dom says. He points to a tall brownstone just ahead of us with an ornate stone stoop. There's a pretty gray cat sitting on the center stair and it doesn't run away. When we get close enough, Dom bends down and scratches it under its neck. The cat closes its pearly-blue eyes.

Instead of watching the slow movements of Dom's fingers in the cat's thick gray fur, I look up at the pretty building.

"This is home," he says.

THE GREYSTONE

"Pop's still at the diner. But you're going to love my Lolly," Dom tells me as he pushes open the front door of the brownstone. The cat strides in like she owns the place. "That's Stormy Skye, by the way," he says, pointing to her. "You can call her Miss Skye. Or Stormy, but only if she says it's okay."

Dom's house, is, well, a *house*. There is a small foyer, and tall windows with lacy curtains, and stairs that lead not to more apartments but to more of *his house*. The long hallway directly in front of us leads to the kitchen, which is brightly lit and colorful. It's so warm that my glasses fog up right away, and the whole place smells like spun sugar and butter.

Even though we've had a whole conversation about his names for his grandparents, hearing Dom say "my Lolly" out loud still makes me want to squee. The cat, which seems to follow his every move, doesn't help. As my glasses clear, I watch Dom shrug off his backpack and leave it and his coat on the floor, then kick off his boots. A small, broad-shouldered woman with very brown skin and extremely white hair meets us in the entryway.

She immediately walks over and hugs me, though I've never

seen her before in my life, and the scent of her skin reminds me of Gigi—something sweet mixed with something essential.

"Well, ain't you a cutie," she says. "Where'd you get all them freckles?" She moves a few of the braids that are hanging over my eyes and tucks them behind my ear, and while the gesture feels like a "correction" whenever my mom does it, with Dolly it feels a little like love. She doesn't exactly study my face, but it kind of looks like she's committing something about me to memory. I can tell she's old, but everything about her is sturdy and straight.

After Dom leans down to kiss her cheek, she raises her eyebrows in his direction and says, "Dominic. Manners, baby. Who is your friend, here?"

"This is Cleo Baker. We're in a bunch of classes together at school and she's gonna help me with my *Macbeth* paper."

Miss Dolly touches my shoulder. "Well, Cleo, it's lovely to meet you. Welcome to the Greystone. You make yourself right at home."

I grin because I already feel like I belong here. "The Greystone?" I ask, and Dom laughs a little.

"Oh yeah. When I was little, I thought the individual brownstones were supposed to be named after the people who lived there. Our neighbors' last name was Brown, so I thought that's why their house was a *brown*stone. Ours is Grey, so . . ."

Miss Dolly pats Dom on the cheek and I smile. "That's so adorable I can't even stand it. And sorry, I meant to say it's nice to meet you too, Miss Dolly. Is it okay for me to call you that?"

She pretends to fluff her hair and she flutters her eyelashes. Those are white, too.

"No one's called me that in years, Sweet Pea. You make me feel like a young woman again."

"Well, if you've still got it . . . ," I say, looking her up and down. She's wearing a floral apron over jeans and a black sweater, and she's surprisingly slender. She has the kind of face you can tell was drop-dead gorgeous thirty years ago. She's still pretty now.

She laughs loudly. "I like her," she says to Dom a little conspiratorially. And when I look over at him, he's studying me in the slow way his grandmother was just a few minutes earlier.

"I think the feeling's mutual, Lolly."

"Why don't y'all get set up in the den?" Miss Dolly suggests, and at almost the same time Dom says, "What you bakin'?"

"Smells like sugar cookies," I say.

"Well, ain't you somethin'?" Miss Dolly almost sings. "That's exactly right."

AMBITION

Dom leads me into a small, cozy room with a bricked-over fireplace; a mantel full of tall, dusty candlestick holders; and one whole wall covered with shelves full of books. Without thinking, I walk straight to the bookshelf, pull a heavy volume down at random, and flip through the pages. I inhale the familiar scent of old paper as it splashes over my face with each turning page. When I open my eyes, Dom is right in front of me, only inches away, staring.

I drop the book, but Dom catches it. "Jesus," I breathe, "You scared me."

"Sorry," he says. When I look at his hands, I see that the book is a really old edition of a Shakespeare-quotation dictionary—a sign if ever there was one.

"You got a thing for books, then?" Dom asks, grinning.

"Oh, shut up," I say, only a little embarrassed. "But yeah, I guess. I kind of miss having a ton of books in my apartment." Dom looks a little confused, and I realize he knows nothing about the history of me. "My parents separated in December," I explain. "When my dad left, he took most of his books with him."

"Oh," Dom says. He doesn't look away from me the way some people do when you share sad or awkward information. "Your dad's cool. Sucks he doesn't live with you anymore. That's shitty."

I shrug. "Yeah, it is. But I guess it was fate, or whatever."

Stormy walks into the room and jumps up on the arm of the couch. Dom frowns a little. "Fate?" he asks skeptically. But before I can answer, Miss Dolly comes in with a plate of sugar cookies. She sets it on the coffee table beside the book of quotations.

"Getting started on that project already, huh?" she asks. "I like a girl who doesn't waste time." She smiles, displaying the deepest set of dimples I've ever seen.

"Thanks, Lolly." Dom shoves a whole cookie into his mouth immediately. Then he opens the book, flips to a page, and runs his finger along the columns of text a little too studiously. I grin.

"Well, let me know if you need anything else. Cleo, honey, you thirsty?"

I nod. "Do you have any tea?"

She smiles. "Of course. Do you take it with milk and sugar?"

"Just lots of milk," I say.

"You got it, hun." She nods. "I'll bring some water in for you both too," she says before disappearing again.

For a second, Dom and I just watch each other. I wonder if he's going to ask me more about my parents, and I silently hope that he won't. But he just kicks his feet up. He's still holding the massive book, so he looks pretty silly.

"I didn't know you were funny," I say. I head over to sit beside him on the couch, and I scratch Stormy between her shoulder blades. Then I reach for a cookie. It's gooey and warm, and the crystals of sugar sprinkled on top melt against my tongue.

Dom lowers the book a little, so all I can see are his dark eyes. Even so, I can still tell he's smiling. "You don't know most things about me, Cleopatra," he says.

—

We relocate to Dom's bedroom, which is on the second level of his grandparents' beautiful house. Dom tells me that his grandmother always tries to get him to "entertain" in the den, but the room kind of gives him the creeps and he's more comfortable upstairs. He tells his grandmother there's better lighting, "which isn't exactly a lie," he assures me.

His walls are exposed brick and mostly bare, save for a few framed black-and-white photographs. All of his furniture is large and old, but stacked with things like comic books and half-finished Lego structures, film cameras and goofy oversized sunglasses. There are books everywhere. I walk over to look through his window.

"I think I wanna write about ambition," Dom says. He sits down backward in a spinning desk chair and wraps his arms around the backrest like it's a pillow.

I sit down in his window seat, which is piled with soft, sun-faded pillows. I don't want to be caught staring at Dom's biceps, so I make sure to look straight at his serious, brown eyes.

"Ambition," I repeat as I reach for another one of the cookies we brought upstairs with us.

He nods. "I think Macbeth's ambition is the main reason his life went so horribly wrong. It's his fatal flaw."

"But what about the prophecy?" I say, challenging him. "Maybe his fate was already sealed, so it didn't matter that he was ambitious. It didn't matter what he wanted. Regardless of the choices he made, maybe things would have ended up precisely the same way."

I think about the party where Layla and I met Sloane and how, when I look back, it feels like that day set our unraveling in motion. The signs were all there. Our fate was sealed the second Sloane heard Layla sing.

"I don't think so," he says, slowly.

"But what about the stars?" I say. "What about how they 'govern our conditions'?"

"What about our destinies not being in the stars, but in ourselves?" Dom asks, raising his eyebrows, and I don't think I've ever before been out-Shakespeared by anyone but my dad. For a moment, I'm shocked to silence. Dom stands up and lights an incense stick, and a thin, fragrant wisp of smoke spins into the air. He sits down on his bed without looking away from the falling ash.

"Stars are just random balls of hydrogen and helium collapsing because of gravity. Most stars are dead by the time we see them anyway. It's almost like looking at the past," Dom says, turning to glance at me for a second. "*Not* the future. You're staring at something that doesn't even exist anymore. And all those people making wishes? It's like they're making a wish on a lie."

I lean closer to the window, looking out and up into the sky.

"They're pretty little lies, though," I say, thinking he'll like the turn of phrase. I look back at him and smirk.

He gets up and walks over to open a door in the corner of his room that I assumed was a closet. He flips a switch, and a stairwell that leads farther up fills with honey-colored light.

"If you wanted to see stars," Dom says a little devilishly, "you should have said so."

PRETTY LITTLE LIES

Dom's secret stairwell leads to a small rooftop deck strung with firefly lights and furnished with cute café tables and chairs like the ones in the diner. From up here, I can see what looks like miles of rooftops, plus the ever-darkening sky and Manhattan skyline. There's ivy crawling up the brick walls that box us in and block the wind, so I feel warmer up here than I did on our walk home.

"I feel like I should suggest we work on your paper," I say. I'm nervous he'll say something about not really needing my help, that he'll say something that reveals why he really asked me here tonight, but he doesn't. I pull the sweatshirt he let me borrow a little tighter around my body. I look back at him. "You bring all the girls up here, don't you?" I ask him.

Dom shrugs, but I see that he's smiling. He takes a few steps away from me and walks over to the railing, and I can't help but think about the party at Valeria's where I first met him. We were on a roof then too. He looks out over the city, and I wish he'd take down the hood he flipped over his head before he pushed the door open. I want to see his profile. I want to see the newest design shaved into his bristly black hair.

"We can still talk about *Macbeth* outside, Cleo," he says, and I think this might be the first time he's ever said my name. I like the way it sounds in his voice. He turns around and pulls out a café chair. He motions for me to sit down, so I do and he follows.

"If you're going to write about Macbeth's ambition," I say, "you have to mention the catalyst. I don't think you can say he was a murderous madman driven *only* by ambition. I think you have to start with the fact that it was prophesied. You have to start where things started for him: with the witches."

"I will," Dom says. He nibbles his lip like he's thinking, and I look up at the sky so he doesn't feel rushed. "But do you really think the prophecy would have come true either way?" I nod, without turning to face him right away.

"Here's what I think," I say. "Maybe his actions were influenced by his ambition, but don't you think fate takes our character into consideration? I mean, he was a *soldier*. If anything, he should have had *more* respect for life and duty and honor than the average guy. But he didn't. And if he could be driven to do something so morally wrong so easily, the universe knew he had it in him all along." I realize too late that it feels like a description of me and the stuff I did to Layla. I feel a sudden ache at the back of my throat, but I swallow hard and try to ignore it.

"I think Macbeth would have realized he wanted to be king. He would have told his cray-cray wife, and one way or another, the two of them would have figured out a way to make it happen." I turn to face Dom, and he's leaning forward with his elbows on his knees, watching me. "It was destined to end the way that it did."

"But Macbeth still made certain choices that led to that end, right? I mean, he had the power to change if not what happened, at least *the way* it did. There's no way you think that free will is nonexistent and that the universe dictates everything, like we're puppets."

I shrug. "All I know is there are signs littered throughout the text that makes it read as if fate is running the show, not Macbeth. So." I flip open the notebook we brought up with us. "I think you should start by arguing that—"

I feel my phone buzz, and I reach into the pocket of Dom's sweatshirt to grab it. "Sorry," I say. "It's probably my mom."

I ignore her call. Then I ignore the next one. By the third time it starts to vibrate, I realize she won't stop unless I answer, but I try silencing it one last time. Dom gets curious. He leans over and tries to look at my screen. "Excuse you," I say to him. I push the phone back into the pocket of the sweatshirt.

"Something important?" Dom asks. And I shake my head. I swallow and look back at the notebook, but I've forgotten what we were talking about or why I'm even holding the pen. I know I'll have a fight waiting for me when I get home because I'm technically still "grounded." Dom scoots his café chair forward, and the noise of it scraping the floor slices through the silence. When I look up he's much closer to the table. Much closer to me. The scents of soap and incense are stronger.

"I read somewhere that for every lie someone tells they get a freckle," he says, and I know he's teasing, trying to make me laugh, but I still reach up and cover my speckled face with my hands.

"Shut up," I say. "You know you've never heard that before."

I peek at him through my fingers. He's grinning, and I want to forget about my mom's calls. I want to forget about this stupid Shakespeare paper and just talk to Dom for the rest of the night about anything we want. But then my phone starts buzzing *again*.

When I pick up, my Mom says, "Where *are* you, Cleo?"

I don't want to tell her. I don't want her to know that I'm on a chilly rooftop with a nearly perfect boy, who is smart and funny and who likes to cook and read. I don't want to tell her that tonight is the first time I've felt genuinely happy in weeks.

"I'm on my way home now," I say, instead of a single word of truth. "I'll be there in twenty minutes."

I hang up and look at Dom. I jot down a few quick notes based on what we talked about, and then I thrust the notebook at him. "Sorry, I have to go. Text me if you have questions, though, okay?"

I start walking toward the door that leads back into the house.

"You were wrong about the stars," he calls after me. I look back at him, even though my mother is waiting. I don't want to go home, so it isn't difficult for me to let Dom's voice hold me in place.

"I get it," I say. "Our will governs our fate. Macbeth's ambition ruined him, not the prophecy, right? We'll have to agree to disagree. But I want to read your paper when it's done. I hope you don't have to stay up all night." I turn to leave again.

"Nah, Cleo. I'm not talking about that." He stands up and takes a few steps forward, closing the space between us. He reaches out and touches the tips of his fingers to a few random places on my face: above my left eyebrow, atop my right cheek-bone, just below my bottom lip. I know he's pointing to some of my darkest freckles. I slap his hand away, and he laughs.

"*These* are the pretty little lies," he says. "Not the stars." His eyes leave mine and seem to land on the lower part of my face, close to what can only be my mouth. My lips part, and so do his.

"I gotta go," I say, and I run down his stairs and out of his house as quickly as I can.

PRICELESS PEOPLE

When I get home, my mom is waiting up for me. She calls me into her bedroom and grills me about school and why I didn't come home right away. I settle on the bed beside her to tell her about tutoring. She's instantly less angry. Maybe even impressed.

"Well, I asked you to take an active interest in your future and you really came through." She grips my chin and wiggles my head a little, and that small gesture warms me to her. "I know you have it in you; that's why it drives me *so crazy* anytime you do something that doesn't live up to your potential."

She takes a deep breath and sits up a little straighter. "I had a long talk with your father," she says.

I hold my breath, nervous about what she'll say next. I look through her dark window and listen to the growing and fading siren of an ambulance as it approaches and passes our building. Whenever she talks about Daddy, her eyes get so sad.

"He told me that you've been having a hard time at school because of something that happened between you and Layla?"

I study my fingers—the rings I'm wearing and my chipped nail polish—instead of looking up at her. "Yeah. We're not really friends anymore," I say simply. I somehow manage to keep most of the pain—and rage—out of my voice. "And I don't really want to get into the details of why. I just want to move on with my life. And get *over* it."

But I can't when I'm going to have to tutor her, I suddenly realize. I can't erase someone who insists on writing all over my life in ink. And I feel that weight settle on my chest again. I feel powerless against the stars and how they continue to thrust Layla and me together.

Mom puts her hand on one of my knees and I flare my nostrils to keep the onslaught of tears I feel building at bay. The gesture is so gentle and honest that it makes me want to call her *Mommy,* like I did when I was little, because even though we fight all the time she can always tell when I'm close to crying. For a second, I want to tell her everything.

"I know what it's like," she says too softly, "to lose your best friend." And her voice has a familiar darkness to it. I know she's talking about Daddy.

"Do you think it's worth it," I say a little hesitantly, because I haven't talked to Mom, *really* talked to her, in forever, and this isn't even a question I've allowed myself to entertain inside my own head. She closes the laptop that had been open in her lap this whole time, so I know she's really listening. "Do you think it's worth it to try to make things right? I was reading all this stuff over the weekend about apologies, and friendship dissolution, shame, and vulnerability, and it all seems so overwhelming. So overly complicated."

She lets out a heavy sigh.

"You're a smart girl, Cleo, but sometimes you rely too much

on your head instead of your heart. This may not be something a book will help you navigate."

I hug my knees to my chest. "Daddy said the same thing," I mutter.

Mom nods. "If you love someone," she says, "it's always worth it . . . to try. You only get a few truly priceless people in your lifetime. You should fight like hell to hold on to them."

I'm a little surprised by her earnestness, by the passion rooted deep inside her voice.

"What about you and Daddy?" I ask quickly, because I feel like we're connecting. I've tried having this conversation with her before and she's shut me out, but I still want to know. "Do you feel like you fought hard enough for him?"

Instantly, her eyes go flat, and I watch as all the doors inside her that fell open as we talked slam resolutely shut. She's not *Mommy* by the time I've finished my question—by the time I know it's too late to take any of it back. She's *Naomi Bell* again, just like that.

"What happened between your father and me is different. But I do think making things right with Layla is possible if you're honest with her."

I can tell our moment has passed, and I'm more disappointed than I would have expected to be. The lump in my throat has melted away, and I regret bringing up Daddy. I hurt her feelings, but *sorry* seems like the wrong thing to say.

I stand up. "I still have some homework to finish," I say.

She blinks a few times and smooths a strand of her dark hair. Her ears look naked without shiny earrings dangling from the lobes, and I realize this is the first time in a while I've seen her at home but not dressed for work. "Of course," she says. She gestures at her laptop. "I have some more work to get done too."

She calls out to me before I reach the door. "But, Cleo," she says. I turn to look back at her, thinking that I need to be more careful with how I ask people about the broken pieces inside them.

"I'm still here . . . if you need to talk," she says.

—

In my dim bedroom, I'm more confused than ever. I don't know if trying to erase Layla is right, or even possible. I don't know if I want to be her friend again.

I peer through the low light to my row of snow globes. Gigi gave me a new one every year for my birthday until she died. I hadn't turned twelve yet the summer she passed away, but when we were cleaning out her apartment, we found the twelfth one already wrapped and ready. I lift that one from the shelf now—it's full of a miniature London, with Shakespeare's Globe Theatre at its center.

The following year, on my thirteenth birthday, I was nearly inconsolable until Layla showed up with a small wrapped box. When I opened it, I found a gorgeous snow globe encapsulating a new city I could dream of visiting one day. Layla promised we would fly there together as soon as our parents would let us. I pick up that one next. It's full of glitter instead of white pearls of fake snow.

A tiny Eiffel Tower stands atop a metal miniature of the rest of the city of Paris. I love this snow globe because it has so much weight to it. I wish I could shrink and live inside the scene. I shake it, and as I watch the glitter float and shine, I imagine what it would be like to be honest with Layla. To tell her I'm sorry and to hear her say that she is too.

What if we were fated to fall apart only to come back together again?

I want to believe that we can both be forgiven, but I don't know if, like inhabiting the tiny Paris I hold in my hand, that's just another dream that will never come true.

then:
October

WE SO SUCK AT PARTIES

"We're gonna g-g-go, right?"

Layla convinced me to go to Chinatown with her so we could look for cheap costumey things to wear to Sloane's Halloween party, but I was still secretly considering skipping it. For one, it was Sloane. And two, Layla and I already had a Halloween tradition. But it was starting to feel like all the things we used to do together weren't as important to her as they once were.

"Where to first?" I asked. "And yes, Layla, God. We're going. But only because you promised to do our normal sleepover after."

Layla clapped her hands and looped her arm through mine. "Yay! Ok-k-kay, so. There are g-g-great options nearly everywhere." She waved her hand like she was personally responsible for conjuring up Chinatown, fully formed. Red Chinese characters were on the fronts of all the buildings, and street vendors peddled everything from folding fans and silk scarves to jewelry, handbags, and hats.

"I still have that mask I got when I went to see *Sleep No More* with my dad," I said, picturing its long beak and giant eye holes as we turned onto Canal Street. Autumn hadn't hit the city completely yet, and it was nearly seventy degrees. I knew old Chinese ladies were probably practicing tai chi in the nearby parks, and the thought of their slow movements and wide hats made me smile.

"No way," she said immediately. "We're going for c-c-c-cute, not creepy. It's the first chorus p-p-party I've b-been invited to. We need to look *good*. We need to c-class it up."

We navigated the crowded sidewalk side by side, pushing our way past tourists and experienced New Yorkers haggling over purses and buying fruit. Layla was wearing a pair of pale blue skinny jeans under a knee-length yellow dress with long sleeves, and she looked like a flower in the sea of darker fall colors everyone else was wearing. That included me, because I was in my typical black T-shirt and ripped jeans. I knew whatever costume she ended up with would be full of light, just like she was.

"I think we can fffffind something good for you over there," she said, pointing across the street.

We slipped into one of those pop-up costume stores that seem to appear and disappear all within the month of October every fall. "Luckily for you, I'm g-g-getting a vision," she said. She made a frame out of her thumbs and pointer fingers like she was zooming in on me with a camera. "Maybe something Shakespearean?"

In the end, I found myself standing in my room wearing white satin gloves with a few drops of fake blood on them to represent the blood on Lady Macbeth's hands, a watch necklace for how often she checks the hour, and a lacy black dress I'd never normally have the guts to wear that we found at a consignment shop. Layla helped me pin my braids into a bun, and my mask was thin and lacy too. Layla said all I needed was a little red lipstick to complete the look. I almost never feel that I look exactly as I want to, but with Layla's help, I was perfect.

Deep down, though, I still didn't want to go to the party, no matter how pretty I felt in my costume. And when Layla started humming her chorus audition song to herself it felt like a sign— a bad one. Though I used to love Layla's singing, now it just reminded me that there was this whole new section of her life that I wasn't a part of: she was a Chorus Girl and I never would be.

When Layla asked me to help with her hair, I lifted the flatiron and just tried to think about our sleepover. About how we'd sit in the dark and watch a bunch of movies and creep up behind the couch to scare each other every time one of us went to the bathroom. I'd finally tell her about how my parents had been acting weird and distant with each other lately, using me to pass information between them like I was a carrier pigeon. I didn't want to tell her before the party because she'd want to help. She'd insist we go to my house and somehow fix it all right away.

"So do you think you'd really be able to convince your parents to let you come visit me in London this summer?"

"Maybe," Layla said, "since my aunt is j-just a train ride away." She grinned at me in the mirror. "And then we'd go to P-P-Paris." She hopped up and grabbed my Parisian snow globe. "Think it's a sign that I was the person who g-g-g-gave you this?" she asked, sitting back down with the snow globe still in her hands.

She shook it as I separated another chunk of her hair and said, "Obviously."

"Do you still miss your g-g-grandmother as much as you used t-to when we were k-k-k-kids?" she asked out of nowhere.

I bit my lip and watched her in the mirror. She looked up at me. "Yeah," I said. "I still think about her all the time. Especially when my mom is overreacting about dumb stuff. Talking to your mom helps calm her down sometimes, but Gigi knew exactly what to say to make her chill, you know?"

Layla nodded.

"She flipped out on my dad the other day," I started, but then Layla's phone chimed. I saw what the text said even though I wasn't actively trying to look. It was from Sloane.

What did Mason say about Friday?

In the mirror, Layla's reflection set down the snow globe and picked up the phone.

I draped a handful of warm, straight hair over Layla's shoulder, and I swallowed hard against a sudden dryness at the back of my throat. I wanted to tell her about my parental weirdness. But I also wanted to know why *I* didn't know anything about Friday.

It was a strange feeling—not knowing something about my own best friend.

I watched my own eyes in the mirror, afraid that if I looked into Layla's all the softest parts of me would show, especially since we'd just been talking about Gigi. I wanted to make sure I didn't look like I was already hurt and trying to get to a truth that not so long ago would have been mine without having to ask.

"You think Mason will be at the party tonight?"

Layla put her phone facedown without texting back and reached for her mascara. She stroked both her upper and lower fringes of lashes twice before she answered. "I think so," she said. She screwed the mascara closed, set it on my dresser, and stared at it. "I hope so." She turned around to face me, and hope bloomed in my belly like a flower. But all Layla said was "Can you hand me those earrings?"

Layla was going as a fairy. She was in a wispy long blue dress and had picked out a set of glittery, translucent wings from the pop-up Halloween shop. Her mask was silver, and so was all the jewelry she was wearing. I finished straightening her hair and she showed me how to blot the lipstick I'd messily applied. Layla's parents were not fans of Halloween and thought it was haram (forbidden in Islam), so she'd told them she was just sleeping over again like usual, not dressing up and going out. We couldn't post pictures anywhere that they might find, but we took a bunch anyway.

Layla was quiet while we rode the train to Sloane's. I pointed out some of the craziest costumes, but even a baby dressed like a sushi roll didn't make her smile. I thought she might be worried about impressing the Chorus Girls again.

"They already like you, Layla," I said. I wrapped my arm around her hip and pulled her closer to me as the train rocketed along the tracks. "They invited us to this party, didn't they? And you're in chorus now. You're like, *official*." She squeezed me back, and though we swayed together as the train moved, it felt like there was more than just the fabric of our jackets between us.

She was still quiet as we walked down the darkened streets in Sloane and Valeria's neighborhood. "You okay? We can go home," I said. "We can go to my apartment right now and we can help my dad make his world famous chocolate-covered popcorn."

I started tugging her back toward the train station. "No, no. I still w-w-want to go," she finally said. "I swear."

"We so suck at parties," I muttered.

129

SOMETHING WICKED THIS WAY COMES

It was strange being back inside Valeria's apartment, which I hadn't seen since summer. This time it was decked out with fake spiderwebs, and pumpkin confetti was dusted across the table near the door, a bowl overflowing with candy perched on top. A rap song I didn't know was playing and a bunch of kids were dancing in the center of the living room. It was full but not overly crowded, so it was easy for us to walk down the short entryway. Layla started looking around for Sloane, and when she found her, we made our way over.

"Hey!" Layla shouted. Sloane turned, and when she saw Layla, she threw her arms open wide, almost spilling her drink. "You came!" she shouted, and she seemed so happy to see her that I felt an instant tightness in my stomach. Layla grabbed my arm and pulled me forward.

"Cleo's here, too!" she said, but Sloane either didn't hear or didn't care.

"Hey, bitches. Layla's here!" Sloane shouted over the music to a few girls dressed in the same costume she was. They were all in short, tight black habits; knee-high socks; and heels: naughty nuns. The word "basic" bounced around my head, but I didn't say it out loud. "L, you totally should have done this group costume with us. But, I mean, I get why you didn't," she said, nodding sagely. "Seriously."

All of it struck a wrong note with me. The costumes, the nickname, Sloan's passive-aggressive "I get why you didn't" that sounded like she didn't get it at all. I also didn't like that I had no idea about this group costume. I bet not dressing up like a nun was probably why Layla was so nervous on our way here. *Why didn't she just tell me?*

"Who are you guys?" I asked.

Sloane shook her head and pulled out a pair of sunglasses with round frames. The other Chorus Girls—Sage and Cadence, Valeria and Melody—all lined up beside her after saying hi to Layla. Sloane slipped the glasses on, put her hand on her hip, and said, "We're *Sister Act!*"

I nodded and smiled. I'd seen the movie a few times on cable. I looked at Layla, who seemed a little uncomfortable. "Cool," I said, failing to sound enthusiastic.

"Want to go find Jase and Mase?" I asked Layla, mostly because I wanted to move away from these girls to make sure she was okay.

"Yeah," she said to me, and then, "I'll b-b-b-be back," to Sloane and everyone else.

"You okay?" I asked as soon as there was enough distance between us and them.

She nodded. "I t-t-t-told them I didn't want to do dress up like that b-b-because someone's religious practices aren't a c-costume," she said. "I mean, I'd be pissed if someone threw on a hijab and w-w-was like, 'I'm g-gonna be Muslim for Halloween!'

Plus, I wasn't going to dress up like them when I knew I was c-c-coming with you."

"Oh," I said. "Yeah, that makes sense." I looked away from her for a second, down at my bloodstained gloves as I said what I said next, because it wasn't true, but I didn't want Layla to know. "I wouldn't have minded if you wanted to dress up with them, though."

"I know, but still." She lifted her mask, and her makeup made her eyes shine in the dark room. "I was worried they'd think 'the Muslim girl' was, I d-d-d-don't know, uptight or whatever."

"I get it," I told her, and it was true. We'd always been outsiders, and this was her chance to be a part of something that was very much on the inside. But there were still things about her that made it easier to stand out than fit in. Even if I wanted to, I wouldn't know how to change those kinds of things about myself.

"The offer to leave still stands, by the way," I said. She shook her head, elbowed me, and laughed.

"Would y-you stop with the leaving?"

—

We bumped into Jase a few minutes later.

"Cleo Imani Baker! And Layla Zafirah Hassan!" he shouted. Layla hated her middle name, and I had no idea how Jase had found out what it was. But he was grinning as he said it, and it was hard for anyone to be mad at Jase when he was grinning.

He and Mason were both dressed in all black, and knowing them, they were probably ninjas or something. I didn't ask. I pretended to be annoyed when Jase gave me a bear hug, but truth be told, I was so relieved to see his familiar face in this crowd I could have cried.

Mason looked at Layla like he'd been in a desert for hours and she was a tall glass of cold water.

"Hey," he said coolly. His brown bangs hung over his eyes like the tail of a comma, and he shook them away with a quick toss of his head. His voice seemed huskier than usual, but I just pressed my lips together and didn't say anything when he reached out and pinched a bit of the fabric on Layla's dress, gently tugging her forward.

"You guys want a drink?" Jase asked us.

"I think I do," I said. I normally wouldn't have anything, but with the Chorus Girls in their matching costumes, and with tension coming off Layla in waves, I wanted just a little something to take the edge off. I figured it couldn't hurt if I took it slow. I looked at Layla, who shook her head and moved a little closer to Mason. She tugged on one of the strings hanging from his hoodie. I expected her to say something about me having a drink, but she didn't. Which just made me want it more.

"Come with me," Jase said, grabbing my hand. Ever the wingman, he pulled me back toward the kitchen to give Mason and Layla some privacy.

Jase poured me something using more than one of the tall glass bottles on the counter, and the only ingredient I recognized was Coke. He watched me as I took a sip. "I . . . don't hate it," I told him, nodding my approval as he mixed something up for himself, and he grinned the widest version of his lovely, dimpled grin.

"You know about anything happening next Friday?" I asked him, because Jase had always been honest to a fault.

"I think Sloane is having another thing. Smaller, I think. You coming?" Jase asked. "I hope you'll beeeee therrree." He sang the words to the tune of the song that was playing, and because I didn't want my features to betray me, I laughed a little. I shook my head and took a sip of my drink.

"Can't," I said without further explanation. I swallowed down more of the mixed drink and said nothing else. The truth (that I hadn't even been invited) would have left more of a bitter taste in my mouth than the booze.

We stood together near the kitchen for a while, nodding to the music and looking around the party. Layla and Mason had started kissing. The nuns had all moved into the living room, and they were dancing in the center of everyone.

That was when I spotted him. Dom was standing across the room dressed like a badass warlock, in a hooded black robe, ripped black jeans, and thick-soled combat boots. I wondered if it was a nod to his sleight-of-hand magic. He pushed off his hood, and there was a series of stars shaved into his hair. They reminded me of the ones that topped every page of the Harry Potter novels. He was drinking out of a mug shaped like a mini-cauldron that matched his getup too well for him not to have brought it with him, and he looked really, *really* good. A minute later, he turned and saw me seeing him. He smiled.

I said a hasty goodbye to Jase and started in Dom's direction without hesitation, feeling buzzed, brilliant, and brave.

"Hey," I said. "Can you guess who I am?" I didn't know if Dom knew my costume, but I also didn't know if he knew I was the girl inside it, and for some reason I kind of hoped he didn't. Hiding behind the mask made me feel fearless and powerful.

Dom smirked. "Only if you can guess who I am first."

"Easy," I said. I sipped my Coke-and-who-knows-what-else. I pulled on the edge of his robe, and it sort of flopped open because he didn't have it zipped up. "And not that creative, considering you do magic all the time. Warlock."

"Close. But not nearly specific enough," he said, leaning closer to me so I could hear him over the music. This must have been what it looked like when Dom flirted. I liked it.

"Can I have a hint?" I asked. He nodded, and the rush of his breath against my neck gave me instant goose bumps.

"Something wicked this way comes," he whispered, and then he leaned his head toward the side of the room, where I saw that Jase had rejoined Mason. It took me a second, mostly because they hadn't committed nearly as much as Dom had (the robe made a huge difference), but then I realized that they too were holding cauldron-shaped cups. I was so surprised that I nearly dropped my unidentifiable drink.

Gondor bont weird sisters "No way," I squealed, completely losing my cool. I immediately wanted to grab and shake him for being so damn brilliant, because I knew Jase and Mason well enough to know that those knuckleheads didn't come up with these costumes. It had to have been all Dom. Overexcited, I blurted, "I'm Lady Macbeth!"

He took a step back and looked me over, a smile spreading slowly as he took in the small details of my costume. I flushed under his gaze. I could see him still connecting the dots when I got jostled into him as a few girls danced by us a minute later.

"Hi," I said again, this time very closely to his face. I'd put my hand on his chest to stop from falling, and he'd grabbed my elbow. Even after the girls passed, we kept holding on. "Hey," he said. He smelled smoky, like his cup was an actual cauldron, and I wanted to ask him what concoction he was drinking. But before I could take my flirting to the next level, I spotted Sloane and Layla over his shoulder.

Sloane was on the phone, and from her body language I could tell that she was pissed. Layla was in front of her, and she looked pretty concerned, too.

My best-friend alarm sounded somewhere in my head, and it was too loud to ignore, even with Dom only inches away from me.

"I'll be right back," I said to him, and I stumbled away through the suddenly thick crowd of bodies toward Layla.

"Lay, what's wrong?" I shouted, so she could hear me, because it seemed like the party was still increasing in volume. Layla turned as soon as she heard my voice, and she immediately looked a little relieved. "C-Cleo, thank God," she said, pulling me a few feet away. "Look, we have . . . a situation."

I frowned, but then I nodded. "Okay?"

Layla let out a heavy sigh and glanced toward the door. She took out her phone and pulled up a text from Cadence.

"C-C-Cady went outside to take a call and t-texted me," she said, and for a second I wondered when she had gotten on nickname terms with Cadence York.

The screen glowed bright in the dark, crowded room.

Omg!! Sloane's ex is down here. He's wasted. And I think he's coming up.

TODD

"Why is it a big deal that her ex is here?" I asked.

"I swear I'll explain later, b-b-but right now I just need you to *help* me."

"Okay, okay," I said. "But is it something juicy?" I raised my eyebrows.

"Are you g-g-going to be gross and g-gossipy or are you going to help?" Layla asked, putting one hand on her hip.

I laughed. "I was just—"

"Help or not, C-C-Cleo?"

"Help. *God.*" Layla got bossy when there was impending disaster, so I started to get that the ex coming over was serious even if I didn't understand why.

"Go watch the d-door, then. And make sure it's *locked.*"

I started toward the door, squeezing around drunk kids in all kinds of costumes. I tripped over the foot of a zombie cheerleader and got tangled in a Sailor Moon wig, and a sexy vampire almost spilled her drink on me.

When I finally made it to the door, I peered through the peephole, but the hallway was clear. I still had my own drink in my hand, so I took another big sip and turned around, looking back into the party. A *great* song came on, one of the few non-jazz-age ones that I liked, and I started bouncing, loving the light, buzzy feeling that was filling my head. Was this easy slowness, this delightful heaviness, what *drunk* felt like? I drank a little more of my drink, thinking about the music and how my limbs felt like they were a part of the song, and then my eyes popped open.

Oh crap, what if I *was* drunk?

I put down the cup and turned back to the door. I looked out again but still didn't see anyone. My head was all fuzzy. I felt like I was forgetting something.

I texted Layla. I think I'm drunk. I'm not sure I'm the best person for the door job.

Just as I hit send, the door I was supposed to be guarding burst open. The knob hit me hard in the small of my back.

"Ow," I said. And then, "Don't you knock?"

The boy standing in front of me was bleary-eyed and pretty. He had thick brown hair and bright green eyes rimmed in red, and he was almost as tall as my dad. He had a little bit of blond stubble on his chin and cheeks, and I spent more time than I'd like to admit thinking about how I didn't understand white people's coloring. (I didn't know a person could have brown hair and a blond beard. I wondered what that meant for the hair on his legs; the hair on his—)

"Where's Sloane?" the guy said, and I blinked a few too many times, like I was waking up.

My mind cleared, and in a single, horrifying moment I realized that *this* was Sloane's ex, the boy *I* was supposed to be preventing from entering the apartment.

Double crap.

"Um, I think you have the wrong apartment," I said. I tried to open the door and show him back out into the hall.

"I'm not an idiot," the guy said. He stepped around me so easily it was like I wasn't even there.

No. No no no. *Oh no.*

Everyone was still dancing, so I pushed back into the crush of bodies, hoping the guy would have as much trouble finding Sloane as I had making it to the door. I pulled out my phone. I couldn't see where Layla had gone and I didn't know where Sloane was, and the Chorus Girls were all suddenly MIA.

He's here, I sent to Layla. What do I do?

Shit, Layla sent back. How the hell did he get in if the door was locked?

Yikes. *That* was what I was forgetting. Triple crap.

It may not have been?

Jesus, Cleo. You had ONE job.

I could see Sloane's ex making his way through the party much more efficiently than me.

Where's Sloane?

She's in the bedroom with me. Valeria's coming out to try and get rid of him.

What does he even want?

"Sloane!" the guy yelled then. "I just want to talk to you! Sloane, where are you?!"

Valeria came into the room and tried to quiet the guy down

139

and usher him toward the door. Then Dom and Jase and Mason were there too. The party had gotten significantly quieter.

"Bro," Jase was saying. "You don't want to do this."

"You know you can't be here," Valeria said softly, and I wondered what she meant by that.

The guy pulled away from them all. "Sloane!" he shouted again.

Girls backed out of his way, and after a while, so did most of the guys.

"What the hell are you doing here, Todd?"

Sloane was standing near the back hallway, and I guess the other Chorus Girls had been trying to keep her in her bedroom until the situation was under control, but with Todd screaming, she couldn't be contained.

Her normally rosy cheeks were bright pink, from the wine coolers she'd been sipping all night or from the situation, I didn't know.

"I just want to talk, babe. That's all. Let's just talk, okay?"

Sloane looked around quickly, and maybe it was all of us staring at her, but something inside her seemed to snap.

"Everyone needs to get the hell out of here," she said.

When no one moved, she got louder. "Did you losers hear me? Get the fuck *out!*" She was bordering on hysterical, and even though she sounded mad as hell, there were tears in her eyes. Layla had her hand on Sloane's shoulder, and I could tell it was meant to be a comfort, but Sloane shrugged her off.

Some people yelled "Booooo," or "Worst party ever." Sloane disappeared into one of the bedrooms with Todd in tow.

I went looking for my jacket and found it on the floor near the chair I'd thrown it on when we first arrived, then went looking for Layla. She was in the kitchen stacking used cups to throw them away, and waving goodbye to people as they left.

"That was *so crazy*," I said. "But I guess we should go?"

"I'm g-g-going to stay here," Layla said. She didn't stop picking up empty cups or balling up napkins or dumping chips from bowls back into their bags.

"You're . . . staying?" I asked, like I hadn't heard her.

Layla nodded.

"But it seems under control, right? They went to go talk." Jase nudged me as he and Mason headed toward the door, and I reached up to hug him goodbye. Mason leaned forward and kissed Layla on the cheek.

"Sloane's . . . upset," Layla said to me as the guys left. Her mouth flopped open but no sound came out. I waited as she took a deep breath and started again. "I d-doubt she's g-g-going to want to be alone once T-Todd is finally gone."

"Of course she's upset. But why do *you* need to stay? Won't Valeria and Cadence and Melody *and* Sage be here?"

I listed them off on my fingers. Sloane had plenty of friends, but Layla was my only person.

Layla looked around at the emptying apartment. She took a deep breath and sighed before saying, "I just do, okay?"

"Is it because I forgot to lock the door? Are you pissed?" I felt my chin wobble a little bit. Yep, I was definitely drunk. "I told you. I think I'm kind of drunk."

Layla grabbed my hand and pulled me into the bathroom. She closed and locked the door and slipped off her mask before she said anything.

"Yes, okay? I'm p-p-pissed that you forgot to lock the d-door, but that's not the only reason. Some b-bad shit went d-d-down at Sloane's old school."

"Bad how?" I asked.

Layla hopped up on the sink and I sat on the toilet. She pulled out her phone, which she sometimes did when she had a long story to tell. She hated her stuttering even more when she had a lot to say. Layla typed for a long while, texting me detailed secrets about Sloane and Todd, and all that had happened at Sloane's old school. Things I had to swear I wouldn't tell anyone . . . ever. Things, Layla told me, no one knew except her and Valeria.

Layla took a few deep breaths as I read and read, letting all the information wash over me.

"Whoa," I said. "That's really messed up."

"Yeah," Layla agreed. "And she still loves him, C-Cleo. Even after everything."

Her nostrils flared, and she looked away from me. "I probably shouldn't have t-t-told you any of that. Swear it, C-C-Cleo. Swear you really won't t-tell anyone."

I swallowed around a sudden lump in my throat because I didn't know how long she'd known Sloane's history, but I did know we never used to have secrets. She was still the keeper of mine, but it seemed she'd become the keeper of someone else's too.

"I swear, Lay. I'm so sorry. I wish you'd said something sooner. I had no idea."

I wasn't used to sharing Layla, but after that story, even I could admit that Sloane needed her more right now than I did.

Layla reached out and touched my shoulder. "I know. My

mom thinks I'm st-st-staying over with you, though, so if she calls, c-c-c-can you like, c-cover for me?"

I hated lying to Mrs. Hassan, and if my mom picked up the phone it would be all over. But I sighed and agreed. Layla smiled sadly, and hugged me.

"Thanks. I'll t-t-t-text you later."

EMPTY THREATS

"So it was *you*?"

Sloane stormed up to my locker on Monday, right before homeroom. I had no idea what she was talking about or why she was even talking *to* me at all. She had barely ever spoken to me directly since the day we'd met.

"Uh, hi?" I said. "What are you talking about?"

Sloane looked behind her and stepped a little closer to me.

"Layla just told me she told *you* to lock the door at my party, and you didn't. That *you* were the one who let him in," Sloane whispered. She was standing so close to me that when she said the word "party" she spit on my face a little. I reached up to wipe it away.

"Oh," I said.

Sloane crossed her arms. Her cheeks had gone ruddier than they usually were under her freckles, so I could tell she was really mad. "Are you stupid? Were you really so wasted after one drink that you couldn't even figure out a lock?"

There was danger in the way she was looking at me. A little too much intensity for me to brush her off.

"Sloane," I said seriously, "Look. I'm really sorry. But if you didn't want him there, why didn't you just kick him out?"

She didn't look away from me, and her pear-green eyes felt almost sharp. I took a step back from her and hooked my thumbs under the straps of my backpack. I tried to look around her, to see if Layla was at her locker, but Sloane stepped into my line of sight.

"Are you really that dumb?" she said. She smirked and looked evil as hell. "You know what? You must be. Can't even lock a fucking door. Dumbass bitch."

The words landed like a punch. I was so shocked that I didn't say anything back right away. I stared at Sloane and she stared right back at me. She looked fierce, like a bird of prey or a big cat. *Vicious.*

"This isn't over," she said. I felt my mouth drop open, but before I found my voice, Sloane stormed away from me.

I stood there for a long time, stunned at her reaction. I knew I was officially on Sloane Sorenson's shit list, and I felt terrified, embarrassed, and so mad I could barely stand it.

Before, I'd felt a little guilty about letting Todd in, but now I didn't at all.

Fuck her. Her drama wasn't *my* fault.

I pulled out my phone. I speed walked to the closest bathroom, and my heart was pounding as I typed out a message to Layla. I couldn't believe she'd throw me under the bus, and I needed to know what really happened. I stayed huddled in the stall until I was almost late to class, waiting for her to text back. But she never did. And when I got to homeroom, she wasn't even there.

I was on edge for the rest of the morning, just waiting for Sloane to retaliate. I'd been bullied in middle school, but people calling me *Weirdo* or *Nerd* or *Freckle-Freak* hadn't prepared me for the vitriol I'd heard in Sloane's voice. And to make matters worse, I still couldn't find Layla, who had been my protector back then, whom I urgently needed to speak to now.

I'd been looking forward to lunch, knowing I'd see Layla there despite our differing schedules, but when I walked into the cafeteria, our table was empty.

I looked around, thinking maybe she got held up after class. Or thinking (somehow for the first time) that maybe she was home sick today. But then I saw her. She was sitting with Sloane and Melody, Cadence and Sage and Valeria. And I was so shaken that I almost walked right up to her to demand to know what the hell was going on. But Sloane was there. And I wasn't ready to face her again.

So I hid. I found an empty table in a far corner of the cafeteria and I sat down all alone.

I didn't eat. I typed out an angry series of texts to Layla. Then I watched her. She pulled out her phone and looked at it. She glanced around, but since I wasn't at our normal table, she had no idea where to find me. Then Sloane said something to her. I watched Layla shake her head and slip her phone back into her pocket without texting me back. And the hurt of seeing her ignore me in real time was worse than Sloane calling me a bitch. It was like a hot blade through the center of me, sharp and piercing.

—

146

I spotted Layla at her locker with Sloane and a few of the other Chorus Girls right after lunch. I hung back until they broke away from her, and it felt strange that I had to be strategic about approaching and talking to my own best friend. I didn't know when this change happened, but maybe it had been happening for a while, in tiny shifts that were too small to notice.

Layla was humming as I approached her. Her back was to me, so all I could see was her sleek black hair and hunched shoulders. I didn't tap her to get her attention, I just leaned against the locker beside hers and said, "Did you hear about what Sloane said to me this morning?"

Layla closed her locker and turned to face me. She acted cool, like she hadn't been ignoring me all morning. "I wanted to t-t-talk to you about that later."

I scoffed. "Layla, are you kidding? You told her I was the person at the door? The way she was freaking out, it's like she thinks I did it on purpose or something."

Layla threw her bag over her shoulder. She crossed her arms. "I d-didn't think she'd flip out on you, ok-k-kay? And I just said it in p-p-passing, that I'd asked you to lock the d-door. I didn't think she'd b-blame you for him showing up in the first place."

"Well, she clearly does," I said, and my voice caught in my throat.

The truth was, I was more hurt by how often Layla was breaking *her* promises lately, and the way she'd ignored me all day, than I was by Sloane's cruelty. I could feel us getting away from what I really wanted to ask her: Did she see what was happening to us; did she know why she was choosing these new friends over me again and again?

"But, Layla," I said, hating how pathetic I sounded. "What are you doing, sitting with them instead of me at lunch? Not texting me back all morning?"

"I'm sorry," she said. "It's just that Sloane's g-going through a tough t-t-t-time, okay? She really needs me right now."

But what about me? is what I thought. *What about Y.O.E.? What makes Sloane more important than us?*

"She basically *threatened* me," I said, and I immediately felt ridiculous saying it out loud, even though it was true.

Layla turned back to her locker. "Don't b-b-be so dramatic. She's just mad right now. She'll get over it. Can we t-t-talk about it more tonight? I c-c-can c-come over."

She hadn't answered my question about sitting with them instead of me at lunch. She hadn't given me an answer about why she hadn't texted me back. And my throat was constricting to hold back tears; it was getting harder and harder to swallow. I felt the tiny betrayals filling me up like poison, and I needed Layla to reassure me. To act like the best friend she was supposed to be.

But she didn't. And the longer we stood there, the clearer it became that Layla wasn't coming to my rescue this time.

I coughed to clear my throat, and when I started talking again I sounded almost normal. "I'm not sure. I have a lot of homework."

And she just nodded like this was okay. She nodded like everything was perfectly fine.

"Let me know, K?" she said. Then she closed her locker and walked away, leaving me behind.

now

LUNCHTIME BLUES

Another way Layla's absence has destroyed me? I no longer know where I fit in the minefield that is our high school's cafeteria—haven't since she started sitting with the Chorus Girls more and more back in November. Lunch used to be solace for me. Now it's torture.

For the last month or so, lunch has gone the same way: When I get to the cafeteria, I'll open up *Othello* or whatever book I have with me, eat, and awkwardly people-watch. I'll always see Jase and Mase walk past. They'll go to sit with the Chorus Girls because Mason always sits with Layla now. It makes me wonder how things are going with the two of them. The not knowing hurts more than it should by now.

Jase's bag lunch will still be in his backpack when they pass me by, some delicious mix of ginger chicken and rice or a beefy Chinese stew. He'll drum his fingers across my table, and Mase will lift his head to acknowledge me. "Hi. Bye," I'll say, a little embarrassed by how badly I wish they'd sit down and eat with me. I'll try not to think about how Jase used to share his lunch with me and whisper the Mandarin names of the foods into my ear whenever I asked, or the stories he'd tell me about the kids who made fun of his lunches when he was little. I'll wish there were a way to shift my thoughts permanently out of the past.

But today, when I walk into the caf, there are two people already waiting at my table. Sydney is leaning across her lunch tray saying something to Dom that's making him laugh. I feel instantly hot thinking about hanging out on his roof; how I wore a sweatshirt of his and how I'd recognize the scent of him anywhere. But I try to shake myself out of it. At least I don't have to eat alone today.

I smile as I approach the table. "Hey," I say, happy and confused all at once, but not wanting to question their presence.

"Dude!" Sydney says as soon as I sit down. I open my bag and pull out my food. "I heard you're cheating on us."

I frown and look up. "Um, what?"

She does her white-girl-hair-flip thing and her curls cascade down one side of her head like weeping willow branches. She's wearing complicated-looking earrings today that are made up of metal rods and circles. They glint and swing as she moves her head. "You're gonna tutor someone else, right? Because you skipped school?"

"How on earth do you know that?" I ask her. But she just clasps her hands together and tucks them under her chin. "Oh, I know people."

"So who is it?" Dom asks next. "I saw you in Novak's Hot Seat the other day, and I forgot to ask you about it last night. I knew something was going down."

I look down at my lunch tray. "It's Layla," I say. "And I'm not *cheating* on you just because you guys were the last people I tutored."

Sydney responds by pulling out her *Macbeth* paper, and it's clearly a revision. "This is the version I turned in to Novak, and she stopped me on my way to lunch and told me she'd read my introductory paragraph and she found it fascinating. She said she was *looking forward to seeing how my argument came together.*"

Sydney raises her eyebrows.

Dom nods, agreeing. "What we talked about really helped me pull mine together last night too," he says.

His dark eyes are aimed straight at me, and for a second, I'm back up on that roof with him, talking about fate and lies and stars. But then I remember how Novak said he didn't need a tutor.

"Why'd you even ask me for help?" I finally ask Dom. "Did you know he's second in our class?" I say to Sydney. *"Second."*

"Right. And *you're* first," Dom says. "Which means you're literally the only person I could go to for help other than Novak. And you're . . . how can I put this? More my type." He smirks.

I press my lips together and look away because I can't believe how overtly he's flirting with me, *right in front of Sydney.* I turn to her because I can't look at Dom.

"This thing with Layla is different, though," I start to explain. "We used to be friends, but she's . . . kind of a bitch to me now."

I chance a glance in the direction of her table, and she isn't looking my way. I shouldn't be surprised. I basically don't exist to her anymore.

"Oh, that's nothing," Sydney says. "See them?" She points across the cafeteria to a table where Willa Bae is twirling a piece of Lark Dixon's long blond hair.

"Yeah," I say.

"You see how she's, like, all over Lark?"

Dom kind of laughs and I say, "Yeah, Syd. It's not really surprising."

Willa is the biggest player at our school. In addition to having dated or kissed just about every queer and questioning girl at Chisholm, she's straight-up stolen a few guys' girlfriends. Still, she's almost universally loved, probably because she's the president of the GSA, captain of the softball team, and drop-dead gorgeous. Her black hair is short but the cut is so haphazard that it looks a little like the start of some kind of dark fire, and her nose is pierced, though her ears aren't. You'd expect someone like Willa Bae to hang out with the "Cool Asian Kid" clique, but she's a bit of a free agent. She starts to touch Lark's hands and forearms next, slipping one of nearly a dozen bangles off her wrist and onto Lark's. Lark giggles. Sydney clears her throat so I look back over at her.

"Right. Well, me and Willa have known each other forever, but in middle school we got really close. She'd come over a lot and keep me company because my dad worked all those late hours at the restaurant. She liked to bake and said it was a travesty that we had this amazing kitchen that my dad never actually used."

I nod, remembering. When I was tutoring Sydney last semester, sometimes I'd come to her apartment and Willa would be there. I hadn't noticed, but now that I think about it, Sydney's definitely been hanging out with her less.

"Your dad works at a restaurant?" Dom asks, and Sydney says, "Yep. He's a chef. It *sucks*."

"Really? I kinda think I wanna be a chef," Dom insists. And Sydney scoffs.

"You're too nice. Don't do it. It would ruin you. *Believe* me."

"But wait, what happened?" I ask Sydney, trying to get back to the subject at hand. "Between you and Willa, I mean."

"Um. I'll tell you *later*," she says. But she tilts her chin in Dom's direction and it's clear she doesn't want him to know.

Dom feigns shock and insult. But Sydney just sips her chocolate milk and stays silent.

After a few seconds, I say, as gently as I can, "So, I kinda want to know. You mind?" to Dom. I can't believe I'm asking someone to leave this table when, for the last month, I would have died for the company.

"You're serious?" Dom asks. And I look at Sydney.

"Why does no one take me seriously?" Sydney wonders aloud. "Is it because I have perfectly conditioned hair and I'm the president of the fashion club? Is it because people assume girls who like makeup and cute clothes are doing it for the male gaze, so it's strange that I don't *always* want dudes around?"

Dom clenches his teeth awkwardly and I stretch my eyes wide. "I think she's serious," I whisper.

"Damn," Dom says. But he collects his stuff and stands to leave. Sydney blows him a kiss and he rolls his eyes.

"Love ya, mean it," Sydney calls as he walks away, and I cover my mouth so he doesn't hear me laughing at his dismissal.

"So," I say, turning to her. "What really went down with Willa?"

Sydney sips her chocolate milk again before she speaks.

"We kissed," she says simply. And I wait for her to say more.

"Willa's been out since middle school, and she's been a huge flirt since then too. And for the last couple of years, I was there for all of her epic crushes and kisses and breakups. I've force-fed her ice cream so many times while she cried over all those girls, you know? Because as much as she puts herself out there, she still gets hurt all the time."

I nod. I don't know what it would be like to be that brave when it comes to love. Sounds terrifying.

Sydney tucks some curls behind her ears and looks across the cafeteria again. "But when we kissed, and I, like, *felt* something? I didn't know what to do. I knew that I loved her as a friend, but after that I started falling for her for real. And like, with all the girls she hooked up with or dated or whatever, I never judged her for it. It was kind of what made us work. But after that kiss it started to feel personal. She kissed me and we didn't even really talk about it, and by the next week she was talking about kissing someone else."

I pick at the edge of my sandwich. I rip off a piece of crust just for something to do. What happened with me and Layla is really different from what happened with Sydney and Willa, but we both know the pain of feeling like we don't matter to the person we love most—to these people who were supposed to be our everything.

"So I got mad one day when she was telling me about some new girl and basically called her a tease. Anyway, we had this huge fight right before winter break and we haven't really talked since then."

"Wow," I say. "That's . . . fucking awful." I want to ask her if she still has feelings for Willa, but I don't know if I'm allowed. What she told me already was a lot to share, so I don't want to push for more.

"Do you . . . miss her?" I say instead.

"Yeah. I do. But I don't know how to make it right."

I open my juice and take a deep pull, and the table is quiet for a few minutes.

"I miss Layla too. And part of me has given up a little, on the possibility of that, of fixing things. So I've been . . . trying to make new memories," I say slowly.

"Huh?" she asks.

"Like, there are all these places that remind me of Layla, and I don't want to think of her every time I go to certain stores or hear certain songs or walk past freaking Washington Square Park, you know?"

"Oh, yeah. Totally," Sydney concedes.

"So I've been going to different spots around the city and purposefully making new memories there," I tell her. "My dad thinks it's not going to work, and my mom thinks I should be honest with Layla, apologize and see what happens next. I have to tutor her *tonight*, and I have no idea what to do."

My phone vibrates. It's a text from Layla.

Sydney leans her chin on the heel of her palm, looking down at my phone. "Well, looks like you're gonna have to decide soon." She grabs her tray and stands up to go. Her earrings clink and ring, like bells.

"If you figure it out, let me know, will ya?"

WHEN YOU WERE EVERYTHING

Layla shows up beside my locker after last bell, and something about her standing there makes me more aware of all I've lost. I still remember when her meeting me here at the end of every day was normal.

"What's up?" she says, and I kid you not, Layla has *never* said "What's up" to me. This must be some piece of her new life without me—the way she greets the girls I hate.

"Nothing," I say, and I sound more defensive than I mean to. Layla bites her bottom lip and pulls out her phone. "Whatever, Cleo. Let's just g-g-get this over w-with, okay?"

I'm just about to say how this isn't an ideal situation for me either, when Layla looks back up at me. Her expression softens the tiniest bit. "I know you were assigned to t-tutor me, and I know you d-d-don't want to. I mean, *I* obviously don't want you to. B-but I d-d-do need the help, and I, um. I appreciate you helping me. I know this won't b-be easy."

She says all of this while looking straight at me, and she sounds and looks like my best friend; like *Lay;* like the version of her I used to know. Something like hope flares inside me—a match being lighted in an endlessly dark room—and I think of my mom saying I should be honest, that only a few people in a lifetime are worth fighting for. I think of fate and Gigi and paying attention to the universe. *Is this a sign that Layla is one of those people for me?*

I try to put all the questions I have out of my mind, at least for now. I decide to try, for once, to let my heart lead me.

—

"You're cool with studying at the big library, right?" I ask as we walk toward the exit. It's what I call the Main Branch. It's what Layla used to call it too.

"Yeah, it's fine," Layla says. "And I mean, it'll be g-g-g good to see your dad. It's b-been a while."

On the street, I don't know if I should talk to her, and if I do, I don't know what to say. In addition to the air being thick with awkwardness, the threat of rejection is there too. It lingers in the footnotes of our story in a way that makes me too afraid to add anything new to the way we are now at all.

It feels a little better once we're on a crowded train headed uptown. Here there's so much other stuff to focus on besides the fact that Layla and I have nothing (or maybe too much) to say to each other: a baby crying, a teenager standing to let a pregnant woman sit down, a guy shouting that he's sorry for disturbing our ride when he really isn't. I can watch the people pushing their way onto or off our train car if I don't want to read my book. And in the crush of bodies churning during rush hour, I don't have to stand or sit with Layla, because I have to find my own pocket of space in this human game of Tetris; I have to go wherever I can make myself fit.

The tension and the speechlessness don't let up until we walk into one of the library's small meeting rooms. We enter the tiny space and take seats on opposite sides of the table. I pull out my copy of *Macbeth,* and Layla does the same. Looks like she got that extension from Novak after all.

"So. Was there anything about the play that stood out to you? Any conflicts or moments or things you thought were interesting or that you think someone else would have a different opinion about? We can piece together an argument from that."

She opens her book to a dog-eared page pretty near the beginning of the play. "Well, there was this one p-p-part. Where Lady Macbeth is, like, convincing Macbeth to murder D-Duncan even though they b-b-b-both know it's wrong." Layla tucks her pin-straight hair behind her ears and says, "I g-g-guess I didn't get why he listened to her."

I flip to that page in my book too. "Well, she basically told him he wasn't a man if he didn't do it," I say. I scan the passage and read the line once I find it. *"When you durst do it, then you were a man; And to be more than what you were, you would be so much more the man."*

I look up at Layla and she seems kind of confused. I put the book down and point to the cover like I'm pointing to Macbeth himself. "I think his ego was too big to take being challenged like that."

Layla nods and rereads the lines to herself. "But he obviously *is* a man," Layla says. "He isn't even a c-c-cowardly guy or a loser. I mean, he had j-just fought in this mmmmassive war and *w-won.*"

"Yeah." I shrug. "But imagine doing all that and it *still* not being good enough. And I mean, it hurts when the person you love most in the world says something shitty to you. It's still hard to take . . . hard to not want to prove them wrong."

I realize how this sounds a second after I say it. I think Layla does too, because we used to be each other's most-loved person. Her eyebrows rise a little and I swallow, hard.

"I didn't mean—" I start.

"I know." Layla looks up and away from me. We can't escape our history. It touches every part of us. Luckily she doesn't want to linger on this any more than I do. She picks up her book again.

"There's mmmore, though. Like this 'unsex me' line. It's like, Lady Macb-b beth's definition of femininity and masculinity is so narrow. She needs to h-b-be 'unsexed' in order to convince her husband to murder the k-king, and then she b-b-b-basically calls him a p-p-pussy when he says he doesn't want to. And then—" Layla flips a few pages. "Then Macbeth is all, um, 'I hope you only ever have b-boy babies because you can't give b-b-b-birth to anything ffffeminine with a mind like that.' Pretty messed up, right?"

I want to make a joke. I want to say, "Is that an exact translation?" because her reading is totally spot on. I grin and nod.

"What?" she asks.

"Nothing. I just love that point. Maybe your argument could be about that."

"Like, how traditional gender roles p-p-played a part in Macbeth's downfall?" She looks up at me and I nod.

"Yep. It's kinda brilliant—turning a modern eye on how similarly people still think of men and women even now—what they can and can't do; who they can and can't be."

"Maybe I'll bring Bangladeshi culture into it too," Layla muses. "How d-d-d-different things are for men and women. The things my brother c-c-can get away with that I would *never* b-be able to, and how sssssometimes it all feels so arb-b-bitrary. Some people even think the inequalities are *b-b-because* of Islam, but Islam actually sssays the opposite—that men and women should b-be equal."

I nod more. "Yeah. I'm sure Ms. Novak would appreciate that personal touch. I doubt she'll get a paper about Islam and Macbeth *and* sexism from anyone else."

I miss talking to Layla about books like this. I miss talking to her about everything.

We jot down some notes that are the start of a rough outline for her argument. And it actually doesn't feel terrible to be in a room with her for nearly an hour. There are a few moments when we fall into the easy way we used to talk to each other. A few times, we even laugh.

"So why don't you work on the paper tonight and tomorrow? And then I can give it a read and let you know if I think you need to tighten anything up before you turn it in. Novak gave you till Friday?"

Layla nods. "That was sssso easy, with you like, validating what I was saying. And helping me fffffocus my thoughts or wh-whatever." She smiles.

I feel a shift then, in the energy between us. The room is warm and quiet, and the moment feels electric. I think that this must be a sign—or at least an opportunity. I feel brave enough to be honest; strong enough to tell her something real.

She's still smiling at me, and she's saying nice things, and we just had an exhilarating discussion about one of my favorite plays. I frown and look down at my hands where they rest on top of my book. I think of Gigi, of Mom, and then of a line from *Hamlet* about asking your heart what it knows and listening.

"Layla," I start to say, and my voice is already shaking. I look up at her and we both swallow hard. "I . . . miss you," I say, because it's the truest thing I know. "I regret . . . everything. And I just wanted to tell you how sorry I am one more time, about all that's happened."

I don't want to get into fate and signs and the universe with her, because Layla barely had patience for it when we were friends. So I just say, "Do you think it's even remotely possible that we could be friends again?"

Her nostrils flare, which is something that always happens when Layla is trying hard not to cry. I take a deep breath, my mother's voice in my head: *If you love someone it's always worth it. You should fight like hell to hold on to them.*

"I know it won't be exactly like it was before," I continue, "when you were everything to me, and I was everything to you—but I was hoping we might be able to try."

Layla glances down at her book, then up to my eyes again. She shakes her head once, hard and fast, and she starts to look more mad than hurt.

"I thought we weren't g-g-g-going to do this anymore, C-Cleo." Her voice is hushed and icy. "I thought we'd both d-d-decided that it—*we*—were done."

I had. *We* had. But I guess some small part of me still believed in the possibility of us. I try not to let the tightness in my chest overtake me. I try to hold it together as everything inside me goes hot with embarrassment; as every part of me aches with the agony of her rejection.

Layla starts packing her stuff, throwing her book and her notebook and her pens into her bag. Her straight hair is hanging over her face like a heavy curtain as she does it, and I wonder if she'll ever rock her messy waves again. She's not talking to me anymore, just mumbling under her breath like I'm not even here.

"I *knew* this was a b-b-b-bad idea. I knew it."

I stand up. I don't say anything else to her because I'll rage-cry if I do. I just grab my things and head out of the room. I need to find my dad.

I'm on the stairs when I shoot him a text. *Map room,* I send. I want to add an *S.O.S.* but I refrain so he won't be too worried. I rush away from Layla, who is texting pretty passionately on her own phone just behind me, and I wonder if she's telling Sloane about all I've said.

When I get to the map room, I see someone else before my eyes find my dad. Sloane is standing against the back wall next to my father. She's talking to him, and it's so shocking seeing her out of context like this that for a second I can't move. She's leaning against one of the desks, instead of in the hallway at school or at a party surrounded by the Chorus Girls. I hear her say, "So why'd you leave Chisholm Charter? Everyone loved you there," and I want to scream. The sound of her voice is a flint, and her speaking to someone else I love is the only spark it takes. I'm on fire.

My dad grins. "That's so sweet of you to say, Sloane, but it was just time for a change." A shadow passes over his face that I've never seen there when *I* ask about him leaving. A sadness about it that I guess he doesn't want to show me. But just as

Sloane leans forward and asks him another question, Layla walks through the door to the map room too, and almost bumps into me because she's still looking down at her phone. I whirl around to face her.

"This library is huge," I rasp more than whisper. "You could've met *your friend* anywhere. Why'd you tell her to meet you in here?"

Layla looks as surprised to see me here as I was to see Sloane, but she knows this is my and Daddy's spot. She has to know, because before everything changed, I *told* her.

Even before she opens her mouth to say anything, I know she'll answer like New Layla, the one who has no problem being cruel to me. Her nostrils flare again, and she says, "You think you own p-places, Cleo. Just like you think you own p-p-p-people. But guess what? It's a free country. This might come as a surprise to you, but you don't *own* me or this library, or any of the other p-p-places we used to hang out. I can g-go anywhere I want. And so o o o-can my *friends.*"

I had planned to hang out here with my dad for a while, but after those words leave Layla's mouth the room feels instantly tainted. I add the map room to my mental list of places to rid Layla of, and decide to double down on my New Memories Project because *fuck her.*

I quickly tell my dad I'll have to see him later. I pull out my phone and text Sydney.

Can you meet me at Washington Square Park?

LIPSTICK & MONOLOGUES

It's nearly dark by the time I get off the train at West 4th Street.

When I texted Sydney, I was in a blind panic and I didn't know who else to call or where else to go. But now, as I approach the park, I wonder if this was a mistake.

So far, I've made new memories alone, with my dad, or completely by accident, like at Dolly's with Dom. But the only thing I felt I could do as Layla and Sloane closed in on a space that was supposed to be mine and mine alone was to escape, and to race to a spot where I'd have more control over who was there, and over what was happening.

It's just starting to get dark, but the park is still filled with people standing under the arch and staring skyward, teens still in their school uniforms flirting, and tourists taking photos and sitting on the wide lip of the fountain. The park feels alive, its energy like an extra pulse under my skin. With the sorbet-colored sky set alight by the setting sun just ahead of me, I can almost forget the reason I'm here.

When I find Sydney, she's sitting by the fountain, sipping something warm. She pulls off the top to blow on her drink, and steam rises from the cup in white wisps.

"*So?*" she says as soon as she sees me. "How'd things go with Layla?"

I don't mean for it to happen, but at the sight of her, I burst into tears.

"Oh! Oh, honey!" Sydney jumps up, nearly spilling her drink, and wraps me in a hug. I stiffen for a second, unused to being touched, but then I relax and fall against her. I let the tears pour and Sydney doesn't say anything. She just squeezes me even tighter.

"It was awful," I say, pulling off my tear-soaked glasses and rubbing my eyes.

"Here, let's sit," Sydney says. She leads me by the elbow to the edge of the fountain.

"Syd, it was so bad."

Sydney roots around in her purse and produces a small packet of tissues. She hands it to me, and I pull three from the plastic. "What happened?"

"I'm so stupid," I say. "Like, it wasn't so bad, at first, and it even started to be fun, talking about the play with her. Then I started thinking that maybe it was a sign, you know, me being assigned to tutor her? I started thinking that maybe my mom was right, that if I was honest it would make things better. We were talking about her paper and everything was going so well that I got a little too brave, I guess."

"No such thing as too brave," Sydney insists. "Only brave enough."

I tell her how I asked if there was any chance at all for us, and how Layla shut me down immediately. How a few minutes later she and Sloane were in the map room, which had always been this special place for me and my dad. I stand up and pace and tell her that this is what I was afraid of more than anything—that I'd show my cards and Layla would rip my heart to shreds again, and now it had come true.

"I'm mad at Ms. Novak for pairing us up, mad at my mom for telling me to try, mad at myself for believing there was something bigger at work; for being so damn desperate. I'm pissed that I even entertained the idea of forgiveness for someone who had already given up on me, you know?"

I don't tell her about the things I did to Layla and Sloane— the reason we're in this mess in the first place. But when I collapse back onto the fountain's edge, out of breath and still a little weepy, Sydney pulls out a tube of lipstick.

"So you were right, then," she says. She takes the cap off the lipstick, and it's eggplant purple.

"Huh?"

"You. Were. Right. Let's erase her. Eradicate her from your life as much as humanly possible. Sounds like she's over you," Sydney says, and then winces a little. "Sorry if that was harsh. But now, since this is officially over forever, you have to get over her."

She brandishes the lipstick. "Pucker your lips," she says.

"I look weird in lipstick," I say.

She draws back, examines my face like she's an art dealer and I'm an exceptionally valuable painting. "Whoever told you that was a damn liar," she says after a minute. "And Coco Chanel says, if you're sad, add more lipstick and attack. So that's what we're doing. Pucker."

I grin, drag my sleeve across my eyes one last time, slip my glasses back into place, and pucker up. I listen as Sydney explains the way I can find the perfect lip color for my skin tone, along with the best ways to wear it. When she's done, she pulls out a compact and holds it up so I can see, and she's right. Even in the dim light I can tell it doesn't look weird at all.

"Now for a new memory." Sydney looks around, her hand on her chin. "Oh! Let's go streaking!" She stands up and starts slipping out of her jacket.

I stretch my eyes wide. "Sydney, no way. It's freezing out here!"

She shivers and pulls her coat back on, laughing. "Fine, fine. I was mostly joking. But you have to do something really memorable if you're really going to rewrite history, Cleo."

She walks backward for a few steps, smirking at me, then turns around and sprints to the closest park bench. She climbs up to stand on it and grins maniacally. She clears her throat.

"Sydney," I shout-whisper, walking quickly over to her. "What are you doing?"

Couples holding hands and a few old people and kids walking past stare at her.

"Memory-making," she whispers back.

"Then, I confess," Sydney shouts. Her voice carries clear across the park. "Here on my knee, before high heaven and you / That before you, and next unto high heaven, / I *love* your son."

She's reciting the monologue from *All's Well That Ends Well* that I helped her memorize for English extra credit last semester. I recognize Helena's words right away and start to laugh.

She recites the entire two-minute monologue from her perch atop the bench, and when she's done a few passing people even clap. She hops down from the bench and bows, smiling and saying, "Thank you, thank you. Oh, you're so kind," and I'm still laughing.

When we head home a few minutes later, I bump Sydney's shoulder as we walk side by side to the train station.

"You're kind of great," I say softly, wondering how a former tutee has become an almost-real friend. She grins and shakes her curls out of her eyes.

"And *you're* fucking fantastic. Don't let anyone, *ever*, tell you otherwise."

then:
November

LITTLE BETRAYALS

It was slow, the way it all happened. So slow I didn't notice I was alone until I almost *always* was.

One day Layla told me she was going to hang out with the Chorus Girls after their rehearsals, and the next thing I knew, that was what she did every Tuesday and Thursday.

She started randomly eating lunch with them, just like she had the day Sloane lost it on me in the hall, so I never knew if I'd be eating alone until I got to the cafeteria. More often than not, our table was empty when I arrived.

Her stopping by my locker between classes became just as unpredictable: sometimes she did, and sometimes I didn't see her all day. And if there was ever any question of who she'd spend time with, I was usually the one who surrendered. In the game of fight or flight, I *soared* away from my problems. And Sloane and the Chorus Girls were my biggest one.

I'd never done well with gray areas—with *almosts* and *sometimes* and *maybes*. I liked to know who my friends were and that they'd be there if I needed them, no matter what. So it was an uneasy balance—this new half friendship—but it was one I was working at because I didn't think I could handle losing Layla completely.

I no longer expected Layla to be waiting for me near my locker, and that day, like most days, she wasn't. But when I walked into homeroom, for the very first time, Layla was sitting at the back of the class with Sloane.

Something weird happened in my chest when I saw the empty chair next to my normal seat. Some strange, shooting pain that I couldn't ignore. I bit my lip against the ache of it as I walked slowly to my desk and sat down. I could hear Sloane and Layla talking behind me, but I didn't turn around.

The only thing that made me feel better in moments like these was daydreaming about London. When Layla had chorus rehearsals on Tuesday and Thursday afternoons, I added to the growing list of landmarks I wanted to visit. Whenever I ate lunch on my own, I'd read about the history of the Globe Theatre. So that first day when she didn't sit with me in homeroom, I pulled out my phone and did a cursory search for weekend trips you could take from London proper. And at the very top of the list was Paris, France.

I wanted to turn around and confront Layla then. To ask her if she was still planning to come visit me in London, or if she even cared enough to. I wanted to send her a text and ask why she decided to sit at the back of the class all of a sudden, but I was starting to wonder, if I never texted Layla first, would she text me at all?

I didn't turn around or send that text. And I tried my best to ignore the acute and stinging pain in my chest at the sound of their laughter. The second that class was over, I went to my next one without waiting around to see who Layla would choose. I was getting tired of not being chosen, when for so long, I'd been Layla's obvious and only pick.

Still, I kept my eye on my phone all morning, hoping for some kind of explanation, some acknowledgment of this latest, agonizing change. But nothing ever came.

—

I comforted myself with the fact that at least I wouldn't have to suffer through a lonely lunch period today because none of us would be in the cafeteria. I headed to the auditorium the moment my lunch bell rang. Layla had told me that Mrs. Steele was posting the roles for the school musical at noon.

She was already there when I turned the corner, staring in disbelief at the paper taped to the auditorium door. I was ready to comfort her because she hadn't gotten a part, but as soon as I touched her elbow she turned to me and said, "I . . . I can't believe I got it."

I stepped closer to the door to see the list. The production would be a musical version of *It's a Wonderful Life* and Layla had been cast as Mary, the main character's wife. This role had lots of singing, which obviously Layla would blow out of the water. But it also had lots of regular spoken lines too.

I couldn't believe it either. And I knew I should have been congratulating her. I knew I should have been saying *something,* but the truth was, I was still worried that she'd get up onstage and she'd stutter nonstop, or worse: she'd get blocked and not be able to say a word.

She turned to me and said, "Cleo, c-c-c-can you believe it?" She was grinning so widely and there were tears in her eyes. I didn't know why I couldn't just smile and tell her that it was great. It was her dream come true, just like making chorus had been, and that should have been enough of a reason for me to celebrate with her. But a dark part of me didn't want to. A dark part of me thought of Tuesday and Thursday afternoons, of lunch, and now of homeroom. I feared this musical would be another piece of Layla's life I'd be set apart from, and I was reminded of a few lines from Hamlet's most famous soliloquy about bearing ills we already have, rather than flying to others we know not of.

I didn't want to lose any more of her than I already had.

I finally dragged my eyes away from the sheet of paper where I'd read MARY HATCH . . . . LAYLA HASSAN half a dozen times. I looked at my best friend, and I pasted on a smile.

"It's definitely unbelievable," I said. "Aren't you nervous?" My concern about her performance was real, but something else, something darker, was happening too.

I didn't want her to have this because of what it would mean for *me*.

I would love to say that I only realized how terrible my question sounded after I said it. But that wasn't true. I knew the question would wound her ego. I knew it would add to the tally of all the tiny ways we'd been hurting each other for months: She didn't answer when I called, so I ignored her texts. She sat somewhere else during lunch, so I didn't wait for her after school. She ignored the things I said, choosing to trust Sloane instead of me, so I spoke up less and less. She'd broken dozens of promises to me, so now here I was, breaking her heart.

Layla's smile fell and I could see the shock—the hurt—in her wide brown eyes. But I didn't have a chance to fix it, though I almost instantly wanted to. She didn't have a chance to say anything to me either, because a moment later, Sloane was beside us, screaming.

"Holy shit, girl! I *knew* you could do it! This is so freaking amazing." Sloane gripped Layla's shoulders and shook them. "Aren't you excited?"

Sloane had the reaction *I* should have had. She was saying all the things *I* should have said. But fear for Layla's almost certain humiliation was a wretched virus in my stomach, making me feel sick. And all the little betrayals were there too, ruining me from the inside out.

The smile slowly returned to Layla's face, the light to her eyes. She turned away from me so quickly that her bag banged into my shoulder. I stumbled a little, knocked off balance, and she didn't even notice.

It felt like the perfect metaphor for the last few months: me pushed aside again and again, and Layla enveloped in the comfort of new friends.

But that day—that moment—was the first time I felt like I might deserve it.

THE STACKS, PART II

For the rest of the afternoon, it was me who avoided Layla. I knew I needed to apologize for the way I'd reacted to her getting that part in the play. But I wasn't sure what to say to make things right.

She still hadn't texted me, even after seeing her in the hall in front of the auditorium. But I swallowed my pride and texted her first.

> Can you meet me in the library after school? We can do our homework in the stacks.

I stared at my phone waiting for her reply, and to my surprise it came only a few minutes later.

> Sure.

I crossed my fingers that she wasn't as mad as I thought she was going to be. Her answer was short, but she could have easily ignored me, said no, or made up some kind of excuse and she didn't. It was a good sign, I told myself.

After last bell I speed walked to the library, and it was crowded with kids. I hadn't thought about it, but it was finals season. I edged around a few people near the entrance and headed into the stacks near the back of the library, to the corner where Layla and I always studied.

The aisles were a little busier than usual too, with kids checking out books like they'd forgotten the library was there until that day. But to get to Layla I hopped over the dropped backpacks and squeezed by people still wearing theirs despite the narrow aisles.

She broke into a smile the second she saw me, which I wasn't expecting.

"Hey," I said, slipping my backpack off and smiling back. "Crazy how many people are in here, right?"

She was still wearing her bag, like she wasn't planning to stay, and as I slid my notebook out of my backpack, I paused, noticing. I looked up at her.

"So. Chorus g-g-g-got invited to this big C-C-Christmas recital that's going to be at Lincoln Center!" Layla squealed quietly. "A bunch of high schools—" she started, but her excitement seemed to steal her voice for a second. She shook her head like she could shake off the block that was causing an extra-long pause in her speech. She started again. "A bunch of schools are ssssinging and it's going to b-b-be awesome, but Mrs. Steele is adding another d-d-d-day of chorus rehearsals to our schedule to prepare."

Which meant Layla would have chorus practice three days a week, and once rehearsals started for the musical, that would leave no after-school time for us to hang out at all. I felt the disappointment tugging at different parts of my face.

"So I'm basically never going to see you, once the musical stuff starts," I said. And I thought my voice would sound sad. But it sounded like I was pissed instead. I shoved my notebook back into my backpack and didn't look at her.

"Why d-d-didn't you congratulate me? Or, I don't know, say anything nice? It's a really b-big deal that I got that p-p-part. I thought you would understand that mmmmore than everyone— how important it was to me."

That was my opportunity to say sorry. To say that I was proud of her and that I couldn't wait to see her up there, doing her thing. But I was suddenly filled with a hot kind of anger about losing even more time with her—time that she didn't seem to mind not being able to spend with me. She clearly wasn't thinking about that. She only cared that I wasn't immediately over the moon for her regardless of the complications—regardless of what it meant for us.

I couldn't bring myself to say any of the things I knew I was supposed to say. And as pissed as I was about everything, I'd rather she hear the awful truth from me than embarrass herself in front of the entire school.

"You can't blame me for being surprised," I said. And it was like I'd flipped a light switch, the way Layla's face changed. It turned into the hard, mean one she's always used for protection. I knew I would cause her pain, but I kept talking, because for the first time in weeks she was acting like she could hear me.

"I just mean that I wouldn't expect someone with a speech impediment to get a lead role in a stage show. And I know you've been working with this new speech therapist, but that smooth-talking voice you use? How sustainable is it? Can you speak like that for two full hours? Have you thought about that?"

Her face got even tighter, even meaner. I reached out to put my hand on her shoulder. I said, "Layla, I'm asking you this stuff as your friend." I frowned and waited until her eyes locked with mine. "I'm trying to look out for you," I said, lying and telling the truth at the same time. I didn't know you could want to hurt and protect someone simultaneously until that moment.

She moved away from my hand. "Wh-wh-what about all the times when I t-told you I wanted to be on B-B-Broadway and you said I totally could? What about all the times you told me I had a great voice? Was that all a lie? D-did you never believe in me at all?"

"Layla," I started. But she stopped me again with a hand held dangerously close to my face.

"So. What you're t-t-telling me is that you've *never* t-taken me seriously?"

I blinked slowly and took a deep breath as I pushed her hand gently away from me. I said what I said next slowly and seriously, looking right at her.

"I don't think it hurts to dream."

It was the truest thing I'd said to her in days.

"You know what?" Layla said. She took a step away from me. "Sloane was *so* right about you."

I took a step forward to stop myself from talking too loudly. "What does *that* mean?" I hissed in her direction.

"It means since the b-b-b-beginning of the year I've been trying to d-defend you, to tell her that you're a g-g-good person,

181

that you didn't mean anything b-by it when you accidentally let Todd into the party. That she should try to get to know you b-b-because even though you're a little pretentious, you mmmean well."

"Pretentious?" I said, insulted.

"Oh please, Cleo." Layla rolled her eyes. "You listen to jazz-age music almost exclusively and you unironically qu-qu-quote Shakespeare. You don't even watch TV. You're *über* p-pretentious. And look, I'm not j-j-judging you for that. I try my hardest not to-to-to judge anyone ever b-because it's how I was raised, okay? But this? Shooting d-d-down my dreams as they c-come true and assuming I'm going to ffffail before I've even tried?"

Layla's dark eyes filled with tears.

"That's sssomething I *will* remember, Cleo." She picked up her bag.

"I think I need some time to think about all of this," she said, in her high-pitched, singsong stage voice. She didn't stutter at all. "I'm not going to text you for a while. I need time to clear my head and focus on the play."

And all at once, I was as mad as I'd ever been in my entire life. I wanted to rip books from the shelves and launch them at her. But I just spoke in my regular voice instead of whispering. People stared, but I didn't care.

"Whatever, Layla. I'm not always just going to be here, waiting for you like a lapdog or something. You don't get to be friends with me only when it's convenient for you."

She didn't say anything back. She just walked out of the library with her head down, her thumbs moving quickly across the screen of her phone. I knew she was texting Sloane. I knew she was talking about me, telling Sloane that she'd been right to hate me from the start.

So I took out my phone too. But a second later I realized I didn't have anyone to text about her. And that fact made my eyes fill, for the first time all day, with tears.

now

SMALL PLATES

At Dolly's on Sunday afternoon, a man who has to be Pop meets me at the door, seats me, and takes my order. He's the kind of older black guy whose face is covered in moles, and whose large, sturdy frame looks like he can lay bricks as well today as he may have back when he was in his twenties. He smells like peach pie. When I ask him about Dom, his eyes light up and the rust-brown skin around them crinkles as he grins. "He's back in the kitchen. I'll send him out here to ya as soon as I put your order in."

Now that I've decided to double down on my New Memories Project, with Sydney's help, I've laid out a whole map of the city with a place or two we'll need to visit each week. I pull out the notebook I've started carrying around to keep track of what we can do in each location. Sydney also texts me her off-the-wall ideas all the time. I write them down, though I doubt I'll ever *Climb the Alice in Wonderland statue in Central Park and scream, "We're all mad here,"* or *Play the Penis Game at the Met* (two suggestions that she seems especially proud of). If we follow the outlined plan, though, I'll have exorcised Layla from all my favorite places by June.

A few minutes after I put my notebook away, Dom slips into the booth across from me.

"Hey," I say.

He grins and says, "You're here," like I'm some kind of miracle instead of an unremarkable sad girl.

"I told you I come here every Sunday, Dom," I reply, but I won't lie—it's nice to feel wanted.

He pulls a few thin, folded pages from his apron pocket and slides them across the table to me. When I unfold them, I see that it's his *Macbeth* assignment. I read the title, and it surprises me: "A Madman or a Man Driven to Madness? The Roles of Fate and Free Will in *Macbeth*."

I look up at Dom and he has a smirk on his face that just about ends me.

"I thought you were going to write about ambition," I say.

"Yeah, I was. But after our *rousing* debate, I was inspired," he muses, and I laugh. "Plus," he continues, "I still get into the role of ambition in Macbeth's downfall. This take on it was just much more complex. And you might not know this about me yet, but—" He leans across the table closer to me and tips his head in a way that beckons me forward. I lean toward him too. "I *love* complexity," he whispers, bouncing his eyebrows up and down.

Dom hops up and heads back to the kitchen, and I start reading. Even when the food arrives I don't put Dom's paper down. I start to see how each of Macbeth's choices played a bigger role collectively in his death than the prophecy alone. But I don't want to tell Dom that.

When I lower the pages and look at the food on the table, I've clearly gotten someone else's order by mistake. Instead of a burger, there are four delicious-smelling, appetizer-sized servings: a few ribs stacked like a log cabin with a sticky, sweetly scented sauce; something round and fried—a rice ball, I think; a few crunchy fried chicken wings garnished with something thin and green; and a miniature pie with a glistening crust. I look around the restaurant, wanting to explain that I didn't order any of this, but Pop is taking an order at a table across the dining room, and the one other server is busy too. I'm just about to stand up to look for Dom when I see him coming around the counter toward me.

"Hey, I didn't—"

"Order any of this? Yeah, I know. I canceled the burger and made this for you instead. I wanna know what you think."

I look from the plates to him and back again. "You made all this?" I ask. "For me?"

Dom nods and steps a little closer to the table. "So I have this idea. When I visited my mom in Atlanta for Christmas, she took me to this soul food place, right? And it was damn good. But I felt so heavy after because the portions were huge."

He rests his arm on the back of the booth where I'm sitting, and his sudden closeness makes me aware of how little space there is between us. I also try not to get too hung up on the fact that he just casually mentioned his mother for the first time ever and I'm dying to know more about her. More about *him*. I just focus on filling and emptying my lungs slowly and evenly, thinking of him under trees hanging heavily with southern humidity because I can't imagine Georgia in winter; his skin deepening under the summer sun to an even darker brown while he eats fried foods and drinks cold, sweet tea with a lady who looks exactly like him.

"So I thought, what if we added soul food to the menu? You know, all the stuff people love: mac 'n' cheese, greens, candied yams, ribs . . . but here we do it in smaller portions, with gourmet presentation?" He gestures to the plates on the table, with their smears of sauces and decorative garnishes, and I can see it: an à la carte menu where you pick as much or as little as you want. Regulars would love it, and the change might attract new clientele too. It's a great idea, and I want to marvel at him, but I'm worried if I look up, I'll forget how to breathe again.

"Pop thinks it's 'too newfangled.' Those were his actual words. But Lolly told me to work on getting my recipes right, and that we could feature one of my mini-plates as the special once a week as I work them out." Dom nods at the four plates on the table. "These are the first few recipes that I think are in good shape. And I'm hoping if the rollout of the specials goes well, they'll let me do more revisions to the menu."

He rubs his hand over his hair and I get a whiff of that Dom-scent, with a little flour and butter mixed in.

I reach for a wing. I take a bite and it is crispy and juicy, still hot, and packed with flavor. I was planning to talk to Dom about his *Macbeth* paper, but now I can't even remember why.

"Damn," I say.

"Good?" he asks.

I nod, and, after I finish the wing, I reach for the tiny pie. It's peach, and when I bite into it, it's syrupy but somehow not overly sweet. The thing that I thought was a rice ball is a "hush puppy," Dom tells me—a small fried knob of cornbread. I eat it all. And when he tries to reach for the last rib, I give him a quick evil eye that makes him laugh and snatch his hand away. They're cooked so well that the meat nearly slips away from the bone as I lift it to my mouth, and the sauce is tangy, with a slight kick that lingers on my tongue even once it's gone. It's all so good that it's a little devastating.

"So your mom's still in Atlanta?" I ask as I napkin off my fingers and dab at my mouth. "You used to live there with her, right? I think I remember you saying that over the summer."

Dom yawns and looks around the now mostly empty restaurant. "Yeah," he says, but he doesn't say anything more about her.

"I think being up all night finishing that paper is catching up to me." He crosses his forearms and rests his chin on top of them. He closes his eyes for a second, and I take the opportunity to unabashedly stare at his pretty face. His skin is the color of the fire-stained bottom of a copper pot, and his eyelashes are so thick and black it looks like he's wearing mascara. The sharp angles of his shaped-up hairline and the elegant swoops of his wide nose make me want to write poetry, and don't even get me started on the pouty curve of his lips. . . .

He opens his eyes and catches me staring. He grins and I look down at my hands. They've come to rest on his paper. I slide the nearly forgotten pages slowly across the table. But I don't say a word, embarrassed he caught me watching him, unmoored by his paper, which was so much better than I expected it to be.

"So?" Dom says. I take a sip of my milky tea, the only thing I ordered that I actually got, and reach for the last hush puppy. "You can't just read my whole paper, a paper you pretty much inspired, and then not tell me what you think."

I still don't say anything because I'm disarmed by him a little, by the way he's looking at me, by the way he can cook and write. A small part of me is also still a little too proud to admit he was right about Macbeth's free will versus the witches and fate. I jokingly lift my hand and look around the restaurant like I need the check, and he rolls his eyes. "Nah, you're not getting out of this that easily, Shorty." He reaches across the table and pulls my hand down, and his palm is warm and rough on my arm. I shrug and grin, staying quiet.

"You're impossible," he says, and he stands to leave.

I let loose the laugh I was holding in. I shove the last bit of food left on the table, a quarter of the mini-pie, into my mouth. "You were right," I mutter. I hope he doesn't hear me since I'm talking around crust and fruit and a smile I can hardly hide, but he turns around almost instantly.

"I was *what?*" he says. He squats next to the table with his elbows along the edge like a server trying to make sure he hears an order correctly in a crowded, bustling dining room. But Dolly's isn't either of the two, so I know Dom just wants to hear *me*.

I roll my eyes even though I'm thrilled about every part of this situation—the food, the conversation, the closeness. I swallow the pie. "You were right, okay? Macbeth totally made those choices. Even if the prophecy made him think he deserved to be king, *he* chose to kill Duncan, and everyone else. *He* made the ultimately tragic decisions, not the witches."

Dom bites his bottom lip. "That's interesting," he says. "I was gonna tell you that writing the paper made me realize that it's you who might be right after all."

Before he has a chance to elaborate, Pop is there, checking in on me. "You need anything else, hun?" he asks.

"I don't think so, but do you . . . need any help around here?"

I ask him, remembering how he seated me *and* took my order. It's so nice to be away from home and the drama with Layla; it's thrilling being so close to Dom. I feel like I could talk to him forever.

I'm desperate to have an excuse to hang out with him, and I'm not brave enough to just tell him that I want to. That I *like* him. And while I think we might be becoming friends, I'm not sure if that matters. My faith in friendship has been shaken, and I'm not sure if I'll ever get it back.

Pop looks surprised, but I'm already here every weekend. It wouldn't be much of a stretch for me to come a few days a week too. "I could use the experience," I add.

"We won't be able to pay you very much," Pop says. He rubs a hand over his head the way Dom sometimes does.

"Oh, don't worry about that," I say. I look up at him with eyes full of hope.

"Well, we really would appreciate the help," he says. He looks like he's thinking about it, and when I glance over at Dom his dark eyes are stretched wide and he's nodding a little in Pop's direction. It makes something inside me sprout wings and take flight.

"Maybe you could hostess, and wait some tables too, for tips," he adds. I nod enthusiastically and Pop smiles. "Okay, then! I don't see why not. If you're free now, maybe Dom can show you around?"

HOW IT FEELS TO BREAK

I follow Dom to the front of the restaurant, where I'll spend most of my time. He says hi to a few regulars at the counter and then shows me the seating chart for the diner's ten tables. He introduces me to the only other server they have left on shift today.

"Business has been a little slow lately," he tells me when we walk past the back windows. He points across the street, where a new gourmet burger place has opened, and a trendy tapas restaurant that only serves small Spanish-inspired plates and expensive cocktails. There's construction on a corner opposite Dolly's that Dom points out too. "That place is gonna do ramen," he says, and there's a darkness to his voice I'm not used to hearing. I want to get back to where we were at the table, winks and grins and giggles; him reaching out to lower my hand.

"Do you think Pop would be cool with me only working a couple of days a week?"

"I mean, we had no one, so I'm sure any help will be cool with him. What are you doing the other days?"

"Tutoring, remember?" I say, hoping Dom will leave it at that. I didn't mean to bring up Layla, not here, where everything has been making me smile. I look at the corner table where Layla and I used to sit, and I feel that particular hurt that only comes from falling, unexpectedly, into the past. Sometimes memories are trapdoors.

"Right. Man, I thought Novak was chill," he says.

"What do you mean?"

"I mean, she assigned you to *Layla*. She knows you're not cool with her anymore, right?"

"Sorta. But I think she thinks it will be good for me, you know?" I twist one of my braids around my finger. "She couldn't just give me someone I wanted to tutor when making me do it in the first place was a punishment for skipping."

Dom grins and raises his eyebrows, like something is dawning on him. "Oh snap. Is that why you said my name all loud in class?"

I cover my face, but when Dom laughs I feel like the embarrassment in that moment was worth it for this one. "It's not *funny*," I say, slapping his chest. He catches my hand and holds it, and when I look up at his smiling face, he licks his lips and looks down at mine. I pull my hand away to take off my glasses. I busy myself cleaning the lenses with the hem of my shirt.

"My bad," he says, "if I gave you the impression that I needed a ton of help. I mostly just wanted an excuse to hang out with you."

He says this so easily, like it isn't the kind of thing people are usually afraid to admit. I mean, I just did the same thing asking Pop to be their part-time, semivolunteer hostess, but I wouldn't have been able to say it the way he did. I blush and look away from him at a portrait of an otherworldly Ella Fitzgerald in a long sparkling dress balanced on a seashell, a gorgeous reinterpretation of *The Birth of Venus* on the far right wall.

"Where does all this art come from?" I ask, to talk about anything other than us. Dom covers his mouth and yawns. His eyelids look heavy, but he steps in front of me and clears his throat.

"Different artists in the neighborhood mostly. Sometimes homeless kids. Lolly volunteers and started an art program that they run at this shelter in Bushwick on the weekends. We rotate the 'exhibit,' as Lolly calls it, every month or so. She picks the art," he says.

"That's so cool," I say. There are small price tags beneath the paintings, with the artist's name and age. Ella was painted by a sixteen-year-old named Raymond Poole, and I wonder how someone with so much talent who's the same age as me could end up on the streets. I cross my fingers behind my back, hoping against hope that someone buys his paintings and that it helps his situation, however little.

We pass through the too-warm kitchen, turn a corner, and enter a room only a little bigger than a supply closet. Dom flips a switch and a tiny break room is thrown into harsh, fluorescent light. "So what happened to you two?" Dom asks.

"Me and Layla?" I say, though I know that's who he means.

Dom yawns again and pours himself a cup of coffee, then lifts the pot and offers me some. I shake my head. "I'm more of a tea drinker," I tell him.

"I think I knew that," he says, putting the coffeepot back down and reaching into the mini-fridge. He offers a bottle of water instead and I take it. He doesn't repeat his question about me and Layla, but he looks at me expectantly.

"Lots of things," I finally say. "We crumbled. Or unraveled, I guess. Or whatever you want to call it." I take a sip of my water. The hurt feels so much like when my parents decided they didn't love each other anymore that I can feel a shift in my breathing. "We . . . broke up."

Dom snorts. "It's not like it was a relationship," he says, and I frown, annoyed at his reaction. Perhaps he doesn't know how it feels . . . to break in this particular way. Or perhaps it's different for boys? But girls cling to their friends for dear life as they wade through the rough waters of learning who they are while everything around and inside them is changing minute by minute. And aren't we all a little bit in love with our best friends?

"What would you call it, then?" I say. I don't keep the sass out of my voice.

"If it is," Dom says slowly, realizing that I'm pissed, "can you guys . . . come back together?"

I shake my head. "I thought we could, but that ship has sailed," I say. "Some ugly stuff went down last year."

Dom says, "The Cleo I know wouldn't give up on someone so easily."

"Guess you don't know me as well as you think, then," I say. I take a long pull from my water bottle, and when I put it back down on the table, I see Dom watching me in that quiet way of his. I feel my eyes trace the line of his collarbone. He takes a deep breath, and the hollow in his throat deepens. He's about to speak, but I beat him to it.

"Tell me more about Dolly's," I say, desperate to talk about something, anything, else. "When did it open? How long have you been helping out? What's your favorite thing to cook?"

For the next twenty minutes, Dom tells me more about Dolly's than I expected him to know. He tells me Pop and Miss Dolly were able to open it with money they had saved up and a loan from the bank. Pop had to have one of his white friends cosign with him on the loan, because the bank didn't trust a young black couple to make the required monthly payments in the seventies. He tells me that opening a bakery had been his Lolly's dream, but a burger joint had been Pop's, so they compromised. And that Pop proposed to Miss Dolly by slipping a key ring with a key to this place around her finger instead of a diamond.

Pop loves being "front of house," but he's super-talented in the kitchen too. "If he'd been born at a different time," Dom says, "or maybe in a different world, he'd be the star of his own cooking show, no question."

That's why Dom started in the kitchen—to give Pop a chance to have more face time with customers. And that's how he fell in love with cooking, experimenting with new recipes, and learning the ropes from Pop well enough that he could cover for him whenever they needed him to.

"I love the . . . *heat,* you know? The pressure to perform? The way one decision can change the whole course of a meal, table, or even the whole service." He moves his hands around a lot as he tells me all this—and hearing him talk about this is better than any magic trick.

"That's why I want to add new stuff to the menu. I'm worried that we won't be able to keep up with the competition. The regulars, they're all getting old, and the new people in the neighborhood are hipsters and like, white rich kids who just graduated college, you know?" I nod, because it's impossible not to notice the shifts happening in our neighborhood, the way it doesn't look the same anymore. There are more coffee shops than bodegas, more noodle and cocktail bars than places like Dolly's.

"I don't want this place to get lost," Dom says, his voice a little quieter than it was before. He takes another sip of his coffee and looks at me, like he's making a decision. And when he starts talking again, I can tell he's decided to trust me with something precious to him.

"Lolly and Pop are already having trouble keeping up with the bills. That's why we don't have a hostess anymore. That's why we're down to only two servers."

"I didn't realize," I say softly, and I want to reach across the table and touch his hand. He nods solemnly and his eyes are on fire as he says what he says next. "They've done everything for me, Cleo. *Everything.* Keeping this place afloat is the least I can do."

I think about his paper, and how he was so adamant about Macbeth deciding his own fate. He wants to do everything he can for this place and he's worried it won't be enough.

I follow Dom's sleepy eyes as they look down to check the time on his phone.

"Shit. It's time to close up." He stands and dumps his empty mug into the small sink. He yawns again and stretches and I want him to lay his heavy, sleepy head on my shoulder. I want to put his worries to bed along with him.

"I can walk you out," he says. But I don't know how he could think I'm ready to say goodbye.

I check my phone. There's nothing from Mom, and the lack of notifications feels like a sign.

"You're tired," I say. "And there's only a few people still here, right?"

"So?" Dom says.

"So I can stick around and help," I say. "I mean, only if you want. I'm meeting Sydney later, but I have some time to kill."

Dom bites his bottom lip, rubs his hand over his hair, and grins.

AURAS

Sydney is holding a creamy-looking bubble tea and a sunset-colored one too when I meet her in Chinatown. She's wearing a faux fur coat, sunglasses, and big pearly earrings, and she looks a bit like she could be an extra in an Audrey Hepburn movie, which is to say she stands out quite a bit on the littered, grubby sidewalks of downtown Manhattan.

"Hey, girl," she says. She hands me the creamy tea and loops her arm through mine, and her familiarity makes my heart squeeze. "What's on the docket tonight?"

So far, Sydney and I have done a photo shoot at the coffee shop Layla and I would stop by every morning, beat the high score on as many games as possible at the arcade Layla and I used to frequent in middle school, and ordered milkshakes as big as our heads with ridiculous toppings at the divey burger joint Layla took me to for my fifteenth birthday. We drank them so quickly we got brain freeze, and then we raced to see who could finish the crazy toppings—like cheesecake, M&M's, and brownies—first.

Tonight, a particular corner in Chinatown is on the itinerary: a tiny jewelry store that is more well known for its aura readings and crystals than the necklaces and bracelets they sell, at least among believers in that kind of thing.

"Gigi first took me here when I was ten," I tell Sydney as we push open the shop door. It's tiny inside, and it smells a bit like a library, which is comforting to me for obvious reasons. "Gigi was really into all of this kind of stuff—chakras and horoscopes, auras and fate. She was always saying to listen when the universe is trying to tell you something. She got her aura read once a month, and every now and then she'd bring me with her. Then, after she died, I brought Layla whenever I came. But she was never that into it. I think it's haram, so maybe that's why."

There's a small line, so I explain how it works to Sydney while we wait. "You sit over there," I say, pointing to a red stool with two hand-shaped panels on either side of it. "They take your photo, and then when it develops, you'll be able to see what color your aura is. They tell you what it all means."

Sydney unlinks her arm from mine and walks around the small shop, smoothing her hands over all the huge chunks of rose quartz. She bends down to look through glass cases at dozens of tiny rough pieces of amethyst, smooth stones of jade and jasper, and even asks to try on a turquoise necklace.

"This is the best place you've taken me, Cleo. For real. It's amazing."

I nod. "I know," I say, feeling myself slip into remembering the last time I was in Chinatown with Layla. We didn't even come here, but the sadness can leak into every little crevice of my mind if I let it.

"I was just at Dolly's," I tell Sydney, eager to think of something happy. She spins to face me with a shiny piece of obsidian in one hand, pale opalite in the other.

"Was Dom there?" she asks, and I nod.

"You guys have some cray-cray sexual energy. Tell me everything."

I blush, but then I tell her about Dom and his small plates. I tell her how he showed me around and that I helped them close up. I don't tell her about volunteering to work there, though, because it feels almost embarrassing—that I'm so desperate to hang out with Dom that I'll work at his grandparents' restaurant for practically nothing.

"Sounds like he's as into you as you are into him," Sydney pronounces after I've told her most of my story.

"I never said I was into him."

"Uh-huh." She doesn't even turn around to look at me. "Okay, Cleo." But under her breath she mutters, "*Someone's* in denial."

"Are you buying any of those?" I ask her. She's amassed a small pile of stones that range in color from deep blue to pure, nearly translucent white.

"Depends on what my aura says, I guess."

When it's finally our turn, she abandons her stones on the counter and steps up to the chair to have her photo taken. "You put your hands on the panels," the woman behind the camera tells her, and Sydney settles both her small hands in the right spots on either side of the chair. I go next.

It's not a regular camera. It's a big rectangular box with a string that the woman pulls to open the shutter. And the photos aren't regular photos. They're Polaroid-esque, and the lady who's helping us places it facedown, before inviting us to sit in front of one of the glass cases full of crystals.

When she peels the photos open to reveal our auras, they look very different. Sydney's is mostly red, bursting along the sides with pink and green, while mine is a blindingly bright shade of yellow, with green around the edges, and a tiny bit of light brown and blue over my chest.

"Whoa," I say. Mine and Gigi's never looked exactly alike, but ours were never as different as Sydney's and mine are right now.

Sydney gets her reading first. "Red is a good color," the woman says. "It means you're strong and adventurous—ready for anything." Sydney nods, and I agree, thinking of some of her ideas for my New Memories Project.

"This green means you're very creative, especially when it comes to practical things . . . maybe like hair? Like clothes?"

Sydney stretches her eyes wide. "I'm the president of the fashion club!" she squeals. "And I mean, look at my hair."

The lady smiles.

"This pink, though. This pink means that there is a new person you love. A new friend or a new boyfriend?" she says, and Sydney scrunches up her nose. "Girlfriend?"

Sydney blushes, but not in a way that seems like she's embarrassed. She grabs my hand. "Cleo's a new friend," she says to the woman, but she doesn't look at me as she says it, which makes me think she's probably thinking about Willa.

Then it's my turn.

"This yellow is interesting. Means you're very smart, very heady. But maybe sometimes you use your head a little too much?"

"Does she ever," mumbles Sydney, and I slap her shoulder.

204

"Your green, because it's here, just along the edges at the top, means perfectionism. It means you always want to be perfect, and you expect perfection from the people around you too. And this brown, right around your heart, means you're confused about something. Because it's so close to this pink, maybe you're confused about a friendship. About a person you love or have loved."

I swallow hard, and take the photo when she gives it to me. Sydney's still holding my hand, but I pull away.

—

Back out on the street, everything about us seems a little bit . . . off. I can't stop thinking about my reading. Sydney is quiet (and Sydney is *never* quiet), so she must still be thinking about hers too.

"You okay?" I ask her, and she nods but still doesn't say much. Right before we enter the subway station, she grabs my hand again. She pulls me over to a bench and once we're sitting, she stares at her aura photo instead of looking at me.

"So, there's something I haven't told you," she says.

I feel instantly tense, like I may have to run. I'm terrified of what she's about to say, because our new friendship is still so fresh, so . . . tenuous. I get a horrible feeling that I may lose her before I even feel like she's mine. I busy myself sticking my photo into my bag so I don't have to watch her say whatever's coming.

"That day you tutored Layla? I called Willa. I thought that you and Layla would work things out and then that me and Willa would, and that all four of us could be friends. But when I met you in Washington Square Park and you were so upset about the way things had gone, I didn't have it in me to tell you that me and Willa were okay. That we'd forgiven each other and met for ice cream and that we'd figured most of our shit out in a single afternoon."

Her words wash over me like a wave, and I'm suddenly drowning . . . in fear, jealousy, and something else.

"So you guys are friends again?" I ask, because I need her to say the words. I think of a line from *Hamlet* about things not being good or bad until you think of them that way, but this feels bad. I can't help but fall into the spiral of memories—the way I was slowly replaced in Layla's life by Sloane when we'd been friends for years; how it would be so easy for Sydney to forget all about me if she has Willa again, since we've only been hanging out for a few weeks.

"Yeah," Sydney says, and she actually sounds excited. "Yeah, but it's good, right? Now we can all hang out together."

Sydney's phone buzzes in her hand, and the screen lights up with Willa's face. And that's a sign I can't ignore; a sign if there ever was one.

You say that now, I think. But I know how these things go.

I stand up. "Thanks for coming with me tonight," I say, swallowing hard around the lump in my throat; around the pain of impending loneliness. "And . . . all the other nights. But don't feel like you have to hang out with me out of pity, or anything."

"Cleo," Sydney says, frowning. "What are you even talking about?" I shrug and start to walk away from her. "Where are you even going?" she calls.

"I got curfew," I lie.

"Now?" she asks. Her phone is still ringing.

"You can get that. Meet up with Willa. I'll see you guys at school."

Sydney looks at me and then back down at her phone. "You sure?" she asks. And I nod.

"Text me later?" she says to me as she lifts her phone to her ear. "Hey! Where are you?"

I've seen the way you can lose someone in slow motion, and I know the kinds of things it can make me do, so I keep my head down, listening as her voice fades away. I slip on my headphones, erasing the sound of her, just like I've been erasing everything else that hurts.

then:
December,
week 1

FEELINGS CHANGE

When I got home from school that chilly day in December and Mom was sitting at the kitchen table with a glass of wine in her hand, I immediately knew something was up. I looked at my phone to check the time, but it was as early as I thought it was, just a little after six. I hadn't spoken to Layla since the day in the library, and I wished I could text her to tell her that my mom was home before eight. She would have gotten it. She was the only person other than my dad who would.

My mom didn't turn at the sound of the door opening. Or at the sound of me dropping my keys into the tray beside a growing stack of unopened mail.

"Mom?" I asked, because my stomach instantly felt low and tight.

She turned when I said that. She smiled slow and soft in my direction and I didn't see her work phone or laptop in her immediate vicinity. Which was even weirder than her being home this early.

"What are you doing home?" I asked her.

She moved the base of her wineglass in small, slow circles across the surface of the table, swirling her drink. I could see the liquid leaving little trails along the sides of the glass—"legs," my dad would say.

"Just waiting for you and your father to get back," she said, like this was normal. "We need to talk to you."

I sat down at the table but my insides ignited with worry. So I got up, put a kettle on, and then headed back to my room to change out of my uniform. I texted my dad.

> Get home asap. Mom is here and she's being super
> weird.

For the first time probably ever, he didn't text me back right away.

The kettle screamed just as Daddy walked in—a harbinger of what felt like disaster. He was home too early too.

I nearly spilled the hot water as I poured myself a cup of tea, and I asked, "Did someone die?" as I joined them at the kitchen table. Daddy shook his head and untied his bow tie.

My voice cracked. "Is one of *you* dying?"

"No, honey. No one's dying," Mom said.

Daddy slipped his glasses from his face, but a second later he put them back on, and I braced myself to hear some new and awful truth.

"We're . . . separating," Daddy said, and Mom nodded, looking up. She continued where he left off.

"Nothing beyond that has been decided yet. We'll see what happens after we spend some time apart."

She released the death grip she had on the stem of her wineglass and reach her hand toward mine. But I moved quickly away.

"Why?" I said, turning to one parent and then the other. Daddy's chin trembled and he looked at Mom like he was apologizing to her with just his eyes. People who didn't want to be married anymore weren't supposed to still communicate like people who were in love. But that was when I realized I hadn't seen them in the same room together for nearly a month.

"I found an apartment—" Daddy started without answering my question.

"Already?" I cried.

Daddy reached out a hand to me, but I shrank away from him too. "It'll be available early next month, so that's when I'll be moving out. But until then, Baby Girl, nothing much will change."

"That's not exactly true, Cliff," Mom said. She was so calm. It made me feel worse.

"Right," Daddy said. "Your mother's right. I'm also going to be leaving Chisholm. I won't be returning to work there after the holiday break."

"I don't understand," I said. And then I said it again. "I . . . I just don't understand."

Mom cleared her throat in a way that sounded like she was trying to swallow. When I looked at her, I nearly shattered.

"Sometimes feelings just change, Cleo. Sometimes people . . . outgrow each other."

Defiantly, I shook my head. "No, that's not a thing. If you love someone you're supposed to love them forever."

Mom said, "Sadly, honey, love isn't always enough."

In his Librarian Voice, Daddy said, "One day you'll understand, honey. You're still so young."

I almost knocked my chair over, I stood up so fast. "*You* don't get to say that to me. You don't get to dismiss my feelings based on my age. I'm not a two-year-old who's bumped her head. I'm *sixteen* and"—my voice cracked as tears spilled over onto my cheeks—"my *family* is falling apart." A second later I added, "Everything is."

My dad encircled his big hand around my wrist like he wanted to hold me in place. But I wrenched out of it easily, because he's always touched me like he's afraid I'll break.

I moved away from the table and back down the hall to my room. I slammed my door. I put on Billie Holiday and I blasted it, letting her sultry, soulful voice fill me up. I lay on my bed, staring at the ceiling, wondering where Daddy would go, how far away it would be, and how often I'd get to see him now that everything was changing. For the millionth time since I'd lost her, I desperately wished Gigi were still alive.

I took out my phone, and despite my earlier hesitations, I texted Layla.

Can you talk?

I waited and waited. I texted her again.

Layla, text me back.

An hour went by without an answer. And then, when I heard a knock on my door, I told whoever it was to go away. I curled into myself and I sobbed like someone had just punched me in the stomach, because that's what it felt like. I was losing everything and everyone all at once. I texted Layla one more time.

Lay. I need you.

I hated how desperate the text sounded, but nothing else had worked. When she finally texted back, it was after midnight. I was half-asleep in the dark, and the glow from my phone only roused me because it was inches away from my swollen eyes. I sat up, read it, and then threw my phone across the room. It hit one of my snow globes and I heard something shatter.

I told you. I need some space.

WE'RE GOOD

I woke up early the morning after my parents told me about the separation, and I left before anyone else did. The screen of my phone was cracked from when I threw it the night before, and my floor was wet and covered in broken glass. I'd hit my Peter Pan snow globe when I'd pitched my phone across my room, the one Gigi had gotten me for my eighth birthday. Neverland was in pieces below my shelves.

I caught the train into the city, needing the quiet buzz of early-morning Manhattan, and got off at the stop closest to school. I liked watching the city wake itself up. Delivery trucks unloaded everything from kegs to dozens of cases of Snapple, and no one was honking their horn yet. Trash trucks beeped and clicked and crashed as they lifted and emptied the contents of dumpsters into their stained compactors. And the only pedestrians were construction workers, baristas, bakery owners, and people with giant suitcases on their way to the airport or just arriving in the city.

Etta James crooned in my ears as I sat on a cold bench to people-watch. I looked up and noticed that wreaths had been hung on lampposts and that the trees that lined the sidewalk were strung with tiny white lights. I changed my music to Nat King

Cole's "Christmas Song" and instantly my mood brightened the tiniest bit. For the first time ever, I wanted to skip school. It was unfathomable, the idea of going into that building and not speaking to my dad *or* Layla. Being alone with my thoughts and Nat's voice in this decked-out version of the city was a much better alternative.

Just as I was about to take out my wallet to see if I had enough money to buy myself a cup of tea, Jase surfaced from the subway station right beside me.

"Cleo? What are you doing here so early?"

"I could ask you the same question," I said.

He grinned. "Touché. My dad's going to do some relief work in Cambodia today, so we all got up to have breakfast with him before he had to head to the airport. My mom was afraid if I went back to bed I wouldn't get up in time for school, so she made me leave."

I laughed. It felt strange to laugh, but it was nice.

"She's probably right." I looked in my wallet. I had ten bucks. "Can I buy you a coffee?" I asked him.

"Oh God, yes," he said, reaching out to pull me up.

Inside one of the only open coffee shops, Jase and I found a small table with two chairs. We slipped out of our coats and sat close together as steam from our drinks spun into the air between us. I couldn't decide if I felt older because I was up early, because I was sitting in a coffee shop with a boy, or because something about me was fundamentally changed by my parents' announcement the night before, and I was having to deal with it all on my own. But whatever it was, I felt like a more grown-up version of myself: tougher, more serious, and a little more alive.

217

"So, you haven't told me why *you're* here so early," he said.

I shrugged. "Just couldn't sleep." I looked over my shoulder at the slowly filling streets, still trying to decide what the rest of my day would look like.

"Cleo," Jase said, kind of seriously. I turned back to look at him. "We're okay, right? Like, we're cool?"

I smiled a little. "I just bought you coffee, Jase. We're fine," I said. I took a sip of my tea.

"Okay, good." He sipped his own drink, but as I watched the way his dimples appeared and disappeared when he lifted and lowered his cup, I wanted to ask him something.

"Why did we break up?" I asked. I saw him tense, but with everything my parents were saying last night, I genuinely wanted to know if his perspective of our downfall was the same as mine.

"I don't mean it in an accusatory way. I mean, like . . ." I tapped the table as I tried to figure out the word I was looking for. "Objectively. *Scientifically.* I think we broke up because you were going to soccer camp, and I would have missed you too much to stay together, and because we just worked better as friends. But I'm wondering if you felt the same way."

His shoulders inched back down. "Oh. Well, I do think we're better as friends, but it wasn't just about soccer camp for me."

I kept watching him, taking in the line of kohl along his lower eyelids. He smiled a little, his dimples sinking in and staying put.

"I guess it was like this: you're this super-cute girl, right?"

I shrugged and blushed a little. "I guess I am pretty cute," I said, looking at how his big hands wrapped around the small coffee cup.

He rolled his eyes. "Right. And so, before I knew you, I made up all these things about you. Like, *I bet she likes comics,* or *I bet she watches reality shows,* or *I bet she loves animals.*"

"One out of three isn't bad, considering you were just going by how I looked," I said. "And actually—"

"Jesus, Baker. Let me finish."

I laughed. "Sorry."

"So," he said. He ran one of his hands through his thick black hair. "In my head you were a different version of yourself, right? Like . . . 'Brain-Cleo.'"

I grinned and pressed my lips together. I thought about Gigi saying I was spinning stories whenever I made things up about people in my head.

"But then I started talking to you, and Real-Cleo was supercool in a bunch of different ways, but not the ways I had imagined."

"Okay," I said, lifting my cup.

"So at first I was like, 'Real-Cleo is even better than Brain-Cleo,' right? But here's the weird part: There is a Brain-Jase too. In *my* brain, not just yours. So not only did I think, 'This is how Cleo will be.' I also thought, 'This is how I will be *with* Cleo.' But the problem was, the longer we dated, the less either of us lived up to those versions of ourselves."

I looked at my hands and bit my lip, but I understood what he meant. He wanted us to be these romanticized versions of ourselves and we just weren't—we never could be.

"Damn," I said.

"Maybe I got too caught up in the *idea* of us. I don't know.

You were unpredictable—I never knew what you might want, how you might be. I was too, I guess. I know what to expect from soccer—what everyone wants and how we're all going to be. I know how to do the whole jock thing, but I didn't really know how to be a good boyfriend. If that makes any sense."

"I get that," I said, thinking about how my parents told me that feelings change. But maybe it's expectations that change more than anything else.

Jase sips his coffee and we're both quiet for a beat before he says, "You know Dom asked me about you, right? Like, asked if I'd be cool with him *getting to know you*."

I looked up at him and Jase was smirking. "Really?" I asked. "Yup."

A too-long pause followed, and I punched his shoulder. "And? What did you tell him?!"

"I said he better not be shitty to you or I'd kick his ass."

My jaw dropped. "Jase Lin!" I squealed, and he laughed. I covered my face because I could feel it heating up and I didn't want Jase to see me blushing. He gently pulled my hands away.

We talked for a while longer about everything. I told him about the Shakespeare program and showed him photos of the Globe Theatre. He told me about soccer, about his dad's charity work, and how he might go to Cambodia with him this summer. We talked for so long that we were almost late to school.

We pulled our jackets back over our shoulders and he laughed at me when I stood up too quickly and almost knocked over my chair after I realized what time it was. We pushed our way back outside and despite our rush, he stopped me on the corner.

"Seriously, though. You sure we're okay?" he asked again, and I allowed myself to miss his dark serious eyes looking at me like I was the only person on earth, but only for a second.

Then I smiled.

"I'm sure," I said. "We're good."

ANYWHERE BUT HERE

I decided to go to school after all. And just as I thought she would, Layla ignored me. In homeroom, she didn't even look in my direction. At lunch, she sat with the Chorus Girls. Jase found me sitting alone and asked what was wrong, but I couldn't bring myself to be completely honest. I was dying to tell someone what was happening with my parents, but the only person I wanted to talk to was my best friend.

Just after third period, I spotted Layla in the hall at her locker alone. She had her headphones in and was nodding along to whatever was playing. I knew I only had a few minutes before she'd be surrounded by Sloane, Sage, Melody, Cadence, and Valeria, and probably Mason too. But just before I walked up to her, it occurred to me that maybe Layla's feelings about me were changing because I hadn't lived up to her expectations, just like what had happened with Jase. She was certainly treating me in a way she never had before, and I needed to know if she was only mad for now or if the ground beneath us had shifted in a way that was unfixable.

"Layla," I said. And I was standing close enough that I knew she heard me, could feel me beside her, but she pretended she couldn't. *"Layla,"* I said again, a little louder.

She let out a heavy sigh and pulled out one of her earbuds. "*What*, Cleo? Don't you know wh-wh-what space means?"

Her hostility made everything I'd been holding in all day bubble to the surface. My throat went achy and tight.

"Yeah, Layla. I know what space means," I said. "But I thought we were best friends. I thought if I needed you, you'd always be someone I could count on."

She narrowed her dark eyes. "Oh. That's funny. B-b-because I thought the same thing. I thought my so-called b-best friend would be ssssupportive when something I've wanted for forever happened t-to me. I thought my so-called b-b-best friend would b-b-b-be rooting for me more than anyone else."

Everything in me was so raw that each word felt like salt being rubbed into a wound. And of course that was when I saw Sloane and the other girls approaching. I'd barely recovered enough to try to respond. My window of opportunity was closing before I could think of what to say next. Because they were all on *her* side. To them, I was a pretentious jerk who didn't know how to keep a secret or lock a door; a mean, thoughtless girl who told her friend she was "surprised" she'd gotten a lead role. They saw me as this version of myself that was warped and twisted and untrue. My conversation with Jase came back to me in a bright and sudden flash: their Brain-Cleo was the *worst*.

"Layla," I said. "You *know* me. You know how I really feel."

"Do I, though?" she asked. And then the other girls were there sneering at me, making me feel small, and an instant later, completely invisible.

That time, though, I didn't slink away. Maybe it was the fact that my family was falling apart and it felt like no one understood or cared. Maybe it was the way these girls always made me feel like I didn't matter. Maybe it was the "so-called" that Layla put in front of the words "best friend." But whatever it was, it made me angry enough to be brave.

The Chorus Girls were all talking to each other with their pretty, girly voices. They were talking over and about me, like I wasn't standing right there. I was *Mean*-Cleo, *Harsh*-Cleo, *Dumbass-Bitch*-Cleo. And they must have been right, because I felt like the funhouse version of myself—everything inside me unrecognizable and stretched a little too thin.

Layla turned away from me to face them for roughly the millionth time, and something inside me snapped. A zing of electric rage shot straight through me, quick and deadly, and I was done letting her decide my fate.

There was also something else: a breaking of whatever had held me together for so long; a shattering of the last thing that had kept the pain inside me quiet. But on the outside I stayed calm. On the outside, I smiled sweetly. I understood Lady Macbeth in that moment as I never had before: I looked like the innocent flower, but I was a serpent under it.

"You know what, *L*," I said. The Chorus Girls all stopped their chattering. They turned to look at me like they were all one person, and some thorny part of me was happy that they'd all hear what I had to say.

I couldn't see Layla clearly because my eyes were full, and I was so angry that every part of my body was shaking. "Best of luck with the musical," I said. And she looked pleased. Happy with herself or maybe even with her *so-called best friend*. But there was a crack in the hull of me, and I was sinking. She didn't yet know, but I wasn't going down alone.

"I hope you sing your fucking heart out," I spat, stepping closer to her. I took a deep breath and hissed through my teeth, "And I hope you stutter through *every* line."

I said it like it was a prayer or a promise. I said it like it was a wish. And I hated myself for saying it almost instantly.

Right after last period, I ran down the hall and out into the cold, just wanting to be alone as quickly as possible. But instead of disappearing into the anonymity of the city the way I'd hoped, I almost ran right into Dominic Grey.

"Whoa," he said, stopping me with his hands on my shoulders so we didn't completely collide. "Where you running off to?"

"Anywhere but here," I said, thinking of what Jase told me about him. Knowing that whatever had started at the Halloween party wouldn't have a chance to go further anytime soon. I couldn't imagine kissing anyone when so much of my life was exploding. I couldn't think about trusting a new person when I couldn't trust my parents or the girl who was supposed to be my best friend.

"Are you—"

"No, I'm not okay," I said. "I have to go."

I jerked away from him, and if there hadn't been a mile-long bridge crowded with tourists between my school and my apartment, I would have run all the way home.

now

A CHAPERONE

Over the next few days, whenever Sydney texts me, I don't text back. I avoid her at school as much as I can and even go as far as to turn and walk in the other direction if I see her coming down the hall.

It's not that I'm upset with her—not exactly. It's that I don't need her yet, and I don't want to get to the point where I do. And since she has Willa now, it's not like she needs me at all.

To fill my time and distract myself from my new Sydneyless-ness, I overly commit to my new part-time job. I go to Dolly's almost daily, and get to know Mr. Henry, aka Pop, and especially Miss Dolly really well. They ask about school and my family, what I like to do and read. I ask them about what it was like to leave everything behind and move here with just a dream in the sixties and seventies, and they tell me endless stories about a version of New York I'll never know.

I seat customers and take their orders; crack jokes with the regulars; swap secrets with Dom, leaning across the counter to whisper to him, whenever he and I go on break. And on the slow-est nights, I watch Dom do magic tricks for little kids who are up way past their bedtimes, eating sundaes at the bar.

I fall in love with the diner and all the people in it, and I understand why Dom wants to make sure this place survives.

"I just feel like there has to be something more I can be doing," I say to my dad. It's the weekend, so I'm at his place and we're spread out on the couch tossing popcorn into each other's mouths. I toss a piece that lands on Daddy's tongue and he says, "Nice," before launching his own shot. It bounces off my front teeth.

"Have you spoken to Dolly or Henry about this?"

"No. I don't want them to know that Dom told me the diner is in trouble. It might be something they don't want a lot of people to know. But Dom said—"

"I know, hon, but I wouldn't jump to any conclusions based on what Dom said. He's a kid, just like you."

"Seriously, Daddy? *Ageism?*"

My dad sighs and launches another kernel in my direction. I dive for it, mouth open, and it lands in my mouth.

"I mean, the neighborhood is definitely changing," he says. "No one can deny that."

"Exactly. And I can't sit around and do nothing. Maybe I could run a fundraiser for them? Do you think the regulars would pitch in?"

He just makes his Librarian Face. "It may not be that simple. If they have a backlog of bills, an influx of cash might help. But if it's just that fewer people are coming through the doors every day, I'm not sure a fundraiser will solve their problem long term. You can give a man a fish and all that, right?"

I frown at him. Toss a piece of popcorn. I'm pretty sure that wasn't Shakespeare. "Did you just quote *the Bible?*"

230

Daddy looks slightly disappointed. He opens the eye he'd closed as he prepared to aim and shoot. "You *know* that's not from the Bible. Look, Baby Girl, I just don't want you to get too stressed about this. You have enough to worry about with keeping up with your homework and tutoring."

"Oh crap," I say. I jump up and place the bowl of popcorn I'm holding on the coffee table. "I'm late."

—

Layla and I agreed that the only way we were going to get through this tutoring assignment was if we had a moderator—a neutral third party to basically chaperone what we hoped would be our last session for a while. We also agreed to meet at a completely innocuous location (this was my requirement), instead of Dolly's even though it's a Sunday.

Layla is already seated at a small table at the back of the Starbucks when I arrive, and a second later, our chaperone walks in. Jase throws his arm around my shoulder while I'm still standing near the entrance glaring in Layla's direction.

"Cleo Imani Baker!" he whispers. "What are we doing?"

"We're glaring," I whisper back. He's quiet for a few seconds. When I look up, he's squinting hard in Layla's direction.

"How long are we going to glare?" he whispers next. I sigh. "I guess we can be done," I say.

"Cool. Hey, Lay!" he shouts, and Layla looks up from her phone. She grins at him, but when she sees me, her smile disappears.

I picked Starbucks because I'd otherwise never go to one.

There are just way too many independently owned coffee shops in the city for me to spend my (parents') money here. It makes me think of Dolly's losing out to burger chains and trendy noodle bars. I don't want to buy anything, but I don't want to get kicked out for loitering, so I get a frappuccino (and, I'll be honest, it's delicious).

"So," Jase says, once we're all seated. "The objective today is for you, Cleo, to read this paper and offer our friend"—I glare at him—"correction, *my* friend Layla, here, some constructive feedback. Because, Layla, you can't afford to mess this paper up, and, Cleo, you're a truant who needs to make up the credit you missed while being . . . truant-y."

I nod. Layla nods. Jase smiles. "Okay, then! Let's begin."

Layla hands me her paper without looking at me at all. She says, more to Jase than me, "I think I hit all the p-points we discussed, b-b-but I'm stuck on the b-best way to p-pull off the Islam section without an outsider reading it in a stereotypical way. I w-w-w-want to make sure I'm saying there are b-beautiful elements of Islam, and that even sssso, there are imperfections. Like, the Qur'an says men and w-w-w-women are spiritual equals—it's *people* that mmake up arbitrary rules about wh-what's right for g-g-girls versus boys."

I nod and skim the first half of her paper. Jase plays a game on his phone. "This looks really good, Layla. Maybe just sprinkle the mentions of Islam versus culture throughout instead of lumping it all together in one section as a separate argument. Like here, when you're talking about Macbeth's ideas of manhood, talk about how masculinity is interpreted differently by different people. Or here, when you touch on the fact that they have no children, and how Lady Macbeth kind of holds it against him, talk about the cultural expectations of women versus men when it comes to kids and raising families. Does that make sense? Weaving it throughout instead of separating it?"

I look at her directly for the first time since we got here. Her hair is so straight, and she's wearing dark eyeliner with dangly earrings, and she looks completely different from the girl I used to know. I suddenly realize—or maybe I just finally admit to myself—that this is who she is now.

My best friend is gone, I think as Layla jots down notes based on what I've said. And the acceptance of something so simple, something that should have been obvious to me before now, makes me let go of whatever it was I was holding on to.

"That's all you needed, right?" I say, because I'm overcome with a desire to get away from her. I can feel my chest getting tight with the threat of tears, and my throat feels achy and thick. Layla flips through the remaining pages of the essay and asks me a few more questions that I answer quickly and succinctly. She pulls out her book and asks if I think the quotations she's included to support her arguments are the best ones, and I double-check, feeling squirmy and more ready to leave than ever. Finally, Layla begins putting her things away and I follow suit. She looks up at Jase.

"Thanks for p-p-playing middleman, J," she says, and I want to puke because I know this is something she's picked up from Sloane, who can't be bothered to say people's whole names. I think of them calling her *L,* and then of the one time I did, and I want to run and hide.

But I run to Dolly's instead.

CHARITY

"Hey," Dom says when I walk into the kitchen. His lips slip into a grin.

"Hi," I say back. I take a step closer to him, peering over his shoulder. He's arranging small scoops of baked macaroni and cheese on a bright blue dish—another one of his small plates, I guess. It's slow in the dining room, and sometimes he gives free samples to customers waiting at the counter for take-out orders, or regulars nursing coffees while they read the paper. When I asked Miss Dolly if it was okay to step away and see if Dom needed any help, she grinned at me conspiratorially. I think she knows I just want to talk to him, but she's kind enough not to call me out about it.

"I thought you weren't coming in today," he says. He sets the plate under a heat lamp and turns back to the stove, sliding dirty pots and black-bottomed pans into the deep sink.

"Yeah, I wasn't. But you know Dolly's is like my safe place now." I lean against the counter beside him. "I had to tutor today," I say quietly.

"Uh-oh," he says, looking at me through the fringe of his

lashes as he continues to move expertly around the kitchen. "How'd that go?"

"It could have been worse, but she barely looked at me the whole time. Jase was there, which helped."

"Ahhh," Dom says. He walks over to the fridge and pulls out a fat red tomato and a ball of juicy-looking mozzarella. "Hard to be upset with that ray of sunshine nearby."

I laugh a little. "Exactly. But I don't know. I think today is the first day I realized Layla's totally different now. Like *my* Layla is really, really gone."

He nods. Dom's always focused in the kitchen, but tonight he seems even quieter than he usually is.

I'm about to ask him if everything's okay when he picks up a sharp knife and starts to cut the tomato into thick slices. My stomach growls.

"Want some of this?" he asks, and I wonder if he heard. He picks up the mozzarella next and slices it, then arranges both on a plate, alternating tomato, then cheese, then tomato before drizzling it all with a thick olive oil.

"Duh," I say. He smirks and sprinkles big granules of salt and pepper all over it, and I grab two forks.

We eat standing up, without talking, and the soft sounds of us chewing is drowned out by the dishwasher and the one other cook, who is talking loudly on his cellphone. The cheese is smooth and cold and the tomato is so juicy that the seeds slide down my chin. I wipe them away with the back of my hand.

"So is it over?" Dom asks. He hands me a napkin, but his eyes seem distant even as he looks at me. "Like, are you done tutoring her?"

I nod. "I think so. If she needs more help for the next assignment, I think I'm going to ask Novak to pair her up with someone else."

I cut the last slices of tomato and cheese in half so we can share up until the very last bite. I look around the kitchen at the stainless steel appliances, the stacks of serving plates and spices. I want to believe that truly good things can last forever even if my friendship with Layla couldn't.

"So. I was doing some research about fundraising," I say, lifting the empty plate and used forks. I settle them into the sink and turn the water on, rinsing it all clean. He looks at me blankly, so I add, "For this place. For Dolly's."

"Oh," Dom says. He angles his head in my direction, and his dark hair shimmers as he turns. He looks skeptical. Or I guess uninterested. He grabs a bar mop and starts wiping down the counter, and I thought he'd be more excited by the prospect of raising money for his grandparents—that he'd be dying to hear what I had to say.

I take a deep breath and I pitch him the idea about running a fundraiser in the neighborhood.

"I don't know," he says.

I tell him about the crowdsourcing websites I'd looked up— how successful I read they can be.

"We could post about it everywhere. People love feeling like they're a part of something."

Dom crosses his arms. "I don't really want to do that," he says.

"But, Dom," I insist. "It could be really great. What about

your small plates? We could set up a table out front and give out little samples to encourage people to come in like you do with the regulars now anyway, and maybe have a donation box near the door. Or what about posting SAVE DOLLY'S posters around the neighborhood. People would be so—"

"Look," Dom starts, but he isn't facing me. He sniffs hard and rubs his hand down his face. He stares at the floor, then at the stove in front of him, then at the wall behind my head. His eyes turn stormy and he furrows his brow. "I totally appreciate you offering to help out after school or whatever. Lolly and Pop do too. But this is our *livelihood,* not some part-time gig the way it is for you, and . . ."

I cut in. "Don't worry about it, really. You know I love this place. I'm happy to help. Obviously, I know a fundraiser won't fix everything. We'll need to come up with something more sustainable to get business back to where it used to be, but I think it's a good place to start, and I'm—"

He looks right at me then, and the weight of his gaze stops me cold.

"Cleo. Stop. Just stop. We don't need—or *want*—your charity."

The color of our conversation turns so quickly that I'm a little too stunned to say anything that makes much sense.

"Right," I say, the way he's looking at me hurting more than his actual words. Stupidly, I say it again. "Right. Of course not."

I try to clear my throat a few times, but it doesn't work. Dom doesn't look my way or say another word to me, just keeps cleaning the kitchen like I'm not there. And here I stand again, feeling invisible; feeling forgotten.

Before I walk out of the kitchen, I want to apologize. I want to get us back to sharing a plate, to talking like we're old friends, to *fix* whatever I just broke. But the last time I tried to tell someone I was sorry, they just told me how little they wanted me in their life. And I'm not brave enough to hear that again—that someone I want doesn't want me back.

Now, not even Dolly's is safe.

All this time I've been blaming Layla for the way things are between us. But after her, and Sydney, and now Dom, it's clear that the problem isn't them. It has to be *me*.

I pull on my coat, waving goodbye to Miss Dolly and Pop, wondering if I should bother coming in tomorrow if Dom is still upset with me. It isn't until I'm back inside my own bedroom that I realize I'll be avoiding three different people at school tomorrow—that I'm back to being all alone again.

A CHANCE

I expect Monday to be torture, what with the Sydney and Dom situations, but in homeroom I encounter the perfect distraction: there seems to be trouble in Chorus Girl Land.

When I walk in, Dom ignores me, which hurts, but I expected that. What I don't expect is to see Layla sitting as far away from Sloane as possible in a classroom of this size. Sloane's cheeks are a bright, angry red, while Layla looks like she's been crying. It's strange that it makes me kind of happy, seeing them so *unhappy* But I need to know what happened.

I spend the rest of the morning launching a full-blown investigation, which is an excellent way to avoid my own problems. I ask around in each of my classes. I walk slowly down the hall, listening for whispers. I linger in bathroom stalls. But by lunch I still know nothing.

I'd planned to hide in the library during the lunch period because I couldn't imagine going back to eating alone after weeks of Dom and Sydney sitting with me. But the cafeteria is prime real estate if one wants to hear the latest gossip. Everyone talks about everyone else on a nearly endless loop in there.

So I head to the cafeteria, thinking about where I should sit.

I want to pick the most strategic table, but I have no idea where Layla will be today since she and Sloane are in the middle of a fight. I still haven't decided when I get to the lunchroom and see Sydney sitting across from Willa at my normal table. Sydney spots me and shouts my name across the whole cafeteria. I immediately turn to leave, reverting to my original plan of hiding out in the library, but she comes over and stops me, grabbing my hand.

"I need you to at least listen to me, okay? If you still hate me after you've heard me out, then you can ignore me forever. But I'm not letting you avoid me just because you're scared. I'm not letting you lose out on potentially great friends because you got burned once. And believe me, I'm a *great* friend."

"Sydney," I whisper, looking around and behind her at the dozens of people watching us. "I don't hate you." I know she'd be a great friend; she already has been. What I'm worried about is her disappearing. Her finding out the worst of it—the worst of *me*—and realizing I don't deserve friends. Especially not friends like her.

But I don't argue because too many people are staring. I follow her slowly across the room.

Willa is tossing fries into the air and catching them in her mouth. Her short black hair is in what I guess could be called a ponytail, but it looks more like a tiny sprout surrounded by a million colorful bobby pins growing out of the back of her head. She's wearing her signature bangles—dozens on both wrists—and they jingle as she throws food in the air and dives for it.

"Hey," I say a little coolly to her. But when she looks up, she gives me the warmest smile, despite my chilly greeting. It sends

Layla's words from weeks ago rushing through my head again: *You think you own places, Cleo. Just like you think you own people.*

And I hate to admit it, but maybe she's right.

I clear my throat and work hard to smile at girls with whom I haven't yet ruined everything.

"Yo, you like jazz, right? Sydney was telling me that you're like, obsessed with jazz."

This is the first thing Willa Bae says to me. Her voice is raspy and deep, and it's strange to hear a voice like that coming out of such a small girl. She looks at me expectantly, eyebrows raised. She leans back in her seat, tosses her arm across the back of the chair beside her, and nods like she's listening to music no one else can hear. She reminds me of Ellen Page, if Ellen Page were Korean and had a cool haircut. And dammit, I think I like her already.

"Yeah," I say. "I do love jazz." I sit down slowly, forgetting about Layla and Sloane and whatever their drama might entail, feeling cautiously open, hopeful and terrified and unsure of what she'll say next.

"Sweeeeet," Willa says, dragging out the *e* sound and reaching for a pair of chunky purple headphones. She fits them over my ears like it's her job, then picks up her phone and starts typing, searching for a song, I guess. I look over at Sydney with wide eyes. *What is happening?* I mouth.

"Ugh, Will. I told you *I* needed to talk to her."

"And you can talk as much as you want as soon as Cleo has heard this one song." Willa looks up at me, shaking her bangs away from her narrow eyes. "You *have* to hear this one song," she reiterates.

She presses play and what I hear kind of blows me away.

It's a cover of "Fly Me to the Moon," and the voice is clear and light, full of the kind of passion that only comes from being fully and deeply in love. I close my eyes so I can shut out the rest of the world as I listen, and when I hear Willa's voice again it seems to be coming from somewhere farther away than the three feet between us.

"See," she's saying from underwater, from a galaxy away. Her bangles sing—an added percussion to the song I'm listening to—so she must be gesturing at me wildly. "That's the reaction *you* were supposed to have!"

When I open my eyes, Sydney is rolling hers.

"Who *is* this?" I ask Willa once the song is over. I hand her headphones back though I really want to keep listening.

"It's this jazz cover band called the Cover Girls. This girl I used to see, her older sister is the singer. I've been obsessed with them ever since the first time I saw one of their shows. I was telling Syd that we should go to one."

"Oh my God," Sydney says. "Are you really trying to use Cleo to guilt me into going? She doesn't even know you!"

Willa is unbothered. She turns to me like Sydney isn't even at the table with us.

"But you want to go, don't you?" Willa says, smirking and wiggling her eyebrows. "Don't you?"

I toss Sydney an apologetic look. "Kinda?"

Willa punches the air. "Yes! I knew you would! We're going!"

Sydney covers her face. "Oh my God," she says again.

—

"She's cool," I say to Sydney when Willa goes to grab a coffee. "Confident in a scary kind of way."

"Oh, I know. That's just Willa. She is like, totally cool with who she is and she doesn't hide it."

I nod, watching as across the room, Willa fills a coffee cup and then starts talking to someone in line behind her more with her hands than her voice. She reaches out and squeezes the girl's hand. She fingers a strand of her hair.

"I really do want to go see that band, though," I say. "You really didn't like that song?"

Sydney looks serious all of a sudden. "It's not that," she says without further explanation. When she starts talking again, it's not about the music.

"Look," she says. "What I wanted to talk to you about before Willa derailed my whole plan was us."

I swallow hard and take a sip of water. I haven't touched my lunch yet, and this conversation is making my stomach squeeze with tension, so I don't think I will. Besides, lately all food seems subpar, and only reminds me of my weirdness with Dom. I sit further back in my seat.

"It's kinda messed up that you just wrote me off the way you did. That you just decided to stop talking to me. And I know you had a rough time with Layla, but don't assume things about me just because of stuff that happened with her."

But you don't understand is what I'm tempted to say to her.

"I don't want to hurt you," I mumble instead.

"Do you not want to hurt me? Or are you afraid I'm gonna hurt you?"

I let out a long, low sigh. "Both?" I admit.

Sydney nods, and then Willa is back. She looks at us, taking in the tense way we're staring at each other across the table. I feel like I'm close to tears. "You need some privacy?" Willa asks.

And when Sydney says, "You mind?" Willa shakes her head and slips those giant headphones over her ears. It sounds like she's listening to metal now. She nods to the beat and keeps her eyes and hands busy ripping open creamers and sugar packets for her coffee.

"Look, how about we do this," Sydney says. Her earrings are tiny chandeliers today, and I stare at them instead of meeting her eyes as she talks. "How about you give me a chance, and I give you one? How about we each try our best, but we tell each other if we mess up? How about we don't decide we can't be friends before we even try?"

I blink, looking up and away from her, trying to get rid of tears, but I'm sure my eyes still look glassy. I give a tiny nod.

Sydney clears her throat. "Okay, then. What's the next spot on your New Memories list?"

I take out my phone and pull up my list. But then I glance over at Willa, who is messing around with her phone. I don't say a thing, but I guess Sydney can tell what I'm thinking: Willa is a threat because she's cute and cool and clearly comfortable with herself in a way I'm still trying to become. Why be friends with me, when Sydney could be friends with a girl like her?

Sydney crosses her arms. "Stop it," she says sternly, like she's a teacher, or my mom. "Give Willa, and yourself, a chance too."

then:
December,
week 2

NOBODY

It had been three days since I yelled at Layla in the hallway. Thirteen since she'd texted or called. It was also the day that Daddy was moving out—whoever had occupied the apartment he'd found had decided to move early so they could be settled in their new place before the holidays. My parents thought that this was a good idea—for Daddy to be settled before the new year and his new job started—so we wouldn't even be having a final Christmas together, as a family that lived in the same place.

I could barely *look* at my mother, because it felt like everything that was happening with Daddy was all her fault, and I was upset with myself because Layla's complete and utter silence was mostly mine.

Daddy had already started lining up boxes of his clothes, books, records, and art along the hallway when I woke up.

"You'll have two Christmases," he said when he found me in the hall, weeping with his copy of *Antony and Cleopatra* in my hands.

"God, Daddy. I'm not a fucking five-year-old!" I said, throwing the book back into the box I'd lifted it out of. "You should know I don't care about that."

Daddy looked wounded, and I felt bad for making something that was clearly hard for him harder. I was just about to apologize when my mom stepped out of the bathroom and said, "Cleo, I know you're upset, but we don't use that kind of language in this house."

I didn't apologize then. I just started crying harder.

"Seriously, Mom? You're lecturing me about language when Daddy's *shit* is in *fucking* boxes all along our *goddamn* hallway? Are you even human?"

I slammed my bedroom door, dressed quickly, and ran out of the apartment after that, not looking back at either of them. I didn't want to see the agony on my mother's face or have to deal with my father's sadness. And I knew I couldn't be there when the movers arrived and he and everything he owned disappeared from our home for good.

—

At school, I discovered that the Chorus Girls had rallied around Layla, and because of what I'd said to her in front of them, I was instantly their enemy. Seeing them step into the school building unexpectedly and almost immediately made my bad morning worse.

"Look who it is," I heard a high-pitched voice trill as soon as I closed my locker. A few people snickered, and I didn't need to turn around to know who was speaking. "Chloe Baker the Bitch," Sage whispered as she passed me, still not knowing what my name actually was, and clearly not caring.

"It looks like someone threw up on her face," Melody said next. She spoke quietly, just loudly enough for me to hear. I hadn't heard that one in a while, but my faceful of freckles had prepared me for those kinds of insults. I'd been hearing them all my life.

Maybe starting a day cursing in front of my parents had made me ballsy, had made me stupidly brave. Because without looking at them, I said, "Funny. That the best you got?"

"It looks like she just came from a shitty funeral," Cadence muttered next, like I hadn't spoken a word. "Do your parents always wear black too? You know, because they're mourning your birth?"

At the mention of my parents, I lost most if not all of my nerve. I thought of the boxes back home and my heart began breaking all over again. I started walking a little more quickly down the hall.

"And her hair," Sage said, and I knew what came next would sting, especially because Sage was black too. She knew what it was like to live with black hair—with feeling like it was never straight enough or long enough or good enough—so she knew exactly what to say to cut right to the heart of me, quick and deep. "It's so nappy and gross-looking. Say it with me, Chloe: *Shampoo. Condition. Rinse and repeat.* And have you ever heard of a flatiron?"

They laughed, and I wanted to pull *their* hair out at the roots. I clenched my fists so tightly that I could feel my nails digging into my palms.

I looked up then, because I knew that Layla had to be with them. My chest felt heavy, and I couldn't get enough air into my lungs when my eyes met hers. She wasn't smiling and she wasn't adding to the flurry of insults they were hurling in my direction, but she wasn't doing anything to stop them either.

"Come on, guys," Sloane said. And I thought, *Is it really going to be her that puts an end to this?* I made the mistake of looking hopeful—of glancing over at her instead of keeping my eyes on Layla, or looking back down. Sloane stared right at me, *through* me, and said, "Anyone who says the shit she said to their 'best friend' isn't worth our time." She turned to Layla. "She's . . . *literal trash* and you don't need her." And then, to me: "Fucking *nobody.*"

I was hot with fury, cold and achy with hurt. And I didn't know a body could contain such a storm of feeling until they kept talking; kept laughing. Sloane threw her arm over Layla's shoulder, and Layla looked down at her shoes, her curtain of too-straight hair falling over her face. And still she stayed quiet. Her silence was the worst part of all.

When they passed, I waited, and eventually the icy flames inside me passed too. And though I was hurting like those girls had punched me and kicked me and left me for dead, I was somehow still standing. If anyone saw me, there'd be no evidence that anything had even happened.

That's the thing about words: they can leave you both unscathed and completely gutted.

Girls wage endless wars with their voices, tearing you apart without touching you at all.

—

I spent all of homeroom trying hard not to listen to every word Sloane was saying to Layla a few feet behind me, but I heard most of it anyway, and plenty of it was awful things about me.

About halfway through the period I couldn't take it anymore, so when my phone buzzed with an email notification that my application status for the Shakespeare program had changed, I was so relieved I lost my breath. I raised my hand and asked for a hall pass, and when Mr. Yoon granted me my freedom, I raced to Novak's classroom desperate for some good news.

I couldn't help but imagine the open-air performances I'd attend in London; the people I'd meet and what their accents would sound like. I daydreamed constantly about being away from this place—away from Layla and Sloane and all my family's drama. And here it finally was—my way out. Ms. Novak was just as excited as I was.

"Well," she said. "Open it!" And so I opened the email so we could read it together. I logged into the application website and we both held our breath. But instead of seeing words that would give me an escape from everything that was going wrong, I was only offered one more disappointment.

"I . . . didn't get in," I whispered, and the words were like a tiny tornado in my subconscious, knocking things off shelves and shattering all the windows in my mind. I wasn't going to London for the summer when it was the one thing I'd been counting on as every other part of my life spiraled out of control.

I stood there in disbelief, rereading the screen, though there was nothing confusing about the words *We regret to inform you . . .* I looked at Novak, feeling like this was all her fault in some way. *She* was the one who had told me I was a shoo-in. *She* was the reason I'd known about the program at all.

"How is this possible?" Novak asked herself, or maybe the air around us. I knew she wasn't talking to me. She lifted the phone from my hands and scrolled through the entire length of the rejection, like reading it again would change what it meant. "Your application was perfect. Your statement was brilliant. I wrote you that recommendation. I just . . . don't understand."

But I hadn't understood most of what had happened to me lately. It felt like my life was turning into a bit of a joke. So I laughed a little. I actually laughed.

"It's okay," I said to Ms. Novak. I let the blow of this settle in my gut with the rest of the hurt that was eating me alive. "It's fine."

"Let me make a few phone calls," Novak said, but I shook my head.

"Don't worry about it." And just as I turned to leave, Layla burst into Novak's class, grinning.

"Ms. Novak, you're not g-g-going to believe this, but—"

When she saw me, she fell silent. Her smile disappeared, and she crossed her arms. I wanted to know what she was about to say, but I knew she wouldn't say more while I was standing there. I ached to apologize for what I said, but after this morning I felt she owed me much more than I owed her.

"I gotta get to class," I said to Novak. But when I stepped past Layla and into the hall, my feet carried me elsewhere.

I went to the library. I hung out in my favorite corner for the next two periods, rereading *King Lear,* and then I skipped lunch too. The substitute librarian didn't know that people hid in the stacks and that she'd need to do hourly rounds just to make sure no one was making out or skipping classes on her watch. So there I stayed, undiscovered for hours.

—

At the end of the school day, I didn't even stop at my locker. I just needed to get out of the building as quickly as possible. But I bumped into the Chorus Girls as I was trying to make my escape, and they started up again, laughing at me and saying impossibly horrible things that shredded whatever was left of my insides.

I stood there and took it. I didn't say a word, because I hoped there was a finite amount of meanness they could send in my direction before they got bored. And there was. They stopped and walked away from me after a few nauseating minutes and I could breathe again, if only until I thought about Layla's silence, my dad's boxes, the Shakespeare program, and as always, like a current under everything, Gigi.

The Chorus Girls were trying to ruin me. But they didn't realize that I had nothing left to lose.

THE PATRIARCHY

It was actually pretty simple to ruin another person's life, once I decided to do it. All it took was a moment, a few words sent to the wrong people, and a little bit of nerve.

After a week of being tormented in big and small ways by the Chorus Girls, my patience had run out. I'd tried ignoring them. I'd blasted my music to drown out the sounds of their voices, but they just got louder, or they stopped and waited until they could find me when I didn't have the protection of headphones. They continued to whisper terrible things in my ears and leave nasty comments all over my posts. When I blocked them everywhere so they couldn't even see anything I shared, they created new accounts to torture me. My stuff started disappearing, too—a book here, a water bottle there. Layla had probably told them my locker combination. And then there were the rumors, which were both true and untrue, but all of which made me feel like my skin wasn't my own anymore, or like I didn't deserve to have a day free of sadness.

I couldn't tell my mother about any of it because we still weren't speaking, and I didn't want to bug my dad, who was still in the midst of settling into his new apartment, what felt like his new life. There was no way I was going to tell a teacher—it would just make everything worse. So I had to take matters into my own hands.

I drafted an email to send to the full student-body email list from the school library, on one of the computers. I figured that way, no one would be able to find out it was me who sent the email—it could have come from anyone. I made a new email address and composed a message that included everything I knew about Sloane Sorenson, Todd Wellington, and their illicit romance—everything that Layla had texted me in the bathroom after Todd showed up at Sloane's Halloween party.

When they first started dating, I typed, Sloane was only a fourteen-year-old freshman, and Todd was a seventeen-year-old senior and star player for her old school's basketball team. I wrote about how Sloane felt special—that this senior who could have had anyone picked her. She got instantly popular, I wrote. She started partying a lot and skipping school, so much that her parents started to worry. They found out about Todd after they saw a dirty text he'd sent to her.

I wrote that they forbade her to see him and that she snuck out to meet up with him anyway.

And then came the day her father walked in on Todd in Sloane's bedroom. In her bed.

I explained how her dad went completely apeshit and told Todd that if he ever came near his daughter again he'd press statutory rape charges against him, because of course, by then Todd was eighteen. And that was enough to keep him away.

Todd already had a scholarship to his
first-choice school to play Division 1
basketball. He couldn't risk that, not
even for the girl he loved.

Somehow, everyone at her old school found out about her father's threat. And they made Sloane's life a living hell. How dare she, a freshman, threaten the future of such a talented young man—a beloved star athlete, the boy next door, the all-American Todd Wellington? He was from a good family, and who was she? Just some slutty fifteen-year-old. A fucking nobody. And in an instant, all those "friends" she'd made when she started dating Todd were gone, if not complicit.

The patriarchy, I typed. Am I right?

She became severely depressed, because of all the bullying. Had to leave school in the spring and be hospitalized. Then she moved in with her aunt and uncle and cousin Valeria; transferred to Shirley Chisholm Charter for a fresh start.

But I didn't stop with the hard-and-fast facts, because Sloane never had. I made the story better, or maybe a tiny bit worse. I added details that I didn't know were true but could have been. I kept my lies small so they'd be more believable.

I stared at what I'd written. I read it over and over again—secrets laid out for anyone to see, anyone to repeat. The thing was, there wasn't anything inherently bad in any of it—a girl falling in love with a boy; a girl being victimized until she broke; a girl who was sick and who needed to start over. But Sloane would never want to be seen as weak, and I knew she thought these experiences made her look like she was.

She'd ruined my whole world, even after she knew what it was like to be hurt in this exact way, so I didn't hesitate. I didn't care.

Feeling diabolical and pissed as hell, I enabled a tool that scheduled the email to send over the weekend. I didn't want anyone to be able to use the time stamp to figure out who was in the library when it went out.

I hit send.

I didn't know how many kids even checked their Chisholm email inboxes, but I was betting that my plan would work. At least a few people would read it and tell *everyone,* and in addition to ruining Sloane, it would ruin Layla too. Because, according to Layla, Sloane had told no one this information except her and Valeria. Then Sloane would know what I was just learning—Layla wasn't loyal to anyone.

I stood up. I looked around, and it was strange that the world around me had remained unchanged. My backpack was still heavy, and my weathered copy of *Othello* was still beside the keyboard. I shoved it hard and low into my bag before I walked away, thinking about jealousy and lies and betrayal—all things that had felt so far away from my life the last time I read the play. All things that were consuming me now, from the inside out.

now

THE BEST FRIEND I CAN BE

I don't want to drag Willa along on a new-memory-making errand just yet. I'm not sure I'm ready to tell her about my plan, about my past, about how I've been systematically undoing the last few years of a now-dead friendship. When I whisper this to Sydney, the fact that I'm not ready, she understands. But I want them to know I'm making a real effort. I want Sydney especially to feel like I'm not running away from her again.

So I invite them to come with me to Dolly's after school.

This isn't a completely altruistic move. I'm thinking that if Dom is there, he'll have a harder time being pissy to me if Sydney and Willa are around. I might even be able to squeeze a word or two out of him. But I want them there, too. I want them to experience the beauty that is Miss Dolly's pies and Pop's fried chicken. And if Dom is there, maybe even a small plate or two.

When we walk in, I seat them at my favorite table, the one in the corner near a window. Then I head to the break room to drop off my stuff. There's no sign of Dom's backpack or coat, and I feel a little bad about that. I hope I'm not encroaching on a safe space that was his first. I know how much I hate it when that's done to me.

"Hey, Mr. Henry. Where's Dom?" I ask Pop when I step back into the dining room. He's behind the counter, refilling a customer's mug with fresh coffee.

"Oh, he said he had a bunch of homework," Pop says. "But I'm glad you're here." He squeezes my shoulder and hands me two glasses of water.

I carry the water over to Willa and Sydney's table and they're arguing about something, which is nothing new.

"There's no way in hell I'm letting you call me Cox the Fox," Sydney is saying.

"Come on, Syd. It's the perfect nickname for you." Willa looks up at me. "It's perfect, right?"

I laugh and set the glasses on the table. Sydney grabs one and takes a big gulp. "Why does she need a new nickname, exactly?" I ask. "You already call her Syd."

"Yeah, see? I'm fine with Syd. Can't I just stay Syd?"

"No," Willa says. She looks away from Sydney and over to me. "This is her *jazz* nickname. You know, like if the three of us were in a jazz band, what would our nicknames be?"

I grin. "Oh, you mean like how people called Billie Holiday Lady Day and Sarah Vaughan Sassy?"

Willa points at me. "See! Cleo just gets it." She grabs my wrist and pulls me down into the chair beside her. She throws her arm over my shoulder. "I think your name would be Cleo the Kiddo. We'd call you Kid for short. You'd be on the keys, and Sydney would be the singer. I'd be drums."

"I don't hate it," I say. I like this game. "Willa, your nickname could be The Big Bang, if you're the drummer. Willa 'The Big Bang' Bae. Goes with your epically long bangs too," I say. Willa shakes them out of her eyes with a flourish and Sydney tosses her curls too.

"It's perfect. And fine, Sydney, you can just be Syd, but only because it would make our intro sick as hell." Willa stands up, like she's introducing us at a gig. Her bangles ring like bells. "We're Big Bang, Syd, and The Kid, and we're excited to play for you tonight."

Sydney and I look at each other and crack up laughing.

For the rest of the evening I bounce between Sydney and Willa's table and the front of the restaurant, where I greet customers as they come and go. It's nice to be here—to be distracted from what might be happening with Sloane and Layla, to not have to think about Dom being mad. All the little hurts building up inside like block towers get pushed into a little corner of my mind as I show Sydney how to roll silverware, and talk to Willa about music, and tuck a few customers into the diner's coziest corners.

When it starts to get really slow about an hour before closing time, Pop lets me hook my phone up to the sound system they normally only use to play the radio, and when "La Vie en Rose" comes on first, he eyes me like I'm an alien.

"*This* is the music you like?" he asks, his hands flat against the counter like he can't believe it. I shake my head and spin around on one of the barstools.

"It's the music I *love*," I correct him, and he laughs. "My Gigi listened to it all the time," I say, remembering her collection of records, her rough hands and how they'd lay the disc on her record player as gently as she braided my hair when I was small. Pop pulls Miss Dolly from the break room and dances with her in the narrow space between the barstools and the back windows, and for a second I'm sad my phone is playing the music, because if it weren't I'd be taking photos of them.

It's nice, sitting there watching people who have loved each other longer than I've been alive. I feel something that the last few months have left wrecked and ruined being restored little by little.

Before Willa and Sydney get up to leave, I ask Willa for her number, because she's promised we'll all go see the Cover Girls together. "I'll text you, okay?" I promise. "And I'll see you to-morrow."

They wave goodbye when they head out and I feel warm and fuzzy inside, and so much better than I did when I first arrived. I secretly hope that the three of us will sit together in the cafeteria tomorrow, but I try not to set myself up for disappointment if we don't.

When "Feeling Good" by Nina Simone comes on a little while later, the few customers left in the diner start singing along, and I wonder if *this* is a better idea than just doing a fundraiser for Dolly's—playing music, or maybe bringing in a live band. Maybe even the Cover Girls, if they're as good live as they sound recorded. I look around, and there's enough space near where Miss Dolly and Pop are dancing for a singer and a keyboard. I make a mental note, but I have no idea if Dom will think of this too as charity he doesn't want or need.

As the dining room empties, I walk over to Pop where he's counting the cash in one of the registers. "Need help closing up too?" I ask. I already let Mom know I'd be late. Pop writes some-thing down because he still does all his math on paper.

"Why don't you go back and grab a broom from Dolly? You can get started sweeping the dining room floor." I nod and head to the back, my music still playing over the sound system even though we've already locked the front doors.

"Hey, Miss Dolly?" I say just before I walk past her. I place my hand on the knob of a small closet just outside her door. "Is this where you guys keep the broom?" I glance into the break room from the hall and I see a photo I didn't notice the first time I was in here with Dom. It's of a pretty, dark-skinned woman and a baby, and once I step a little closer, I can see that the woman looks a lot like Dom. When Miss Dolly sees me looking at the photo, she smiles. Maybe I shouldn't, but I take her expression as an invitation.

"Is this . . . Dom's mom?" I ask. Miss Dolly nods.

"Yep. That's my baby girl. Mallory. Pop calls her Molly. So we were Dolly and Molly."

I bite my bottom lip and step farther into the room. I point to the baby in the photo. "Is that . . . ?"

"Baby Dominic? Sure is." Miss Dolly picks up the photo and looks at it a little more closely. She smiles, but her eyes look sad.

"Molly got pregnant with Dominic when she was eighteen. She'd already been accepted into Brown, and we weren't going to let that opportunity pass her by. So when she told us she wanted to keep the baby, we told her to defer a year, and we'd help take care of him while she went to school. Dominic's dad, John, was around too, but he had just joined the military. So off they both went—Molly to school and John to basic training, and somehow . . . they just never got back to being full-time parents. Something would always come up. First Molly wanted to get her graduate degree, then John got deployed. Then Molly met someone while she was in grad school, and when John found out, he took on another tour. We didn't want Dominic to be jerked around—to have to move from place to place while they figured their lives out—so we just held on to our boy. By then we were pretty attached anyway. And by the time they had both settled enough to handle having a child, Dominic was nine or ten, and mostly as uninterested in living with them as they had been in him."

"You'd already made a life here," I say, because I get that part at least. They have a house and the diner and each other. They're happy.

She nods. "Yeah, and it's a good one, too."

But then I remember Dom at that party in the summer, how he said he'd just moved here. "But I thought Dom just moved back to New York this past summer?" I ask.

"Ah, yes. He usually spends his summers in Washington, D.C., with his dad, so after middle school that's what he did again. But then he wanted to give living with his mom a try. Henry and I were upset, because we had a feeling Molly wasn't ready. I don't know how the girl thought she could go from no children to raising a teenager. But I didn't let Dom know that I felt that way. I just hoped for the best. So he moved to Atlanta with Molly. He started ninth grade there with her, but unfortunately I was right. She couldn't handle him. He started acting out, and she didn't know what to do. I honestly think Dom missed New York and maybe us a little too, though he would never in a million years admit it." She chuckles and I smile. "We didn't want to pull him out in the middle of the school year, though, so I let him finish out the year before he came back. I'm not letting him go again, I can tell you that much right now."

266

She reminds me of Gigi, the way she talks about Dom like he's everything she ever wanted. It's how my grandmother always made me feel when I was with her.

I swallow and dip my head a little, so happy to be in this small room with her and so grateful for her story, but a little sad that Dom isn't here with us.

"Dom's . . . upset with me," I say. "And I really don't want him to be, because I've had a pretty rough couple of months and he's been kind of great about it all."

Miss Dolly looks concerned, but I want to make it clear to her that this isn't about me. "What can I do to make things better between us? I'm still learning how to be his friend." And as soon as I say it, I know this is what I failed to do with Layla—she changed and I didn't adapt. Maybe I changed too, and she didn't try to learn what the new me needed either. I don't want that to happen with Dom. "I don't know how to give him what he needs, I guess. I want to be the best friend I can be."

"He's very proud," Miss Dolly says, without asking for any more details even though she's just basically given me her entire life story. "He's very stubborn," she continues. "And he's a little too smart for his own good," she finishes. "Sometimes, with Dominic, the easiest thing to do is to let him figure things out on his own." She leans back in her chair and squints at me, and her dimples pop into her cheeks even though she's only smiling a little. She wags her wrinkled finger at me. "He likes you, I can tell."

I blush a little, and I can't help but smile even though Dom didn't talk to me all day. I don't know if she means as a friend or more, but either is fine with me.

"He'll come around," she says. "Just give him a little time."

THE RUMOR

When I walk into school the next day, everyone is staring at me.

I know I've been more paranoid about a lot of things since I lost Layla, afraid that the whole world could turn against me at any moment because my best friend did. That's why I'm not sure I can trust my heart around Dom. That's why I don't always answer Jase's, Sydney's, and now Willa's texts right away—I'm still a bit afraid of letting any of them get too close. But I don't think I'm hallucinating when I say *everyone* is staring at me.

I want to think it's because I'm wearing a new sweater over my uniform shirt. It's tighter than the things I usually wear, and bright white against my eggshell-brown skin, in sharp opposition to my normal black hoodies. My boobs look great, if I say so myself. And my nails are painted white too, or "Love, Lilly," as Sydney read off the bottle before letting me borrow it. She said she'd only wear the color in summer but she thought I could pull it off year round. "You need to lighten up," she'd said. "Figuratively *and* literally."

So I try to ignore the looks, or chalk them up to my new clothes, my bright nails. I open my locker like everything is normal.

The truth is, the stares and whispers remind me of the day everything between Layla and me started to go really wrong—when Sloane called me a bitch and Layla didn't seem to care. And when I get to homeroom, people are still staring, and it's harder to ignore in a small classroom than it was in the long, wide halls. I notice something else too: Layla and Sloane are sitting side by side again. I never did find out what happened yesterday to briefly pull them apart.

Mr. Yoon takes attendance and when I raise my hand and say "Here," it feels like the whole room goes silent.

I stare at my book. At my white nails against the pages, which have yellowed with age, and I read the same line of *Othello* over and over and over:

Men should be what they seem. Men should be what they seem.

Dom is late. He comes in a few minutes after the attendance has been taken, and though I look right at him, he avoids my gaze. He sits a few feet away, despite the open seats on either side of me. I gave him his space all day yesterday, so today I planned to apologize. I wore my cute sweater and painted my nails and hoped it would make me brave. But with everyone staring and him still keeping his distance, I lose my nerve. He doesn't want to speak to me, just like Layla. I swallow and look down at my desk, pretending to read the words on the pages in front of me, until I feel my phone vibrate in my pocket. When I look down at it, it's a text from Sydney.

Meet me in the second-floor girls' bathroom, like NOW.

Why?

I'll tell you when you get here.

269

I raise my hand and ask Mr. Yoon for a hall pass, and as soon as he gives me one, I walk quickly to the bathroom to meet Sydney.

I push open the door and she's pacing, arms crossed, her crazy-curly hair everywhere.

"Holy shit, Cleo," she says. She doesn't stop pacing. "Holy *freaking* shit."

"What?" I ask.

"Have you noticed anything weird today? Like are people treating you differently?"

I don't want to talk about everyone staring at me, when yesterday I was invisible. I don't want to say *Yes, of course, how could I have not?* I shake my head. Then I kind of shrug and nod, because I'm not sure I want to know why.

Willa bursts into the bathroom a second later. She reaches out and pulls me into a hug and her armful of bangles are cold against my neck. "It's so awful," she says. And Sydney gently pulls her away from me.

"I didn't tell her yet, Will."

"Tell me what?" I ask, officially freaked all the way out.

"You know what everyone's saying, right?" Willa whispers, and I instantly feel shaky and all wrong inside. My sweater feels too tight; my nails a little too white.

"No . . . ?"

Willa storms through the bathroom like a whirlwind, knocking all the stalls open, making sure we're alone. Once she's confirmed that we are, she crosses her arms like a bouncer at a club and nods at Sydney. I can see that they have the kind of connection

Layla and I used to—they can communicate without any words at all. It makes my chest ache in a peculiar and lonely way.

"Someone sent around a text . . . about your dad," Sydney says.

I frown. I was expecting it to be something horrible about me: about how I skipped so many days the last two months, or that someone saw my mom riding the train with me, dropping me off like I'm a little kid. I even thought that maybe it would be some lie about me and Dom, since he's sat at lunch with me a few times and anyone who saw us could have decided to tell the world that we were secretly dating or something worse. But my dad?

"He doesn't even work here anymore," I say.

"Yeah, that's what everyone is talking about. Look, I don't believe it, okay? I want to make that clear first. I don't think it's true."

"Me either," Willa says. She rolls her eyes and shakes her head. Her choppy hair swings. "It's totally ridiculous."

"Sydney," I say, stepping closer to her. "You're freaking me out. What are people saying about my dad?"

She takes a deep breath and nervously flips her hair. She looks down and up and all around. And just before I'm about to scream at her to *just tell me,* she does.

"They're saying that the reason he doesn't work here anymore is because he . . ." She squeezes her eyes shut. "He hooked up with a student."

I lose my breath. I blink a half-dozen times. And then Willa is beside me, with her arm wrapped around my shoulder. It feels like the weight of her is the only thing keeping me from splitting apart.

"*What?*" I ask, and my voice comes out almost as a whisper. "What the hell? Why would anyone say that about him?"

Sydney opens one of her eyes, and I guess I look calm enough because she opens the other and shrugs. "No idea, dude. It's also kind of weird that's it's happening now, right? Almost two months after he quit. Like, if this was going to be a rumor, shouldn't it have started a long time ago?"

I can't think straight. I can't even really *see*—I'm that unsettled. I push Willa roughly away. I lean against the wall and close my eyes, and I desperately want to scream. At anyone who believes this horrible lie; at Sydney for telling me about it; at the monster who could invent a rumor this cruel. But more than anything, I want to disappear.

The last time I felt like this was right before Layla and I fell apart for good. I feel the punch of tears at the back of my throat, but it's not because I'm sad.

This is pure, unadulterated rage.

"*That's* why everyone is staring at me," I say. "*That's* why people are acting like I have the bubonic plague. They think my dad is a . . . pedophile?"

I look at Sydney, like she needs to confirm this any more than she already has, but she just tucks her hair behind her ears and looks at the floor. Her earrings today are spirals, tiny tornados I wish would pick me up and carry me away. I look at Willa and her dark eyes are fierce, like she's as angry about this as I am. She reaches out and grabs one of Sydney's dangling hands—it's like she always has to be holding on to someone else.

"What are you going to do?" Sydney asks. And I make a mental note that she said "you" instead of "we." Layla would have said "we," and something about having to endure this alone is too much to take. I grit my teeth and step into a stall, slamming the door closed behind me.

"Cleo," Sydney says. "Cleo, are you okay? I mean, I know you're not, but—"

"Just leave me alone," I mutter.

I hear Willa and Sydney whispering, and then Sydney tries to talk to me again, but I stay silent. After about ten minutes a few other girls come into the bathroom, and under the door I see Sydney's riding boots and Willa's checkered Vans shuffle to the other side of the bathroom. When it sounds like the other girls have left, Sydney tries one last time.

"Cleo. It's almost time for first period. Do you want me to stay in here with you or do you want space?"

I want her to stay, but I don't want to have to ask. I want her to go, but I can't send her away.

I don't say anything, and when I hear Sydney swing her bag back over her shoulder, my throat gets achy, and my eyes fill.

"If you need us," Willa says after a few hushed minutes pass between us, "just text, 'kay?"

"We'll come right away," Sydney adds, and she drags her feet a little as they turn away from my stall. I hear Willa's bangles jingling, and then they're finally gone. I open the door of my stall the tiniest bit to peek out and make sure the bathroom is completely empty. It is.

I kick the stall door a few times until it swings all the way open. Then I sit there until I feel calm enough to go back to Mr. Yoon's class and grab my stuff. I can't go to first period—I can't do the rest of today. I know there will be consequences, but there's no way I can sit in a room with twenty other people who think my dad is a perv. I want to find out who did this to him—destroyed his reputation with a heinous lie—so I need to find out who sent that text message.

The second I step out of the girls' bathroom, Jase steps out of the boys'. He's looking down at his phone, so I try to skirt by him, but he must recognize my braids or hear the clomp of my boots.

"Cleo Imani—" he starts, but I cut him off.

I spin and I say, my voice hissing through my teeth, "Not right now, Jase, okay?"

He looks surprised. His ever-present, dimpled grin falls off his face and his brow crinkles, his dark eyes taking in my war-torn face. "Oh shit, are you all right?" I swallow hard around the hurt and shake my head, because I could never lie to Jase.

"But I don't want to talk about it, okay? I just need to get back to class."

He reaches for me then. He reaches in that particular way that he used to whenever we'd had a fight back when he loved me. He'd put his big hand out and I'd put my smaller one in his and he'd pull me to his chest. I would complain or cry and he would kiss me until it was all better. But he can't fix me with kisses, because he doesn't love me anymore. And even if he did, this isn't something his gentleness would make better.

"I have to go," I say, so softly I'm sure he doesn't hear me. I leave his hand outstretched, dangling in the space between us.

When I walk back into class, Dom has moved into one of the empty seats closer to where I was sitting. And while this would

274

have been exciting to me ten minutes ago, now it just pisses me off. Why should *he* get to decide when he wants to be my friend? Why does everyone else get to pick when they want to be close to me and when they don't? I'm sick of it.

I sit down, and I pretend Dom isn't there, less than a foot away from me, though the sweet-smoke-and-nutty-soap scent of him is hard to ignore. I start packing up my stuff, the lump in my throat swelling so large that I have to bite my tongue against the pain of it.

Dom leans across the space between our desks. "You good?" he asks, and I know my jaw is clenched tight and my eyes are probably glassy behind my glasses, because not even my best Poker Face could hide this kind of pain well. I've been so used to going it alone that I forgot what it was like to have someone else care. Like Sydney and Willa in the bathroom. Like Jase in the hall. Like Dom now. Having people who notice when you aren't okay complicates things.

I take a deep breath and nod, hard. I sneak a glance at Dom, because I want him to believe me. I want more than anything for him to go back to being mad, just so he'll leave me alone. But he persists. He leans in again and says, "You sure?" And I just lose it. I slam down the book I'm holding hard enough on my desk that the people around us look at me even more intently than they've been staring all morning.

"Jesus! I'm fine. Why are you suddenly acting like you care?"

Dom frowns at me. He doesn't roll his eyes or change his posture at all. He just keeps looking at me, and eventually he looks away.

"I don't know," he says. "My bad."

As soon as the bell rings, I shoulder my bag and fly from the room. I push my way through the crowded halls thinking about nothing but the irony of that line from *Othello* when I'm questioning everything.

Men should be what they seem.

I need to find a place to hide so I won't have to endure everyone's stares for the rest of the day. So obviously I head straight to the library, to tuck myself away in the stacks. I push my earbuds in and turn the Cover Girls all the way up, and I don't stop when I think I hear someone calling my name—I just walk even faster. I'm only a few feet away from the library door, inches from freedom, when I feel a hand encircle my wrist.

I turn to see who's grabbed me and it's Valeria. Her cheeks are blotchy like she's hot or upset, the same way Sloane's get, and her fluffy auburn hair is falling out of its ponytail.

"Valeria?" I ask. I pull my wrist out of her grip and yank out my earbuds. "What are you doing?"

She's out of breath. She must have seen me as I passed through the senior hall and run after me the whole way from there.

"Hey," she says. "Gimme a minute." She bends over, her hands on her knees, her breath coming in quick bursts, and I wonder how she sings the way she does if jogging down a hallway winds her like this.

I say, "Valeria, I gotta go."

I turn and open the door to the library, but she follows me in. "Wait," she says.

"What?" I whisper. Ms. White, the librarian, shushes us anyway.

She looks behind her, like she's making sure no one else hears what she's about to say. But the library is nearly empty because most people are in class, and the halls are too since first period starts in just a few minutes.

"I've been looking for you all morning," Valeria says. She pulls the ponytail holder out of her hair and twists her giant curls into a messy topknot, roughly securing it like an animal she needs to tame. "I thought you were in Mr. Yoon's homeroom?"

"I am. I was in the bathroom for most of the period," I tell her. Sydney and Willa's concerned faces flash in my mind but I force them away.

"Oh," she says. "Well." She smooths the sides of her head and tucks errant strands into the bun.

Valeria has maybe said three words to me since Layla joined chorus, but she's always seemed nicer than the other girls. I sigh through my nose, because if she ran all the way down the hall to tell me something, the least I can do is listen.

"Don't freak," she says, slipping her thumbs behind the yellow straps of her backpack. "But I'm pretty sure my cousin started the rumor about your dad."

YOU DESERVED TO KNOW

I've never been in a fight before.

I'm not really the fighting type. I like books and jazz-age music and hugs. And I'll admit I like talking shit, but rarely do I do it to anyone's face.

But Sloane is testing my nonviolent nature for the second time in the span of a few months. She is still changing things about my world that I knew to be true: that Layla and I would be friends forever; that people are basically good. And she is dangerously close to making me into the kind of girl I never thought I'd be: the kind of girl who punches other girls right in the face.

"What," I say to Valeria, hoping that I heard her wrong, though my *what* doesn't sound like a question. My next sentence is punctuated with hard blinks and pauses between my words. "What. Do. You. Mean?"

Valeria is speechless at first. And the longer she doesn't answer, the more I start putting things together myself.

Sloane swore she would get revenge for letting Todd into her house back in October. She threatened me, if only with a look and an implication, and so for a while I was expecting some kind of retaliation. Once everything happened with Layla, I'd thought it was over. But she waited until my guard was down before she attacked for real because she's pure evil. Still, I feel like I'm missing something.

"I don't know how else to say it," Valeria mutters. "I'm almost positive it was her. She's had it out for you for months, Cleo. You know that as well as I do. And when she found out you were the person who sent that email about Todd . . ."

"Wait. How does she know *I* sent the email?" I realize too late that I've just admitted to it; that if there was any question that I hadn't sent it, that uncertainty is gone. Valeria doesn't even blink.

"Sloane had this theory for a while that it was you. And then, the other night, she was on Layla's phone looking through her texts and saw that Layla had texted you basically the whole story the night of the Halloween party. She threw Layla's phone against the wall, and they were screaming at each other in my room so much that I thought they were going to literally kill each other. It was a mess. But now they seem fine and Sloane's not mad anymore and *today* this rumor surfaces? It seems too convenient not to be connected. It seems like Sloane."

I pace a little and Valeria just stands there as I process everything. That's what she and Layla were fighting about—my email and all the big truths and tiny lies I told. That Layla had given me the information that became my only weapon against Sloane. And now Sloane was trying to ruin me, just the way I'd ruined her. The only difference is my email only hurt one life, temporarily. Her text could hurt two, for good.

"Why are you telling me this?" I ask, because Valeria is Sloane's cousin. She should hate me for sending that email and airing all of her relative's dirty laundry.

Valeria shrugs. "Sending that email was wrong. But her saying this about your dad is next-level evil. I can't get with it, and even though Sloane's my cousin, she's always been kind of a bitch. Besides, I never spoke up while everything was happening in December. I didn't, like, *contribute,* but I didn't stop it either. My mom always says *If you grin, you're in,* and I never got what she meant until now." Valeria takes a deep breath and fiddles with a tiny stuffed monkey hanging from her backpack strap. "Anyway, I thought you deserved to know," she says without meeting my eyes.

I nod.

"What are you going to do?" she says. I'm so sick of people asking me that, but I swallow hard and look right at her.

I used to have Layla to fight my battles, but I haven't had her for a while. I think it's about time I learn to fight for myself. "Thanks for telling me, but now this is between me and Sloane," I say. I force myself to smile.

"Since your cousin knows about the email, she should know by now—I'm not a girl to be fucked with."

then:
December,
week 3

WHAT'S DONE CANNOT BE UNDONE

Just like I'd hoped, by Monday, everyone in school knew Sloane's deepest secrets. But I hadn't predicted how awful people whispering about *her* would make *me* feel.

While I was at my locker, I heard someone say that after everything with Todd had happened, Sloane had attempted suicide, which was *not* something I put in the email. "Who told you that?" I asked the girl I heard say it, but she wouldn't reveal her source.

In the bathroom, I heard people whispering that Sloane's father had gotten a restraining order against Todd and that if he violated it, he could be arrested (that part was one of my lies).

By lunch I'd heard everything—from one version where the cops broke up Sloane's Halloween party to one in which Sloane's parents actually pressed charges against Todd and he had to drop out of college because his parents needed his tuition money to pay lawyers' fees. I was horrified. But as Shakespeare wrote, *What's done cannot be undone,* so I just gritted my teeth, waiting for what I knew was coming.

It took longer than I expected. In the hallway, Sloane's eyes and cheeks were bright red. She was surrounded by the Chorus

Girls, and they barely reacted when I walked by. I only glanced at her for a second, but when I did, she glared at me *like she knew*. But Layla was still standing beside her with one arm tossed over her shoulder. Layla sent daggers my way from her eyes too.

"Shit," I said once I turned a corner and found myself alone. "Shit, shit, shit." I ran through the details of the email again, piece by piece. I'd been careful. She couldn't *know* it was me, even if she suspected it was.

I was walking by the library, Sarah Vaughan's "Black Coffee" streaming into my ears, when someone yanked on my arm pretty violently. I spun around and there she was. Layla.

"In," Layla said through her teeth. And then she shoved open the door of the library. Reluctantly, I followed her.

"It was you, wasn't it?" Layla said the second we were in what used to be "our" corner of the stacks. I didn't say a word.

"I can't b-believe this," Layla said. "I told you not to t-t-tell anyone any of that!"

I crossed my arms and stared at her. I stayed quiet the same way she had when her new friends were torturing me.

She opened her mouth, but she got blocked. I just kept staring, waiting. I had nothing to say to her.

"Seriously, C-C-Cleo. That was so low. For you t-to send that around? I thought you were b-b-better than that."

"And I thought you were my friend. But I guess we both thought wrong, huh?"

"You know, Sloane already knows you d-did it."

I felt a little scared, but I didn't let the fear show. My heart was pounding, but I laughed in her face.

"Prove it," I whispered.

Layla squinted at me and turned, like she was about to leave. "So I'm guessing Sloane doesn't know that you're the one who told me," I said.

She spun back around. "Keep your voice *down,*" she hissed.

I grinned. "That's what I thought. If you don't want her to find out, I suggest you don't confirm anything. And tell all your bitchy friends to leave me the hell alone. If they don't, I'll send another one naming you as the source."

Layla's wide eyes grew even wider. "You wouldn't," she whispered. For one absurd moment, Layla looked like a Disney princess, with her silky hair and her eye makeup, her smooth skin and the shocked look on her face. She looked like she *wasn't real,* which made it easier for me to stand my ground.

I took a step closer to her. "Try me," I said through gritted teeth.

Layla really did leave then. And the second I couldn't see her in the aisle anymore, I fell against the shelves and sank into a crouch. With my face in my hands, I cried, letting all the tension pour out of me like rain.

—

For the rest of the week, Layla brushed past me in the hallway, so close that our shoulders touched, like she wanted me to know she saw me and she was snubbing me on purpose. Sometimes none of the other Chorus Girls were even around, so I couldn't tell myself her coldness was for their benefit—it was all just for me. But dealing with her passive nastiness was a small price to pay, because the rest of them had stopped their whispering. I could go to my locker and not worry about being accosted. I could use the bathroom without worrying about being locked inside. I could post a selfie and know that no one would call me *hideous* or *freak* in the comments. It was blissful. I went to class and settled back into my life mostly as it had been before . . . minus Layla. And it was, if not nice, at least better.

On Thursday, when I saw all of them clustered just outside homeroom, though, I got nervous. But as I approached, they didn't turn to jeer or leer at me. It was like they didn't see me at all, which was a significant improvement from my life pre-email, so I continued on my way.

As I passed, I couldn't help but overhear what they were talking about. It was the last day of classes before winter break and they were all aflutter, excited about the musical's premiere that night. In the midst of everything else that had been happening, I had totally forgotten about it.

I watched Layla closely, but she seemed fine—not the least bit nervous. I watched the way she turned as various girls called out, "L, did you figure out that note in the third song?" and "L, are you free to run lines at lunch?" and "L, your stage makeup at dress rehearsal was *lit*. Can you do mine tonight?" She nodded and said yes and pulled eyeliner from her bag and waved it in the air and I could tell that they all loved her. I despised them.

Then Sloane noticed me. She suddenly couldn't stop saying my name. She hoped *Cleo* didn't have the nerve to show her face tonight. She hoped *Cleo* at least had the decency to let Layla make her debut in peace. "You're going to kill it, and you shouldn't feel like you have anything to prove to anyone, especially *her*."

THE MUSICAL

I hadn't been planning to go to the musical. But Sloane's words had been swirling through my head all afternoon, and when last bell rang I decided that I would. Because *fuck Sloane*. I'd let her dictate how I moved through this school for long enough.

And I was sick of Layla too. I *wanted* her to fail. She'd stood by for days while her new "friends" made my life hell and didn't even have the decency to ask them to stop until I blackmailed her into it. The more I thought about it all, the angrier I got, and as time crept closer to curtain, the fierceness in my chest built into fire. By the time Jase and Mase showed up in the balcony, where I had gone to sit alone, I could barely sit still I was so mad, so ready for a fight.

They sat down on either side of me right before the lights dimmed, and when Mason's elbow touched mine I said, "Watch it."

"My bad," Mason said. "Jeez."

"Cleo Imani Baker," Jase stage-whispered. "How the hell are ya?"

He wouldn't want to know the honest answer to that question, so I took a deep breath trying to calm myself. *They're not the enemy,* I repeated inside my head. I knew I had a right to be angry, but none of this was their fault.

"You cut it pretty close," I whispered to them both. I nodded at Mason, apologizing for flipping out about his elbow, and he nodded back and immediately started texting. He had a small bundle of wildflowers tied with twine, and I knew they were for Layla. The sight of them made me feel petty and pissed all over again. I wanted to knock them off his lap and stomp them into the floor.

"Yo, that light is gonna be mad distracting for the actors," Jase said to Mason.

"Who made you the phone police?" Mason asked him with a grin, but he put his phone away a minute later, before reaching behind me to tug at one of my braids, clearly trying to make me loosen up.

"Ow!" I said, and Jase started laughing. "I'm not in the mood for your crap, Mase. Seriously."

He put both his hands up like he was under arrest. "My bad, Baker."

God, boys were so annoying.

Music began to swell and I trained my eyes on the stage. "Shut it. It's starting."

In the dark of the auditorium, sandwiched between Mason and Jase, I could easily pretend that everything was fine—that I was just a normal girl at a school play with friends. But seeing Layla up onstage when there was a whole theater between us felt like a sign, or at least a metaphor: there was an impossible distance between us, a tear in the fabric of who we were to each other, a displacement of what and where we used to be. Things would never be as they were again.

When Layla came out onstage, I sat up a little straighter, and for almost an entire act, she was absolutely flawless. She flirted with Trey Parsons, the kid playing George Bailey, slapping him across the chest and fluttering her eyelashes. They sang a song and I could feel how surprised the audience was at the power and clarity of Layla's voice.

"Damn, she's good," Jase whispered, and I didn't know how to feel. Part of me was enjoying the show, and I couldn't help but feel happy in the way you always do when you're wrapped up in a story. Maybe a small part of me was proud of Layla too, despite our ongoing problems. But dark thoughts about the Chorus Girls and all that had happened between us snuck in and hovered over everything like a shadow. I crossed my arms and kept watching.

Layla stepped forward to deliver her next line.

"George Bailey, you are some t-t-t-t—t."

She stuttered even though she was using her singsong, smooth-speech voice.

"Oh no," I muttered. Sweat pricked along my spine and my heart picked up speed. She tried again.

"George Bailey, you sure are some ta-t-t-t-t—"

Then people started whispering, and it sounded like a soft wind sweeping through trees.

"Fuck" is what Mason whispered. He shoved his hands into his messy brown hair. *"Fuck."*

Then Layla got blocked. "George Bailey, you are some—" she started, but her mouth just flopped open and shut like she was a beached fish. She was trying to talk, but her voice was stuck somewhere deep inside her throat, and when she got like this she had to relax in order to get her voice back.

But how do you relax under hot stage lights, in full makeup, with a hundred classmates and strangers staring at you?

"No," I said again, and then, "Shit." I wanted to do something because this was exactly what I'd wished on her. It was exactly what I'd feared. Jase shifted uncomfortably in his seat.

I didn't think it could get any worse once she was standing there, frozen. But then it did. Someone in the audience shouted, "You sure are some t-t-t-t-t-t-t-t-t," in a high, mean voice and a few people even laughed.

Layla's eyes went wider than they already were—huge and round and frightened. She was a deer in headlights, a kid whose recurring nightmare was coming true. A moment later a teacher rushed down the side aisle looking for the culprit, and someone else said, "Shut up, asshole," but the damage had already been done.

Trey Parsons cleared his throat and whispered something to Layla that shook her out of her frozen state. She took a step away from him, swiped a quick thumb under her eyes, and said, "George Bailey, you are some *talker*."

She pretty much sang the whole sentence, though I was almost certain it was supposed to be a spoken line. Then Trey said, "It's not just talk, Mary," and they were back on track.

But my heart still skipped a beat every time she had to speak for the rest of the show. And whenever I looked over, I could see Mason gripping his armrest like it was the edge of a lifeboat.

—

I went looking for her after the show. I didn't know if she wanted to be found, but I felt like I had to make sure she was okay. She probably hated me, but some things, like public humiliation on what's supposed to be the best day of your life, were more important than everything else. Especially after what I'd said. I suddenly wanted her to know I hadn't meant it. I needed to say I was sorry for that, if nothing else. I waved goodbye to Jase, and though Mason had flowers for Layla, I knew she wouldn't be rushing into his arms anytime soon.

I found her exactly where I thought she'd be, in the very corner of the library where I went whenever I wanted to hide. She was sobbing and alone.

"Lay?" I said softly. I heard a faint buzzing, but I didn't know where it was coming from. I leaned against the nearest shelf and kept some distance between us. "Are you—"

"Are you happy?" she hissed, cutting me off. "I bet you're ec-c-cstatic right now."

I frowned and shifted a little farther away. "Of course, I'm not happy, Layla. I was coming to apologize. And to make sure you're okay."

She stood up and swiped her sleeve across her eyes, smearing her makeup so much that she didn't look like herself anymore. I heard the buzzing again and I wondered if there was someone else, one aisle over in the stacks, texting or getting a call.

"You're apologizing *now*?" she asked.

"I wanted to do it sooner, but after Sloane . . ."

Layla crossed her arms. When she spoke again she mostly sounded exhausted. "But after Sloane *wh-wh-wh-what*, Cleo?

You say that . . . that *awful* thing t-t-to me and then you say nothing else? For weeks?"

"*You* let Sloane and all those other girls say awful things *to me!*" I countered. "And *you* said nothing to me for weeks either! Not to mention all the stuff that happened before that. Leaving me behind. Leaving me out. You've been leaving me bit by bit for months. So don't pretend this is all my fault. It isn't, Layla. And you fucking know it."

I was breathing heavily when I finished talking, my chest moving quickly up and down. I hadn't planned to say all that, but once it was out, I realized it had been building for forever. And it was all true.

There was also so much about my life now that she didn't even know. At this very moment, my father was unpacking boxes in a different apartment and it felt like nothing would ever be the same again with us or with my family. I hadn't gotten into the Shakespeare program, and I felt inadequate in every way a person could. I was lost in my own life, and I didn't know how to get found.

Layla shook her head, and something about her face turned hard and apathetic. "You're right," she said softly. "And you were right about me. You said this w-would happen and you were right. I knew it could happen t-t-t-too, you know. I'm not an idiot. But I was trying to b-be b-b-brave."

She shrugged. And I could tell that she'd given up on this conversation, on *me,* from the way her arms flopped at her sides.

"Maybe we c-c-could have forgiven each other if you'd apologized b-before it all c-c-came true and if I'd stopped Sloane when she t-told me they were going to g-give you a taste of your own

292

medicine. But I *wanted* them to hurt you, b-because you hurt me. And now that this has happened, I d-d-don't know how to t-talk to you, C-C-Cleo. Do you get that? I don't even w-want to."

The worst part was that she didn't even sound mad. She sounded like she was explaining something simple to someone who didn't understand. Like she was tutoring me on the basics of intricate and unforgivable things.

"If you never wanted to speak to me again, why'd you come to the one place you knew *I'd* be able to find you?" My voice was thick with the beginning of tears, and I sounded weak and desperate. It was embarrassing, but I didn't stop talking. "Of all the places you could have gone, you came here to *our* spot."

Layla picked up her coat. She slipped her arms into the sleeves without looking at me. "I came b-b-b-because I knew no one else w-w-would know to look here. Not b-because you *would*."

I realized then that the faint buzzing I'd been hearing was her phone. People were looking for her, to congratulate or comfort her, and she was here hiding from them. She wasn't in this half-hidden corner of the library because she needed or wanted me, but precisely because she *didn't*.

She walked past me then, brushing my shoulder the way she had in the hallway. Like I was anyone. Like I was no one at all.

My eyes filled, but I didn't turn around to watch Layla leave. I took out my phone and I texted her instead. Because texting had always been the way we could communicate best. Even if we were mad. Even when we were in the same room.

Lay, I typed out. But I didn't know what else to say.

Just like the time in the cafeteria, when I first realized something had gone wrong between us, I watched as she looked at her phone, then at me, and shoved it back into her pocket without writing me back.

I watched Layla's back, her black hair straight and falling against her jacket like strips of ribbon. I didn't want her to go and I didn't want to go home. But a second later, she was gone and I knew I'd have to face everything I'd been avoiding.

—

That night, Layla finally wrote me back. I was sitting on the couch and I'd actually been laughing at a funny commercial on TV when my phone buzzed. I looked down at it and the smile fell from my face.

You don't get to call me that anymore.

now

SHE TELLS ME EVERYTHING

I go back to class.

Now that I know exactly who my anger should be directed toward, it's easier to handle the looks and whispers. I'm calm and collected as I take my seat in first period, and I actually listen and pay attention to most of the physics lecture. I raise my hand to answer a question Mr. Frick asks about friction.

"Pressure is the force exerted divided by the area of contact," I say. "The amount of friction can increase or decrease depending on how small or large the area is between the two objects that are in contact." As soon as the words are out of my mouth, they feel like a sign.

"That's exactly right, Cleo," Mr. Frick says, and I don't look at anyone else as I copy down the equation from the whiteboard, because I'm laser-focused on getting through this class and getting to Sloane.

The second we're dismissed I'm up and out of my seat, thinking about friction. I pack my bag quickly and swing it over my shoulder, and I walk down the hall to where I know Sloane will be. There has been a palpable tension between Sloane and me since the day we met, and this rumor might be the last straw.

When I turn the corner, I hear her voice, high and clear over the other voices in the hall. She's calling out to Layla, who's approaching from the opposite end of the corridor as me. Layla sees me but doesn't let her eyes linger on my form. She probably thinks I'm just passing through, the way I normally would be.

"L!" Sloane calls, and I want to shout back, *That's not her damn name.* "Oh my God. You're not going to believe what happened to Cady in first period."

I'm getting closer. In a few steps I'll be right beside them, the Chorus Girls, with their perfect hair and fake smiles. I'll be right next to Layla, whose hair is always straightened now; whose eyes are always made up and whose tongue is quick and cruel. *New* Layla, the one who doesn't look like she ever would have hung out with someone like me—someone unrefined and geeky and weird. But I can't think about Layla right now.

"Sloane," I say when I'm close enough. The other girls, including Layla, look at me like I'm not worthy of speaking to her. They collectively shift their weight—taking a step back or pushing out a hip to get a little farther away from me—like the unworthiness is catching.

Sloane turns around, and her smile falls from her face the second she sees it's me calling her name. Her features rearrange themselves into what I can tell is her own version of a poker face, but hers isn't as good as mine. I can see the anger brewing just beneath the surface. I can tell she's seconds from losing her cool.

Good, I think. *So am I.*

"It was you?" I ask, the irony not being lost on me that this is exactly what she said to me when she found out I was the one responsible for letting Todd into her party.

But unlike me, hers wasn't an honest mistake, so she knows exactly what I'm talking about right away and she doesn't deny it. She slips a notebook into her backpack and closes her locker.

"I only told Melody," she says guiltlessly. But that just makes me angrier. Everyone knows you don't tell Melody anything you want to stay secret.

"Well, it isn't true," I say. "And I'd really appreciate it if you didn't go around talking shit about my family."

Layla's looking at me. I can feel her eyes, and the weight of them makes my blood feel like it's on fire. This is as much her fault as it is Sloane's.

"How do you know?" she asks next, and I'm caught completely off-guard.

"What?" I say.

"*How* do you know it isn't true?"

"I just do," I say. "I know my dad."

"Do you, though?" she asks, tilting her head, and I frown at her. I feel my resolve wavering, because she has a glint in her eye that makes me wonder if she knows something that I don't somehow. But if that's really the case, I don't want it to be revealed right now, in front of all the Chorus Girls. I don't say a word more, but Sloane fills up the silence.

"I mean, he left school in such a hurry and without any explanation, really. Didn't you ever wonder why?"

She shifts her weight and gestures with her hand like she's talking about the weather and not the downfall of the most important person in my life. I want her to stop talking, but I also need to know what she's acting like she knows.

I swallow hard, and a drop of sweat trickles down my spine.

"What are you talking about?" I ask quietly.

She squints at me. "Did you even see the text?"

"No," I say, "but that's not the—"

"I never said he hooked up with a student," Sloane explains, cutting me off. "I said he left Chisholm because of an *illicit relationship*." She raises her eyebrows like I'm supposed to know what that means. "But you know how facts can get distorted. You know how these things can take on lives of their own." She studies her fingernails like they're infinitely more interesting than I am.

I blink away from Sloane and look around at the other girls. They've shifted away from us the tiniest bit, and they're all huddled around Layla's phone like they're watching a video or something, but I can tell they're still listening. My throat feels tight.

I was sure that it was all made up. That Sloane was just being bitchy and that my dad was the victim. I wanted to be right, but suddenly I'm not sure I am anymore.

Sloane says, "Well, I don't want to be late to class," knowing she's clearly won our little standoff, if you could even call it that.

When the other girls turn and start to walk down the hall away from me, Layla looks back once and her eyes seem sad. But I don't want her pity. I don't want a thing from her anymore.

Just before Sloane leaves me behind too, she takes a step closer to me and leans down to whisper in my ear. "Your mom and Layla's mom are still tight, right?" She barely pauses long enough for me to nod. "Well, Mrs. Hassan tells Layla a lot more than she probably should. And Layla? She tells me *everything*."

I jerk away from her, and I try my hardest to keep my face composed. To keep myself together while she's watching me, clearly looking for a reaction. I don't give her one even though alarm bells are ringing through every inch of my body. I'm almost shaking trying to keep my cool.

Sloane smirks. Then she jogs a little to catch up with her friends. She tosses an arm around Layla's shoulder, and it only sharpens the pain that is slicing its way through me. The second they're out of sight, I lean against the lockers to try to catch my breath.

I don't believe the rumor—no way—but there's clearly more to why Daddy left Chisholm. If Sloane isn't lying, Layla knows something, and that makes me more upset than maybe anything else. That she kept something this big and painful from me but told *Sloane*. And while I'd love to say I'm surprised, I'm not. At all.

I want the truth, so I know I need to go straight to the source.

MEN SHOULD BE WHAT THEY SEEM

All the days that I've missed this month were days when I didn't enter the building at all. So I'm not the kind of kid who would normally need to know how to sneak away from school—how to skip, say, one class—and I have no idea how to get out of here before last bell undetected.

I know I can't use the front door, so I head to one of the side stairwells. Some of them have emergency exits, doors that have to remain unlocked in case of a fire or some other disaster. But this feels like an emergency to me. Bits and pieces of my life have been going up in flames for months, so I need to get out of here to save myself, to get away from everything that's burning.

The first stairwell I check has no exit at all, and the next one has a sign that says an alarm will sound if the door is opened. In the third one I find two people making out against the only way out, and while I'd normally pretend I hadn't seen anything and keep moving, I'm desperate.

"Hey, look, I'm sorry," I say. A brown-skinned guy with curly black hair pulls away from the person he's kissing—another guy, with cornrows and a round hickey on the left side of his neck. Looks like they've been at it for a while, but you wouldn't know

it by the annoyed expressions on their faces. "I just need to—"
I point to the door behind them.

They both move, as one, to make room for me to pass.
"Thanks," I say. I don't look back, but I bet they're making out
again before the door even closes.

The subway isn't crowded because it's only a little after eleven
a.m., so rush hour is over, and no one's headed out for lunch yet.
My mood lightens a little as I fade into the bigness of the city and
become just another face in the crowd. On the platform, no one
is staring at me. On the train, no one knows what the kids at my
school are saying about my dad. On the windy sidewalk, I'm just
like everyone else: cold, busy, and on my way.

I don't text him. I don't want to give him a chance to know
I'm coming, or a chance to charm me with one of his all-caps
replies. Once I get there, I skip up the library stairs two at a time
and head straight to the ground floor.

This part of the library is never exactly quiet, but it seems
oddly empty today with the riot going on inside my head. I step
into the reading room, and he looks up from the computer on his
desk and smiles.

"Well, this is quite a surprise," he says softly. He doesn't scold
me for being out of school like I thought he'd do right away. He
doesn't ask why I've come. And instantly, just from the sight of
his crooked glasses and bow tie, and the sound of his Librarian
Voice, I feel the ice around my heart start to melt. I don't want
to cry here, but the weight of it all comes crashing down at once.
I sniff, and before the first tear falls, Daddy is out of his seat,
stooping in front of me.

"Baby Girl," he says. "What's going on now?"

I don't want to ask him, because I feel like I should know that this isn't true, not about him. That this is an evil rumor made up by someone who wants to destroy me. But I'm so unsure of everything now. Every piece of the life I knew has turned out not to be true. So I have to ask. I have to hear him say that I'm not an idiot to think I know the man he is.

"Someone at school started a rumor about you."

"About me?" he asks, and I watch his face closely for anything that lets on that he might know where I'm going with this. I don't feel any twitches in his fingers, which are holding mine. He isn't avoiding my eyes.

"Yeah. They're saying . . ." And I don't know if I can say it out loud. I don't know if I can speak of this in front of him. He squeezes my hand.

"It's okay, Cleo. Whatever it is, we'll figure it out together."

"They're saying you left Chisholm because you had an affair. With a student."

He blinks a few times. He slips his glasses from his face and my heart seizes. I'm no longer someone he can see clearly, and blurry daughters are easily lied to. He says, "Honey. I swear. That isn't true."

"Why'd you leave, then?" I ask. And I watch him even more closely. The second he looks down, away from my eyes, I know I won't be able to believe whatever he says next.

"Hon, we've been through this. It was time for a change. Your mother and I are going through a rough patch and we thought it would be best, for *you*, if I worked . . . elsewhere."

And this is how I lose whatever's left of me: I don't ask if he's had a relationship with someone else, though I suspect, now more than ever, that Sloane wasn't lying.

I just nod and say, "Okay." But the sight of the few freckles that dust his cheeks hurts me, because they're a reminder that I come from him—someone who lies; someone who wrecks and ruins. Someone who can betray his family and keep it quiet.

I turn and walk away from my favorite person, away from my favorite place, to the person I normally avoid at all costs and the place I like least, knowing that at least I can trust her to do me the small kindness of telling me the actual truth.

I realize in that moment that I never actually asked my mom about what happened between them. I blamed her for the separation without knowing the truth about anything. I feel guilty about that now, but I hope it isn't too late to make things right.

—

I don't know how I get home as quickly as I do, but the subway ride is a complete blur. After leaving the library, that line from *Othello* is all I can think about: *Men should be what they seem.* One second I'm in Midtown Manhattan, and then, suddenly, I'm in Brooklyn, walking through the cold to my apartment.

The two flights it takes to get to my floor have never felt so long. I'm choking back tears and hating myself for the way I treated Sydney and Willa, Jase, and Dom. I'm hating my father because he lied to me, and I'm already hating my mother for telling me some still-unknown truth.

I reach my door and push it open and I nearly faint I'm so

distraught and overcome with emotion. I sink onto the couch and take one last deep breath.

"Mom?" I say. My voice comes out shaky and quiet. I should have known she wouldn't be here. It's the middle of the day, but I clearly wasn't thinking. So I call her. I dial her work number instead of her personal one, and I lift the phone to my ear and wait.

"Naomi Bell," she answers. I guess she doesn't have my cellphone number saved in her work phone, and something about that makes me tremble. There's noise in the background, like she's at a busy restaurant. And it is lunchtime, so maybe she's meeting with a client.

"Mommy?" I say softly.

"Cleo? What's wrong?" she asks. And her knowing just by my voice that something isn't right tips me over the edge. A sob escapes my throat before I can stop it.

"Hold on," she says. I hear her excusing herself from the table. I can imagine her in a tight pencil skirt and blazer, in red lipstick that matches her nails. She's a woman who still gets catcalls on the street even though she's well into her forties. She'll tell the guys off, too. She is a force to be reckoned with, made of beauty and power and smarts. And that's why I feel like a near-constant disappointment to her.

I came from a storm of a woman, but I'm just a drizzle of a girl.

Daddy would be a fool to cheat on her with *anyone*. He has to know that.

"Honey, what's wrong? Where are you? Are you okay?"

I cough until my voice works again. "I don't know. There's a rumor going around at school that Daddy . . ."

I can't bring myself to say it, but Mom starts speaking for me. "That he had an affair with Ms. Novak?" she offers. I'm so shocked at her words that I stop crying.

"What?" I say.

"Is that the rumor? Is that why you're so upset? Well, it isn't true, honey, okay? He didn't *do* anything with her, but they were getting . . . inappropriately close." On that word, I can hear a change in Mom's voice. A crack that tells me it hurts her to say this. "That was why we decided he shouldn't stay at Chisholm. We didn't want the students to start to talk." She clears her throat and I can see her perfectly in my head. She's probably looking skyward, the hand that isn't holding the phone bunched into a tight fist and slammed against her hip. "We were trying to protect you."

"Oh," I say quietly.

"So don't listen to them, okay? If those kids are spreading some lie about your father having done something with your teacher, it isn't true. Do you hear me?"

I nod, though she can't see me. "We can talk about it more later," she says. "I'm at this lunch and . . ."

"It's okay, Mom. I'm sorry."

"But you're okay?" she asks, and suddenly, armed with this new information, I'm at least a little better.

"I'm good," I say. "See you tonight."

DUH

I'm pacing around the living room trying to digest what my mother just told me. I'm relieved this is the half-truth my father was keeping hidden: that he *was* involved with someone else. At least it wasn't a student, but the fact that it was my favorite teacher feels like an even bigger betrayal. I'm still trying to figure out how to deal with that part of the puzzle when our apartment buzzer rings. I don't answer it at first, assuming it's a delivery person paging the wrong apartment. But then it rings again and again, so I go to the door and press the button for the intercom.

"Hello?" I ask.

"Oh, thank God," Sydney replies. "I thought I was going to have to search the whole damn city for you."

"Let us up," a second voice says. Willa.

"What are you guys doing here?"

"What do you think, ya weirdo? There's an awful rumor going around about your dad. You locked yourself in the bathroom. And then you disappeared from school and you haven't been answering any of our texts!"

"We sent a lot of texts," Willa adds.

"You didn't have to come," I tell them, my voice getting a little shaky. Truth is, I'm touched. "Everything's fine," I lie.

"Oh my God, Cleo," Sydney says. I can imagine her rolling her eyes. "I can't with you."

I look through my window, but I can't see them. They must be right up against the door. "Yeah, sorry. That isn't even remotely true. Everything's a mess," I say, leaning my head on the wall above the intercom.

Willa starts to chant. "Let us up, let us up, let us up!"

I let them up.

When I open the door, Willa immediately slips off her shoes and leaves them by the door. Her socks are covered in smiling avocados. She wraps me in a hug.

"Jeez, kid. We were worried about you," she says.

Sydney doesn't wait for her to let go before she wraps her arms around me too.

"You left school?" I say, my voice muffled by the wool of Sydney's peacoat and the puff of Willa's parka. "For me?"

"Duh," Sydney says.

Willa coughs. "Syd, I can't really breathe?"

Sydney lets us both go. "Sorry."

They take off their coats, tossing them onto the couch, and I lead them down the short hallway to my room. Willa pads over to my shelf of snow globes and shakes one right after the other, so that by the time I settle beside Sydney on my bed, the fake flakes and glitter in all of them are swirling.

Willa sits cross-legged at my feet and leans her head against my knee, and Sydney scoots closer, slipping her arm around my shoulders. We watch the snow spin, and I don't realize I'm crying again until Sydney uses the edge of her sweater sleeve to wipe my cheeks.

"I'm so glad you guys are here," I whisper. And they both, somehow, move even closer to me.

I'm not ready to tell them what my mom told me about Ms. Novak, but I do tell them that the rumor isn't true.

"We never thought it was," Willa says softly.

I tell them what Valeria told me—that Sloane started the rumor about my family to get back at me for the email I sent months ago.

When Sydney says, "That email came from you? That . . . doesn't seem like you," I realize I never told her the whole story. And in that moment I decide to, because keeping secrets and telling lies is exactly how I ended up in this mess in the first place.

I start at the beginning of summer, at the Fourth of July party where Layla and I first met Sloane. And even though I'm terrified of what they might think of me once the truth is in this room sitting between us, I tell them everything.

"So," I say, taking a deep breath after my whole ugly past has been revealed, "I decided I didn't want to miss her anymore. She wasn't worth the pain, or whatever, and I'd already ruined everything anyway. That's why I started with the whole making-new-memories thing."

"Damn," Sydney says. "That's . . . way worse than I thought things had been. It was fucked up for you to send that email, but also, I kinda totally get it. I'm so sorry, Cleo," she says, reaching for my hand and squeezing it. She tosses her hair and then looks up at me. "So when are we going to murder Sloane?"

I laugh a little, but Willa doesn't say anything. She's picking at my carpet.

"There's this Shakespeare quotation," I continue. "*Make not your thoughts your prisons.* And I guess I was just trying to stop that from happening, you know? I was trying to think less about Layla and everything that happened. I'm always trying my hardest *not* to think about it. You're actually the first people I've ever told the whole story to, and I'm terrified you'll see me differently now." I take a deep breath and steady my nerve. "Do you?" I ask.

Sydney shakes her head and smiles slowly. Willa just rolls her eyes.

"Nah," Sydney says.

"You're stuck with us now," Willa agrees.

Sydney asks where the bathroom is a few minutes later, and I point her in the right direction. Once she's gone, I slide onto the floor to sit beside Willa.

"You okay?" I ask her. She's been quiet for a while now, and even though it feels like we've known each other forever, we haven't really. I don't know her moods or what they mean yet. She looks at me, shrugs, and then lies down and stares up at the ceiling. I follow suit, our heads side by side, our bodies pointing in opposite directions.

"You ever feel like you can't miss someone without missing every person you've ever lost?" Willa asks. I twist my head to look at her. Because of the way we're arranged on the floor I can't see what her face looks like, only her profile—her messy, too-long bangs getting tangled in her straight eyelashes; her small nose and the pointed corners of her mouth. She keeps staring at the ceiling.

I think of Gigi. "That's exactly what I feel like," I finally say. "That's exactly what I feel like all the time."

"Shit's dark," she says. "So I get why you wanted to like, *erase* Layla, by going to all those places and doing more memorable stuff."

I nod, my braids dragging a little on the carpet.

"Thing is," Willa continues, "you kinda have to go through the dark to be sure you're okay. And like, while I get the sentiment behind your project, why not just make brand-new memories instead of overwriting old ones? You don't have to erase the bad things to be happy. Besides, the dark shit is important to remember too."

I look at my snow globes. I blink away tears as I think of all that I've lost. Willa props herself up on her elbows and shakes her bangs out of her eyes.

"She hurt you bad. Let yourself feel it, and everything that comes with it."

When I glance over at her, she puts her hand on my shoulder. I just nod.

"Oh my God, guys," Sydney says, rushing back into my bedroom.

I sit up fast. "What?"

"Someone posted about the rumor!"

Willa hops up and snatches Sydney's phone from her.

"Shit. This is bad. If anyone sees this . . ." Willa glances at me through her bangs.

"What?" I ask, my eyes flying from Sydney's face to Willa's and back again. "What would happen?"

"There would probably be some kind of investigation if like, *authorities* saw it, right?"

"No way that would happen. It's not even true," I say.

Willa shrugs. "I don't think that matters, dude. Can we prove that it isn't?"

They both stare at me, and the one person who can prove it pops into my head like lightning.

Novak.

ONE MORE TERRIBLE TRUTH

Willa puts on one of her favorite Korean dramas, and the three of us watch it together and hang out for most of the afternoon. Once they leave, though, I barricade myself in my bedroom for the next few hours, trying to decide what to do. Maybe I won't need to do anything. Maybe this will all blow over and no one will see the post or even care about it. But what if someone *does*? What if my dad gets into serious trouble over a lie?

I lie in the center of my bed, trying to make sense of what I know. Of what Mom meant by *close*. Of what could have been happening between my father and Ms. Novak that was so intimate that my dad needed to change jobs, and that, even after everything, my parents still split up.

Soon, exhaustion from all the emotional stress of the morning sets in and I fall asleep. I don't wake up until a reminder in my calendar chimes, telling me that I'm supposed to go to the diner tonight. But with this rumor going around, and after I yelled at Dom, I know I'm not going to.

I call Dolly's. Pop picks up. "Dolly's Diner. How can I help ya?"

"Hey, Pop," I say. My voice sounds all croaky from crying or sleeping or both. "It's Cleo. I'm not going to make it in to help out tonight. I'm not feeling well. Is that okay?"

"Of course, honey. Dom mentioned you had to leave early from school. Anyway, take all the time you need."

I say thank you and hang up before I roll over to stare at the wall, praying that I can fall back to sleep and pretend everything that has happened today was a dream.

The next time I wake up, my window is dark and Mom's warm hand is on my shoulder.

"Cleo, honey, how long have you been sleeping?"

I glance at the time on my phone. "A while," I say. I sit up and stretch and I watch my mother slip off her high heels.

"What really happened with Ms. Novak?" I ask right away.

She reaches up and pulls down one of my snow globes. It's the one of Hogwarts. She shakes it and then crawls into bed with me. We watch the fake snow as it swirls around the miniature castle. I haven't seen my mother this still maybe ever. I search her face and then her eyes find mine.

She looks as if she's sizing me up. She's studying me like I'm a gas tank and my face is the gauge. Even though I called her a few hours ago sobbing, I still myself, putting on the best Poker Face I can muster. I try to look as tough as I can. And I guess she decides there's enough room inside me for one more terrible truth.

"Your father is in love with her, Cleo."

"In love . . . with Ms. Novak?" I say, stunned.

She nods. "He came home one day and told me that he felt we'd been growing apart since your grandmother passed away." She looks down at the snow globe again. "He said I'd been working like a fiend and that he felt like I had no time for him. He said I made him feel like nothing he did was ever good enough. And maybe I did throw myself into work after we lost her, but he got a little bit lost too." She takes a deep breath, and I put my hand on hers where it still holds the snow globe. "I think he'd already decided to move on, and a bigger part of me wanted him to be happy than to stay with me if I made him sad. He could tell I wasn't my best self with him either. So separating just made sense."

"So . . . did he cheat? On *you*?" I ask. I touch her perfect hair. I think of her intense and steady devotion to everything.

"I wish it were that simple, Cleo. But no, not exactly. We were changing, or maybe we'd already changed. And I don't think either of us was willing to make the kinds of compromises and sacrifices the newer version of the other person needed."

I nod. I kind of understand that part at least. It's like Layla and all the new music she started listening to, the way she got into makeup and hair and chorus and forgot about the things we both used to love. It's like me wanting everything to stay the same when nothing was ever going to. For a second, I hate my father and Ms. Novak for hurting my mother as much as I hate Sloane and Layla for hurting me. But as my mother continues speaking, outlining her and my father's slow descent, I see that she made some mistakes too, just like I did.

None of this is as simple as it seems.

"I wish you'd told me," I say.

"I always thought you deserved to know," she says. "That people change. That love and life are fluid. That even your heroes can make choices that fall into shades of gray. But your father thought it was a bad idea, that it might be too complicated for

316

you to handle. Now that I think about it, I wonder if he was just saying that to protect himself. To protect the way you saw him as this great, flawless guy."

I'm a little embarrassed that I was holding on to the childish sentiment of things lasting forever, of people being perfect. Even now, I don't want to let it go.

"He did know Layla and I were fighting, though," I counter. "So maybe he thought it would be too much for me—this on top of everything else." As soon as I finish the sentence, I can hear myself defending him even though I have no reason to. I don't know when my father became superhuman in my head.

—

We shift from my room to hers and order takeout. We're talking and eating, sitting in the center of her big, soft bed, in a pile of bare brown feet and blankets.

"Sorry," I say to my mom, because I don't want her to think I'm taking his side in this. We've all lost something because of what's happened: a love; a life, even my own quiet innocence, though that couldn't have lasted much longer. She smiles softly.

"It's okay. In his defense, I think he was right. After Ma died, I wasn't as emotionally available to him as maybe I should have been."

As if to illustrate her point, her work phone rings and she reaches for it. I move it away from her neat red nails and shake my head.

When we finish eating and I go back to my room to finally change out of my uniform, I'm feeling a hundred times better than I did when I first got home. It's funny how a dose of honesty and Chinese food does that for a girl.

I pick up my phone from where I set it before I fell asleep, and I have a bunch of missed texts from Daddy. I don't think I can answer them right now. I finally read the texts from Sydney and Willa. I even have a few from Jase.

There's just one from Dom: *Just text me back if you're okay.*

I get the sudden urge to right all the wrongs I've committed today. To show up for the people who have shown up for me. I text Jase back and say that I'm sorry for being rude to him in the hall. I text Sydney and Willa, thanking them for coming over. Then I check the time. It's still early enough that if I head to the diner I can help Miss Dolly and Pop close up, so instead of changing into pajamas, I pull on a pair of jeans and the tight white sweater I had on earlier today. I'm hoping I'll have a chance to apologize to Dom in person like I planned to all along.

then:
December,
week 4

ALL ABOUT ME

Cleo Imani Baker

I got this text from Jase almost as soon as I walked out of my apartment building on the first Monday of winter break. It was windy and cold. I couldn't stand to stay inside with all of Daddy's stuff gone, and yet I wasn't ready to visit his new place either. My mom and I had established a delicate kind of peace, me admitting that decisions like marital separations aren't made alone, her apologizing for trivializing my feelings on the day Daddy moved out. We weren't completely healed, but we were getting there, moving a little closer inch by inch. Even though we were back on speaking terms, Mom was still working almost constantly. I was getting used to being alone.

My last conversation with Layla had been on repeat in my head for days, and I wished I could move into the stacks at the library and be rid of everything and everyone else. It was still a few days until Christmas—a Christmas I was confident would suck—which meant I had dozens of waking hours ahead of me without school, plans, or anything else to look forward to.

I stared at Jase's text, wondering what he might want. I was a little afraid to speak to him after what happened the night of the musical. I didn't know whose side he'd be on since Mason was dating Layla now, and he was Jase's best friend. I didn't know if I could handle losing Jase too.

I chanced it. I texted Jase back as I pushed through the turnstile and stepped onto the platform. I didn't know where I was going, and I didn't really care. When I felt lost, I liked to *get* lost, and in New York City it's easy to lose yourself.

Yes, Jase Lin?

I usually did all of my Christmas shopping online, but since I'd waited until the last minute and didn't have anything better to do, I decided moments after boarding the train to brave Fifth Avenue. Even if I didn't find anything, I'd at least be able to take in all the lavish decorations and lights. I thought it would be pretty enough to momentarily distract me from everything. And once I was in Manhattan walking down the bright, crowded city streets, I realized I was right.

New York City in December is pure eye candy. There are old men and women in Santa hats ringing bells as they collect donations in red pails, and even the street performers change their selections to seasonal carols. As I admired the window display at Tiffany's, daydreaming about sparkly jewelry that would probably never be mine, Jase texted back.

Just found out both my parents are on call tonight.
So I'm obviously having a party.
My place. 9 o'clock. You better be there.

322

I smiled. I hadn't been to a party since Halloween, but I was perfectly okay with keeping that streak going. Maybe I would go ice skating instead. Maybe I would get some hot chocolate at a holiday market. The day was already looking up, so why would I ruin it with something as messy and unpredictable as a party?

Oh, idk, Jase. Can I let you know?

I walked farther down the block, thinking about getting my dad a bow tie or my mom a pair of earrings. She'd slipped me her credit card before she left for work that morning, and though she gave it to me for food, I didn't think she'd object to a few gifts. I texted her just to be sure.

No you may NOT lmk, Jase texted back as I walked into a huge department store. A clerk squirted a cloud of perfume right in front of me. I glanced up from my phone just in time to dodge it.

YOU'RE COMING. Even if I have to come pick you up myself.

I rolled my eyes, but his was a kindness I'd missed. I was pretty sure I wasn't going to his party, and I felt like I needed to figure out how to be alone without being lonely. Today seemed like the perfect opportunity to do just that—to spend some quality time with myself. I mean, Sartre wrote *Hell is other people* for a reason.

If you want to hang out tomorrow we can, I sent. But I'm skipping your party. Today is only and all about me.

—

The first department store I walked into had a full wall of snow globes on display, and as soon as I saw them, it felt like a sign. I stepped forward, shaking each one to send its contents spinning, and held tight to one with a miniature of the very store I was standing in at its center. *The thing about snow globes,* I suddenly remembered Gigi saying, *is that they're pretty to look at, but they'd be awful to inhabit. People are like that. Lives too.*

I'd never realized what she meant until that moment, in that department store. How people can look so perfect from the outside, their lives can seem so easy, but really, everything's a swirling mess.

I left with only the snow globe of the store, which I bought for my own collection, and I headed to a holiday market with Nat King Cole's "Christmas Song" playing on repeat through my earbuds.

In the park, there were stands with handknit mittens and tiny wooden toys, gourmet spices and organic lotions. I picked out a pair of delicate freshwater pearl earrings for Mom, and a pink-and-blue knit bow tie for my dad.

I grabbed a hot chocolate with a giant gourmet marshmallow on top, and while it was still too hot to sip, I found a seat on the stairs at the entrance to the park. There were skateboarders, and moms with bundled-up toddlers, and people my age kissing and laughing and goofing off. I sipped my chocolate and it was rich and warm, and a little later, when I found a necklace with a silver snowflake charm, I bought that for myself too. The hours passed quickly in the hustle and bustle of people shopping and laughing and singing, and it was a relief to lose myself in the white noise of the city.

I was starting to get a little too cold to stay outside for much longer. So I lifted my snow globe and shook it, peering through it at the rest of the park, as a kind of goodbye. But I lowered it slowly when, only a few feet away, I spotted a pale girl with flushed cheeks standing next to a brown-skinned girl with long black hair.

LONDON

Sloane was standing there just in front of me, staring at her phone. She hadn't seen me yet where I was perched on the stairs behind her, but the second I started gathering my bags she looked in my direction. I stood up quickly, still planning to turn and run away from them, but she rolled her eyes, tapped Layla's shoulder, and pointed at me before I could make my escape.

"Oh God, L," she said, sounding bored. "Look who it is."

If I hadn't been having a lovely day all on my own, maybe I could have let the dismissal go. But I'd found gifts and had delicious hot chocolate and people-watched, and here she was ruining the happiest few hours I'd had in months. So I didn't. I settled my bags back on the steps and looked right at her.

"What the hell is *that* supposed to mean?" I said.

"Ugh, nothing. It's just that you're everywhere. Like a cockroach."

Oh no, she did not.

"Jesus, Sloane. *What* is your problem with me?" I asked, and my voice sounded annoyed and pleading all at once. Her vitriol couldn't all be because of the Halloween party. The more

I thought about how awful she'd been to me, the less I understood.

Sloane crossed her arms. "You still don't get it, do you? I don't have a problem. I just don't like you. And frankly speaking, Layla doesn't either."

I was shaken even though I shouldn't have been. I felt a pain in my stomach, quick and sharp like a blade of truth. Layla looked guilty for a split second, before her face contorted into an expression I'd never seen her make before. It almost looked like pride, but it was a twinge darker than that. Layla looked self-satisfied. Layla looked almost *smug*.

"It's true," Layla said. She jutted out a hip and twirled a piece of her hair. "I don't."

Sloane laughed. "Tell her about London, L," she said. I swallowed hard and my eyes slid from Sloane's face to Layla's and back again.

"London?" I asked. *What could she have to tell me about London?* But then Layla started talking.

"Ms. Novak wrote me a recommendation for the Shakespeare summer p-p-program t-too, you know. The one at the G-Globe in London?"

This was a turn in the conversation I hadn't expected. My eyes traced Layla's face, slowly. I felt my hands start to shake, so I squeezed them into the tightest fists I could make and shoved them hard into the pockets of my coat.

"Why would you even apply to it?" I asked.

"There's a Young Actors Summer School, j-j-j-ust like there's a Young Scholars one. I applied when you d-did, b-but I wanted

327

it to be a surprise that I'd b-be coming with you if, by sssome miracle, I got in."

I knew exactly where this was going, and even though everything in me was screaming *run*, I was rooted to the spot in front of her. I had to hear it out loud to believe it could be true.

"After y-you ssssaid what you said, I asked Novak if I could w-w-withdraw my application. I d-didn't want to chance it— getting in and b-b-b-being stuck there with you. But she said it was t-too late."

Sloane was loving every second of this. So were Sage, and Melody and Cadence, who were suddenly there too. They were surrounding me, like we were a fistfight waiting to happen. But Layla and I had only ever been a war of words.

"I wasn't g-g-going to t-tell you," she said. "Because Novak t-t-told me you d-didn't get in and that you were really d-d-disappointed. But I g-guess the head of the program was really moved by my statement of interest."

Sage crossed her arms. And Melody and Cadence looked at each other, grinning, like the words Layla was saying were lyrics to their favorite song. I could feel it getting harder and harder for me to breathe, harder and harder for me to listen—to keep my mind where my body seemed to be stuck. The girls, they turned into monsters around me, and the park turned into my own personal hell. I was surrounded by flames, hot and burning, and there was no way out.

"In my statement, I t-t-t-told them that I st-st-stuttered, but that I'd gotten a lead p-part in the school musical; that I knew I'd probably st-st-stutter onstage, but that I was d-d-doing it anyway."

They weren't moving, but it felt like everything was closing in on me. And my heart was breaking all over again. I knew what Layla would say next, but I still wasn't ready to hear the words.

"I g-got in, Cleo," she said. "I'm going to London this summer."

As she'd been talking, my eyes had filled with tears, and at the sound of those words, I blinked and it all spilled over.

Layla started crying too. I knew it was because she cried when she was angry, but I convinced myself, just for a second, it was because she felt as awful as I did. She swiped the tears away hard and fast.

Sloane put her arm around her shoulder. But Layla didn't stop glaring at me. Her dark eyes were the same ones I'd looked into for years. Even with the makeup she was wearing, and with the super-straight hair, her eyes still looked the same. When she spoke, though, she was *New* Layla—a complete stranger.

"I'm so damn glad you won't be there," she hissed.

Then I was completely broken.

Then I was gone.

now

STORMY SKYE

Right before I get to my stop, it starts to pour. Raindrops pummel the top of the train, so that it sounds like pennies being shaken in a tin can above our heads. Other passengers dig around in their bags for umbrellas, but all I can do is tuck my braids into the collar of my coat, and my phone into the front pocket of my jeans. I wrap my scarf around my head, hoping my hair won't get too wet.

I run up the stairs at the stop closest to Dom's house and Dolly's, and burst through the diner doors wet and laughing.

"What are you doing here, Sweet Pea?" Dolly asks.

"I thought you weren't feeling well," Pop says.

I pull my scarf from my head and shake my braids loose from my collar, "I know, but I wanted to help you close up if you needed me."

"Well, ain't you the sweetest?" Dolly intones. She grabs a clean bar towel and pats my braids dry.

"Is Dom here?" I ask, tossing the bar rag into a bucket with other used ones. Pop shakes his head. "I told him to head home and close the windows since I knew it was supposed to rain. Dolly likes to sleep with them open these days. That woman loves the cold." He glances over at her and smiles.

I help lift the café chairs, stacking them on top of the tables, and then I sweep and mop the dining room floor. I turn on a song I know Pop likes and he nods as he wipes down the counter, humming to himself. When I head for the stacks of cloth napkins and clean silverware to start rolling them, Dolly comes over. She places one of her warm, soft hands on mine to still them and leans a little closer to me. "Dom has seemed pretty down these last few days. Have you two made up yet?"

I lift my eyes to meet hers. They're brown, but I don't think I noticed until now that there's a cloudy circle of blue around her irises. "Not yet," I say. "To be honest, I was hoping he'd close the windows at the house and then come back here," I admit.

Dolly grins. "Oh, Sweet Pea. Why don't you just go talk to him now?"

"I'm not done here yet," I say, wanting to put it off, wanting to stay here, where I know I'm wanted.

"I think I can manage rolling the rest of these," Miss Dolly says, seeing right through me. "We still have to count out the register and make the deposit at the bank. That should give you two plenty of time to talk."

I nod and look down at her wrinkled hands—the only part of her that seems at all old. I reach out and give her a hug, and she smells like lavender and home. We're almost exactly the same height, and for a second I forget that there are so many years between us. "Thank you," I tell her. I throw my jacket and scarf back on, and I'm out the door before I remember to grab the umbrella Pop told me to take from the break room.

The rain is still falling in cold, thick sheets, but Dom's house is only a few blocks away. I sprint past brownstones and wide apartment buildings, a small park, and a guy walking a dog in a bright yellow raincoat. There are a few kids in galoshes splashing in puddles on a fenced-in driveway and a woman pushing a stroller covered in plastic, and I marvel at how, even in the rain, the streets here are never empty.

At the end of Dom's block, I spot Stormy crouched beneath a black sedan. I bend low and reach out, trying to get her to come to me so we can both get out of the rain, but she only backs farther into the inky shadows under the car.

I knock on Dom's door loudly, and he answers so quickly that for a second I wonder if he saw me coming.

"Hey," I say. "Your cat is under that car! I tried to get her out, but she wouldn't come to me."

He blinks at me, and I notice his eyelashes are wet. He must have gotten caught in the downpour too. "Yeah," he says softly. His eyes travel from my combat boots all the way to the scarf wrapped around my head. He smiles. "She likes the rain. That's why we named her Stormy Skye."

He moves backward so I can step into his foyer. He reaches up and pulls the dripping scarf off my hair. "Why are you out in this mess?" he asks.

He's wearing what look like the softest pair of sweatpants, a clean white T-shirt, and thick gray socks, and I want to snuggle up to him. To bury my face in his cotton-covered chest.

"I went to the diner to help your grandparents close." He grins and shakes his head a little. "But also," I continue, "I wanted to apologize. For earlier today when I yelled at you. And also for suggesting the fundraiser thing. You told me about the restaurant in confidence, and the first thing I suggested was to tell a bunch of other people about it." I look up at him and he bats his pretty, wet eyelashes.

"It's been a rough couple of months," I say. "And getting to know you better has really been one of the best things in my life lately. Talking to you and Jase, Sydney, and now Willa has kind of saved me. The last time I messed things up with someone, I waited too long to apologize. So here I am."

I take a deep breath. I reach out and squeeze his hand once before letting go. "I'm really so, so sorry."

He bites his bottom lip. "I'm sorry too," he says. "For being pissed about your suggestion about the diner. You were only trying to help, and the truth is my dad had just offered my grandparents money earlier that day. He's always doing that shit—sending money instead of coming around. But yeah. It was a dick move to take it out on you."

I look down, and when I look back up he's smiling. The tiniest shiver shakes through me because the rain has seeped into my clothes and onto my skin.

"Do you want me to dry your clothes? I got caught in the storm too, so I was just about to start the dryer with my jeans and stuff."

I don't know if that is what I want, but I know that *this* is what I've wanted for a while: To be close to Dom again like I was the first time we talked about *Macbeth* on his rooftop; to be alone with Dom in an empty house where anything might be possible. I want to trust him, I suddenly realize, in a way I haven't let myself trust anyone since my life started to fall apart piece by piece a few months ago. I want to trust Jase and Sydney and Willa, my mom and my dad and Ms. Novak. I even want to trust Layla again, though I know I probably never will. But Dom is the one I'm standing in front of when this realization hits. And maybe that's a sign. Maybe I can start right here, with him.

I'm terrified, but I take a breath. "Okay," I say.

And when Dom reaches out his hand, I grab it and let him lead me forward.

A NEW BEGINNING

"Why do you like Shakespeare?" Dom asks out of the blue.

After he pulls me out of the rain and leads me up the stairs, he offers me a pair of his sweats and a long-sleeved T-shirt. I step into his room with my dripping jeans and sweater in hand and he takes the wet clothes from me and dumps them into the dryer in the hall. I'm still wearing my damp underwear because I was worried that either my body touching his clothes directly or seeing his hands on my bra would make me spontaneously combust. I'm barely holding it together with the soft fabric that smells like him touching easy places like my wrists and the backs of my knees. I wouldn't be able to handle much more.

When he steps back into his room, I'm standing in one corner near the window looking out at the rain. His clothes are all way too big, and a part of me wants *him* to occupy the space my small body has left in the unrolled sleeves of his shirt, the drooping fabric of his pants.

"Why do I like Shakespeare?" I repeat, turning slowly to face him, because I'm surrounded by too much Dom-ness for my brain to operate at full capacity.

He nods. "Do you like it for its beauty or for its meaning?"

There's a light in his eyes that isn't normally there, and I want to give him the answer that will make me seem smart and interesting and worth knowing. I've decided to trust him, and I want to prove that he should trust me too.

Somehow I am a girl who makes all the wrong choices, but I am also a girl who aches in every way to be wanted despite my mistakes. I'm about to answer when he steps closer to me and keeps talking.

"Pretty words are easy, Shorty," he says, reaching out to me. He rolls up the sleeves of the shirt I'm wearing, revealing one of my small hands and then the other. "But the stories are the complicated part. They're messy and tragic and funny and broken." Dom licks his lips and something inside me falls off a cliff.

"Shakespeare, he used a lot of pretty words, and sometimes he used them to obscure the truth a little." I nod and Dom kneels. He rolls up the bottoms of my (his?) too-big pants, and his warm thumbs graze my ankles. He looks up at me from the floor.

"You just said a lot of pretty words to me," he says, his eyes not wavering from mine, like he's trying to see inside me. He sits back on his heels. "So I'm just curious," Dom continues, "what it is you like most about the plays. Is it their elegance or their . . . deception?"

I swallow hard. He stands up slowly and he's so close to me that I can see his individual eyelashes. They're dry now. The storm is still raging outside, and I can hear the rain beating on his windows like it wants to come in and cover us. I feel like my answer will matter more than it should. That he's asking because this will reveal something about me that Dom is desperate to know.

"Can't I like both?" I ask, sounding bothered and breathless.

"But which," Dom asks, "do you like *more*?"

I reach up to adjust glasses that aren't on my face. I must have left them in the bathroom when I changed. I drop my hand, unsure of where to put it. I want to touch him, but I just hold on to my own fingers again.

"I like that he can use beauty to reveal the scariest, worst parts of being human," I say, watching Dom's dark eyes. "I like that the truth is only hidden if you don't read closely enough." I think about Ms. Novak and my dad—there were signs everywhere that I ignored. Dom's eyes flicker, and he kind of grins.

I want to know why.

Dom nods and moves a single wet braid from where it hangs over my forehead, and every part of me is aflame. And then, all at once, I can't take it anymore: the smell of his skin on the clothes that I'm wearing, the inscrutable look in his eye. The way that I decided to trust my heart and him tonight over everyone and everything else. I lean forward without thinking and kiss him.

He kisses me back. Dom puts his warm hand on the back of my neck and I reach around him and wrap my arms tight around his torso. I haven't kissed a boy since last summer, and even though it's a freezing cold night instead of a humid, hot day, I'm so glad this is happening now—in Dom's warm bedroom, in the middle of a storm—right after he asked me why I love Shakespeare.

He backs me toward the door and I trip over my wet boots, and when I almost break away laughing he doesn't let me. I'm glad. His lips curl against mine in a smile, but we keep kissing, all hot mouths and wet hair and hands. We make out against the door, and his arms rest against the wood on either side of my head, making his body feel like it's filling the whole room. All I can see is him. When I lift my hands to wrap my arms around his neck, I accidentally hit the light switch. The room goes dark, and then I do break away, giggling. I say, "Oops," and I feel his flirty whisper against my cheek in the sudden darkness.

"You move fast," he says.

"It was an *accident*," I reply, slapping at his chest, and then I blindly grope the wall for the switch. But when I find it, it's already flipped up, in the on position, which is strange. I flick it down, but the room still stays dark.

"Oh shit," I say. "I think the power's out."

I feel more than see Dom grin. "Nice," he says, and for a second I'm laughing too hard to kiss him more.

Dom has his phone in his pocket, so he pulls it out, flips on the flashlight, and shines it above us, so we can see each other's faces.

"Hey," he says.

"Hi," I say. I feel exposed and suddenly shy in the bright light from his phone. I don't know what I'm supposed to say or do next. My face is burning because I can't believe what has just happened, but I hope Dom can't tell.

He reaches out and puts another rogue braid behind my ear. He kisses me again, soft and slow, and I close my eyes until I feel like I'm sinking into the floor. He pulls away for a second, and I go up on my tiptoes to give him another peck on the lips. He says, "As much as I want to do this until the power comes back, I think Lolly and Pop will be home soon, and I don't want them to trip on anything downstairs. I was supposed to come home to make sure all the windows were closed against the rain, and since I've been a bit . . . distracted, there could be puddles."

I nod. "Oh," I say, and then I blush at the fact that I can distract Dominic Grey. "Sorry. Let's clean up, and find candles and stuff."

He pushes away from where he's leaning against the door, and I step forward, but he doesn't go any farther at first. "Just one more," he says, and before I can ask *One more what?* his lips are on mine again.

"Okay," he says a few minutes later. "Okay, what were we doing?" I grin a little. I press my thumb against my lips, then dip my finger into the hollow in his throat before tracing a long line of gentle pecks across his collarbone and up his neck. It's as magical as I thought it'd be. I look up at him and his eyes are closed; his brow is furrowed like he's genuinely confused.

He stares down at me and I stare right back. I can tell already: he's going to be another end to everything I knew to be true.

But maybe a new beginning is exactly what I need.

"Making sure your grandparents don't break a hip when they get home?" I answer.

"Right," he says, nodding. But he doesn't move.

"Dom. We need towels or a mop. We need to find candles."

He points at me, his eyes coming into focus a little more. "Right, yes. Mop. Candles."

He takes my hand again and pulls me forward, and I'm surprised that a touch as casual as this one makes me feel almost as heady and lost as kissing him does.

SPINNING STORIES

We fill his hallway with light. Candles glow softly from every corner of Dom's entryway, the kitchen, and atop the bricked-over fireplace in the den. I think, but don't say aloud, a line from *The Merchant of Venice* every time a wick catches and brightens another corner of the house. *How far that little candle throws his beams!*

There is only a slight spray of water under two of the upstairs windows, and I leave Dom downstairs to clean that up with the thick towel I used to dry off.

My phone buzzes and it's Sydney.

Ok. I think I know how I'm going to murder Sloane

But I'm Dom-drunk, and the rumor feels like something that happened a lifetime ago.

I send a cry-laughing emoji. Let's talk about it later. I'm at Dom's.

She sends back about eighty-seven exclamation points, and I smile and click my phone's power button so that the screen goes dark.

Dom finds me a few minutes later, and kisses me hard and long against the damp curtains.

We put small tea light candles on the right side of each stair so Lolly can pick her way up without any trouble. For Pop, we leave a battery-operated lantern on the kitchen counter so he can make his way through the house regardless of where he decides to go. And in each bathroom we leave a scented candle so that they smell sweet and are lit with a soft, golden kind of shine. In Dom's room, along with candles, we light incense.

"Good job," I tell Dom once we're back upstairs. Watching his steady hands light dozens of candles hasn't done much for my psyche. If anything, I want him more now in this dimly lit dark.

He turns after lighting a candle that sets the last corner of his room aglow.

"Thanks for the help, Shorty," he says.

He looks over at me, and for the first time since he asked me about Shakespeare I purposely look away from him, out at where the rain still pours. I squint at a nearby lamppost that's as dark as all the rooms in Dom's house. The power lines that lead to it are strung with a few pairs of sneakers. The wet shoes shine in the moonlight.

Dom sits on his bed, and I walk toward him slowly. He swallows, and I feel the possibilities opening up before us like a book that is filled with blank pages. Instead of kissing him again, which is what my body is screaming to do, my eyes land on an old copy of *The Secret Garden* that's sitting on his nightstand. And once again, something about Dom surprises me.

"No way," I say, reaching for it. "You're reading this?" He looks a little embarrassed for a second, but then he admits it with a nod. "I haven't read this book since I was a kid, but I loved it when I was younger," I tell him, turning it over in my hands.

His copy is well worn, with yellowed pages and a frayed paperback cover, and when I flip it open, I see THIS BOOK BELONGS TO *Dominic A. Grey,* written in a child's scrawl. It makes me smile to imagine him writing his name in this book, proclaiming it his because he loved it so much.

"Lolly got it for me the year I turned ten," Dom says. He looks at me closely, like he's making a difficult decision about something. He takes the book from me and picks up one of my hands. He plays with my fingers and then, it seems, he decides to trust me with another small piece of his story.

"When I was ten, I was kind of a little asshole," Dom says, and I laugh. "It was the year when I realized my mom and dad weren't ever going to show up in the way they had been promising to since I was little. They would call all the time and promise that the next time they visited it would be for forever. Or that I'd come to live with them soon. They'd send me birthday cards and Christmas presents but never actually stick around. And I think when I turned ten I figured out that everything they'd been telling me was all . . . bullshit, you know? So I was kind of a shithead to Lolly and Pop for like a year. I took it out on them since I couldn't take it out on the people I was really pissed at."

I look down at our hands in his lap. He twists the ring I'm wearing on my thumb around and around. He presses our palms together, then laces his fingers through mine before he starts talking again.

"So, I think she got me that book to try to shake some sense into me. Mary, the main character, is a bit of a bitch at the beginning of the story."

I laugh again and nod. From what I remember, he's right.

"And like, then everyone she's ever known dies and she has to go live with strangers. I don't think Lolly meant it as a threat— like 'if you don't shape up we're all going to die.'" I chuckle and so does he. "But Mary, she doesn't have any friends until she stops being shitty, and then she finds this badass garden full of magic."

I unlace our fingers and take his forearm in my hands. I trace his veins from the base of his wrist up to the crook of his elbow. He squirms a little, I guess because it tickles, but he doesn't pull away. I want to study every inch of his skin.

"I obviously now know how fucked up it is that the garden 'fixed' Colin, the kid who had to use the wheelchair? And there were some other pretty problematic things in that story. But over- all, I still totally relate to that book, and to Mary. Her parents didn't give a shit about her and it pissed her off, so she was a crappy kid for a while. But then she realized that there's still so much good in the world, you know? There's still a chance for things to be amazing even if your life didn't start out so great. But it's kind of up to you to build the life you want."

He's killing me with this history of his—the way it's all tied up in books and his philosophy about everything. And now that we've been touching for the last hour, I don't know how I'll ever survive not touching him again. I throw my legs over his lap be- cause even though I'm right beside him, it's not close enough, and everything that is happening feels like the beginning of our story. The end of the prologue to the short past we've shared.

"Cleo," he says seriously, and I don't think my name has ever sounded quite as good as it does when Dom speaks it aloud. I'm lost in him, but he's trying to tell me something, so I pull myself out of my own head and listen more closely. "Yeah?"

"You're doing that thing you do."

"What thing?" I ask.

"That thing where you start telling yourself a story about what's happening instead of paying attention to *what's actually happening*."

I blush, thinking of Gigi. "When I went dreamy and silent around my grandmother," I tell Dom, "she'd say I was spinning stories."

"You miss her?" he asks. And I nod.

"All the time."

"I can't imagine not having Lolly," he says softly. "So I get it. But maybe stop spinning stories for a second?" He smiles a little. "I'm trying to tell you something."

"I know. I'm listening."

He looks up at his walls, then back down at where my legs are flopped over his. "It's like this," he says. "I saw you that first day in Mr. Yoon's class, right? On the first day of school? And you were sitting there with your freckles and your purple glasses, your fresh braids and those ridiculous boots. I remembered you right away. And bumping into you like that—ending up at the same school and in the same homeroom against all odds—it made me wonder about fate. It made me rethink everything."

I think I see where he's going with this, though I feel like we're in a philosophy classroom instead of on a bed. I feel like there should be books in front of us instead of sweatpants-clad legs, tingling skin, and our own urgent fingers. "Like how you wouldn't be a person determined to *take* control if it weren't for the things that happened to you that you *couldn't* control?"

He nods. "Kind of. And then, after we talked about *Macbeth* and I started writing that paper, I realized it's not one or the other: fate or free will. It's *both*. Things you can't control happen all the time." He shifts, moving closer to me, just as we hear his front door open and Pop call out to us from the entryway. Dom's voice is soft and urgent when he speaks again.

"But you *can* control what you do next." He picks up a card from a deck on the table behind him. He holds it, waves his hand, and makes it disappear. I grin.

"Action is eloquence," I say, quoting *Coriolanus,* a play I've only read once.

He moves his hands again, in a way that's too quick for me to see. The card reappears. "Exactly," he says back.

still now

THE HOT SEAT, PART II

I can't stop thinking about Dom or what he said as we sat together on his soft bed. How we talked endlessly about fate and free will, helplessness and control. I might not be able to control what's happened with my parents, or anything that Sloane and Layla have said or done to me, but I can control what I do next.

I want to bitch Layla out for telling Sloane about my parents. I still want to punch Sloane right in the face. But I don't do either. I do send Ms. Novak an email, though. I'm tired of hiding—of pretending I'm okay when I'm not. And I have an idea that might be the beginning of fixing everything.

Ms. Novak,

By now you've probably heard the rumors that are going around about my dad. And if I'm honest, I'm worried this could have real repercussions for him if it goes any further. I want you to know that I know the truth, and I'm begging you to set the record straight.

351

Maybe you could write a letter or talk to Principal Davis or something? I don't know what would be best. I just want to make sure his name is cleared. And after all that has happened, I don't think it's wrong for me to say you owe me (and him) this small kindness.

I know I still need to make up the assignments I missed when I skipped school, but I'm not comfortable continuing to tutor Layla. Instead, what if I performed a monologue for extra credit? I can do this just with you, after class, or in front of other students if you prefer.

Please consider coming forward for me and my family. And let me know what you think about the monologue idea.

Thanks,
Cleo I. Baker

Just as I hit send, my phone buzzes with a text from Dom.

Morning, beautiful.

I grin.

We text back and forth as I get ready for school, but I'm still nervous about what shape he and I will take in the hallways of Chisholm Charter. We haven't had time to talk about what happened between us and what it all means. I text Sydney and tell her all about me and Dom while I'm on the train, and the second she sees me in the hall, she rushes over.

"You kissed. In the rain. And the power went out?!?" she squeals, because I pretty much told her everything on my thirty-minute commute. "How was it humanly possible for you to keep that to yourself for the last twelve hours?" She pants with her tongue hanging out of her mouth, and the tiny silver elephants dangling from her ears swing. She fans her face like she's hot, or maybe like Dom is. I grab her hands and squeal a little. Before I can push the huge smile off my face, Willa is there too, wanting to know what we're screeching about.

I pull Willa to me and tell Sydney to huddle closer too, deciding to trust them; deciding that life is hard enough without facing it all alone. I became friends with Layla while I wasn't watching, and we fell apart that way too, but with Willa and Sydney, every piece of us has been a choice.

I will choose them every day that they choose me back, and I'll be the best friend I can. So I tell them more about me and Dom in his dark, empty house, happy with who we all are to each other right now.

Just as I finish my story, I feel a hand slide around my hip. Dom is there, and while we haven't talked any of this through, he looks like he's pretty decided on how things will be with us from now on. He says hi to Sydney and Willa and then a flirty "Hey" to me that feels like a goodbye to everyone else. My girls get the message.

Sydney flips her hair and squeezes my shoulder, and Willa just says, "Make good choices!" before skipping away, her arm hooked through Sydney's. I blush hard and stuff my head into my locker, but I'm secretly ecstatic to have a boy to be teased about— and to have new friends to do the teasing.

Dom pulls my hands away from my face and makes me re-emerge. He says, "You told them already, didn't you?" And when I shake my head, he touches my face and mutters, "Pretty little lies, I swear."

"Do we need to talk," I say, "about all of this? Us?"

Dom shrugs and leans against the locker beside mine. "Not really," he says. "We're a thing, right?" And it's such a Dom answer.

"Yeah, Dom," I agree. "We're definitely a thing." I hook my finger into a belt loop of his khakis, tugging him a little closer.

"Good," he says, pressing his lips to my temple.

In homeroom, Dom sits just in front of me and turns around every time I touch his shoulder or elbow or the smooth dark skin on the nape of his neck. There's a series of spirals cut into his hair this week, and when I trace them with my fingertip, he shivers.

"You *have* to stop touching me," he whispers as Mr. Yoon takes attendance.

"Make me," I say, and when he playfully grabs my wrist I let out a little yelp that earns us a few stares.

They're not the kinds of stares that followed me because of Sloane's rumor. Like most things in this school, the episode was short-lived and seems to have already dissipated in the collective consciousness. But I don't think I'll ever forget that Layla told Sloane desperate details about my family that I didn't even know. That she willfully handed over something that could wound me so deeply, knowing that it would be used to do just that.

I'm still vaguely aware of the two of them, where they sit at the back of class; still vaguely angry every time I hear the thin tones of their voices. But for the first time in a long time, I'm not at all concerned about what they might be saying or thinking about me.

I spend most of the period flirting with Dom and group-texting Sydney and Willa under my desk until Layla taps me on the shoulder. When I look up and see that it's her, part of me seethes.

"Thanks for th-th-the help with that paper," she says. She lifts her graded essay and a red 92 is circled at the top. For a second, I'm so disoriented by her talking to me in a nonconfrontational way that I don't know what's happening.

"Oh, good for you." I cross my arms. "Thanks for telling Sloane about my dad so she could start that rumor," I say, as casually as she thanked me for my help. "That was *awesome*." It may be a petty response, but I can't believe she has the nerve to talk to me like everything is fine between us. The second I say it, though, I feel like it wasn't worth the energy. Like *she* wasn't. Layla looks stunned.

I let my crossed arms fall back to my sides. "Look. I told Novak to assign you to someone else. So consider us even. Done. Whatever. Okay?"

Layla blinks a few times and something like relief floods her features. "Okay," she says, and nothing else, and something about the exchange feels final. It makes me know that all the crap between us is ending, right here.

I grab my bag at the same time as Dom reaches for my other hand.

Layla's eyes land on our clutched palms. But the urge to tell her about my life, about Dom and me and who we are to each other, is completely gone. I toss her a small smile, and a nod, before I turn and head for the hallway.

The day is full of highs and lows. Mr. Frick's class is awful, as usual, but seeing Willa and Sydney at lunch is lovely. We make plans to go see the Cover Girls, and Willa spills a pack of M&Ms across her tray that we separate by color and eat together. Walking hand in hand with Dom makes it easy to forget that all my problems are still very much my problems. But when he lets go of my hand to head to his next class, it feels like a kind of falling. Every bad feeling comes rushing back, because I have Ms. Novak's English class next.

I think about skipping. I haven't told anyone the whole truth about the rumor yet, and Ms. Novak's involvement feels like a secret I want to keep forever. So I text my mom, because she's the only other person who knows what really happened—how I really feel. I tell her I want to skip Novak's class for the rest of the year because I'm still angry. I expect Mom to send half a dozen texts telling me not to skip, but she surprises me.

So don't.

Don't what?

Don't go. Go to the library or something.

You do realize you're giving me permission to skip a class, right?

Life is short, and you're sad. If you go, don't talk to her if you don't want to or can't.

Get out of there as soon as class is over.

> Or just deal with it. Walk right up to her and tell her you
> know everything.
> Even though your feelings are not her responsibility,
> you're allowed to speak your truth.

She's right, and I'm so touched at her giving me permission to do what I feel is best that my eyes well a little bit right there in the hall. I just send, K. **Love you**, and then I lurk until I'm almost late. I decide I want to take the "not talking to her" route, and it goes really well until she calls on me to answer a question when I haven't raised my hand all period. I freeze, and I'm not sure what to do or say, because all I can think about is Ms. Novak leaning over the circulation desk in the library, or the way she cried on my dad's shoulder when she found out he was leaving Chisholm. The lingering glances they shared that I must have missed and all the other time they were spending together that I didn't know about. I can't answer a question about the text we're reading when I have so many unanswered questions about the tiny ways in which she and Daddy ruined my life. I say, "I don't know." Novak frowns a little in my direction, but she lets it slide.

At the end of class, as I collect my stuff to leave, she calls me up to her Hot Seat. I try to get out of it because I'm not ready to be so close to her. If it weren't so late in the year I'd probably ask to be added to a different English class, but we're already well into the second semester.

I say, "Can we talk later? I really need to get to history."

But Novak says, "Don't worry, Cleo, this will only take a second. I won't make you late."

I cross my arms and walk up to the butterfly chair, hoping the barrier of skin and blood and bones will keep my heart safe. I sit down across from her and she smiles at me. I want to hate her. I want to *tell* her that I hate her. But part of me knows what it's like to make the wrong choice just because of how you feel in a single moment.

I can't help but wonder if she's idealizing Daddy the way I was; if the Cliff Baker in her head is anywhere close to the real one. And if he is, how is she not terrified that his feelings for her will fade just as they did for my mom?

"I got your email. And I want to tell you, I really respect how well you're handling this . . . situation. It isn't appropriate for me to really discuss the details with you, but I just want to let you know I'm going to do the right thing."

At the word "appropriate," I roll my eyes. Everything about our *situation,* as she put it, is inappropriate.

"But the other thing I wanted to say was that I never spoke to you about Layla's paper. It was remarkable, Cleo. Such a unique perspective—so smart and well drawn. I knew she had it in her, so I wanted to thank you for helping her. Your influence was most certainly felt."

I nod, and look away from her. "I'm glad. We done?"

She bristles at my coldness, and I feel a little bad, but I don't know how to do this—how to talk to a woman who was my favorite teacher and who is also the person who is partially responsible for my family breaking in half.

"Yeah," she says. "I'm reassigning her to another tutor, as you requested, but I wanted you to know you'd done a great job. And your monologue idea is an excellent one. But instead of

358

memorizing one from a play, how about you write your own?"
Her gray eyes seem darker than usual, and her curly hair is un-
ruly and wild. I see something in her eyes suddenly—some kind
of understanding, but also an assertion that she's still the one in
charge here. I kind of hate it, but I know I can't overtly disrespect
her. My parents taught me better than that, and she *is* still my
teacher.

I stand up, and I relax my arms the tiniest bit. "I can do that,"
I say. "And I really am glad Layla's paper turned out okay."

Ms. Novak shuffles some papers on her desk. She avoids my
eyes the same way I avoided hers all period.

"Me too," she says.

THEY'RE JUST PEOPLE

I ask Dom to meet me in the library after last period. We're both going to Dolly's, but I need to check out a book for a history paper. Plus I haven't seen him all afternoon, and after the day I've had, something about that feels like a crime.

"Hey," he says after I've texted him directions to my favorite corner of the stacks. Without saying hi back, I push him against the shelf and kiss him hard and long. I'd forgotten what it was like to want someone, to know that they want me back. And because I know now how quickly feelings can change, I don't want to waste a second for as long as we last.

"So, can I tell you something that you can't tell anyone?" I ask him a few minutes later. He's a little breathless from making out and he's standing close behind me while I run my fingers lazily over the spines of dozens of books, only half looking for the one I need. He sets his chin on the top of my head and reaches around me to pull a book from the shelf. I feel him nod.

"My parents split up because my dad fell in love with someone else," I say, and it's easier to let the truth fly free than I expected.

He puts the book back and wraps his arms around my waist. "Damn. I'm sorry," he says simply.

I shrug as much as his grip allows me to.

"You don't have to tell me if you don't want, or if you don't know. But did your dad, like, act on it?"

"I'm not really sure," I say. It's easier to say all of this without looking at him, so I keep my eyes on the endless rows of spines in front of me. "I don't think he did anything physical. But he told her his secrets. He spent time with her in a way that a married man in a monogamous relationship shouldn't with a woman who isn't his wife."

I swallow because I feel a soft sadness coming on. "It's just hard, you know? My dad was my hero. He was, like, perfect to me. And now that I know he did this—hurt my mom, hurt our family—I don't know what to think, or how to feel about him."

Dom releases me and with his hands on my shoulders, he turns me around to look at him.

"Remember what I told you about idealizing people? How most of the stuff you thought about me wasn't true once you got to know me?"

I bite my lip. "Yeah."

"Your dad? He's like us. I had to learn that about my parents the hard way. They're just people. They make wrong choices and do stupid things all the time. They're human."

"I know," I say. "I guess I just expect more of the people I love."

Dom glances up at the colorful shelf in front of us and I follow his gaze. "Ever think that you expect too much of them?" he asks softly.

I shrug. I don't want to think about Layla right now, but that's who immediately comes to mind. I feel a little heat creep up the back of my neck—unexpected anger.

"Is it so wrong to expect loyalty, and for love to be unconditional?"

Dom kisses my temple and drapes his arm over my shoulder. "I have no idea," he says.

I take a deep breath to calm myself down. "I guess I'm having this conversation with you," I continue, "because I feel like this thing between us could be something real. And as much as I want things to be a certain way, I don't want my expectations of it to ruin us, okay? I don't want to expect you to be perfect, and I don't want you to expect that of me either." I turn my face toward him. "Does that make sense?"

Dom nods.

As if on cue, my phone buzzes. I take it out of my pocket, assuming it will be my mom. But when I look at the screen, it reads *Daddio.*

"Ugh," I say. I ignore the call. "What am I going to do about him?"

"Take some time for yourself," Dom says. "You don't need to talk to him right away. You gotta sort through your feelings and shit."

I smirk. "Feelings and shit?" I ask.

"Hell yeah," he says. "From what I've seen, you have a lot of them."

I playfully push him away and find the book I need, and we head out into the hall.

The school is mostly empty, and as we walk down the hall hand in hand, Dom starts to hum and I remember my idea about the diner. Live music. Maybe even the Cover Girls. I'm nervous to bring it up since he was so defensive last time I made a suggestion, but I feel like this is a much better idea.

"What would you think about bringing in a live band to play at Dolly's?" I ask as we exit the building.

That shield flickers in his eyes. But I say, "Just hear me out, okay? I was playing my music during my last shift. You know, Nat King Cole, and Nina Simone, and Louis Armstrong? And the customers were so into it. Pop was dancing with Miss Dolly and it just completely changed the energy in there." I stand up a little straighter. "I think live music could be even better," I say. "I'm seeing this amazing jazz cover band with Willa and Sydney this weekend. If they're as good live as they are recorded, it could be really cool."

Dom crosses his arms. But then he looks at me and a slow smile spreads across his face. "I don't know if Lolly and Pop will go for it," he says. "But it's definitely worth a try. Only thing is, hiring a band is expensive if you want a good one." This is a complication I hadn't thought of. But before I can get too worried, Dom keeps talking.

"But maybe it could be an open mic night instead. We can get kids from school to come, and post stuff online to get more of a turnout."

I clasp his shoulder. "You're brilliant," I say, thinking about how this could appeal to the artsy people who go to school with us and also the artsy hipster-types who are new to the neighborhood.

"Maybe we could debut your small plates the same night? And that way, it's like a special menu for a special event. If people don't like it, they'll know it was just for one night. But if they do, you can use that to convince Pop to make some of your recipes a permanent part of the menu."

Dom doesn't say anything. He just smiles widely and puts his hands on either side of my face. He kisses me right there on the sidewalk, and my heart is so full that I laugh against his lips.

THE COVER GIRLS

The Cover Girls crowd isn't what I expect it to be.

Sydney, Willa, and I are shivering on the sidewalk outside a tiny legendary jazz club waiting to get in. The line is full of college kids with undercuts, women in tight dresses who look like they'd be friends with my mom, and guys with goatees and graying hair. This is one of the few clubs in the city that admits people under twenty-one, but we're waiting for Willa's ex, Lulu, who swore she could get us in without paying cover (as long as we bought a drink) and promised she'd save us seats near the front.

"Jesus, it's fucking freezing," Sydney says. She's wearing sparkling eye shadow that makes her look like she's famous, and bright diamond stud earrings in the shape of stars. Willa's pulled her choppy black hair up with dozens of bobby pins and circled her dark eyes with a dark blue liner that matches the night sky. I'm in the lacy black dress I wore to Sloane's Halloween party, because I'm eager to give the dress a new memory, and Sydney let me borrow a pair of her earrings. Soft black tassels swing from my ears.

We huddle closer together with our arms interlocked, and Sydney threatens that her toes and fingers and the tops of her ears are going to fall off. "Nothing's going to fall off," Willa promises. She disentangles herself from us and cups Sydney's hands in hers. As Willa blows on Sydney's cold fingers, her messy bangs blow across her eyes and I can see why girls fall for her by the dozen. I pull out my phone to take a picture of them standing so close together and Sydney grins wide.

"Wasn't Lulu supposed to be here by now?" I ask, just as the side door we're standing next to swings open and nearly hits me. Sydney screams, and I laugh, and Willa says, "Yaaassssss," and pulls a pretty Indian girl with long, straight hair into her arms. Lulu, I assume.

"OMG." The girl actually says the letters, looking at us over Willa's shoulder. "You guys look *hot*."

"Lu, this is Sydney. That's Cleo. Syd and Kid, this is Lucia Gupta, aka Lulu G," Willa says, quickly introducing us. Willa bites her bottom lip and looks Lulu up and down. Lulu blushes. "You don't look half bad yourself. Thanks for the hookup," I hear Willa whisper. We say hello, slide past Lulu, and step inside the warm building.

Inside the club, the show hasn't started yet. We have to buy a drink, so I head to the bar for a club soda with lime. Sydney gets cranberry juice and grabs Willa a Coke because she's still lingering behind us, talking to Lulu. Sydney's face is all screwed up.

"You pissed she's flirting with Lulu?" I ask Sydney.

"No," she says, way too quickly for it to be true. I tilt my head and take a sip of my drink, making a *yeah, right* face. "Maybe," Sydney admits.

"Sorry I haven't asked you," I say, "but how are things with you two? In the *feelings* category, I mean. Do you still like her?"

366

Sydney looks across the small room. Lulu is pointing to three chairs in the second row where she's tented tiny slips of paper that say RESERVED for us. Willa touches her on the elbow and leans forward to whisper something in her ear.

"Yeah," Sydney finally answers. "But I'm trying *not* to."

"How's that working out for you?" I ask. She shrugs and pouts. "Have you talked to her about it?"

Sydney shakes her head. "I can't. Or I guess I don't want to risk it. We're just getting back to being friends. But like, when she grabbed my hands outside, I thought I was going to die."

"They're going on soon," Willa says. She's suddenly just behind me, and she tosses her arm across my shoulders. "It was so nice of Lulu to save us those seats, right?"

Sydney smiles widely. "Sure was!" she says too brightly. I hand Willa her Coke, and as we make our way to our seats, I allow myself to get a little excited. The band steps out onto the low stage, and a tall woman who looks like Lulu will look in a few years pulls the mic from its stand.

"How y'all doing tonight?" she asks in a breathy voice. And soft whistles and applause spill from the audience. I cross my ankles and lean forward, wanting to be closer to the sound of her. Her speaking voice isn't that different from the recordings of her singing that Willa had played for me. "That's Daya 'The Duke' Lopez on the bass. Jimi 'Jax' Coleman on the keys. And I'm Charm. Just Charm." More whistling and clapping fills the small room and I nudge Willa, who is right beside me.

"The nicknames," I whisper. She grins and squeezes my hand.

"We're the Cover Girls. Mind if we play you a few songs?"

They're more amazing live than I could have imagined. Charm sings covers of Billie Holiday, Nina Simone, Bessie Smith, and even a song by Etta James, the opening hook of which appeared in a really popular EDM song.

Sydney says, "Wait, this was an Etta James song first?" and I nod. "Is nothing in this world original anymore?" she whispers dramatically. And Willa shushes her.

Each song spills into the next, and I am completely enraptured. Some are fast, some are slow, and I soon realize that we're in one of those all-night clubs where the music doesn't end until the sun comes up.

"I'm gonna grab another drink," I say to Willa.

"I'll come with you," she says.

"Want anything?" I ask Sydney. She shakes her head, her leg never stopping its steady bounce to the song the band is playing.

At the bar I order another club soda and check my phone. Willa orders another Coke and leans forward to ask the bartender something. I have a missed call from my dad and a text from him too.

> Take a cab to my place after your show.
> Your mother doesn't want you on the subway this late.

I don't want to go, but I've been avoiding him for days. And his place is much closer to the Village than Mom's and mine.

> Fine. But Mom said I could stay out till midnight.

I know, he sends back. And I want to tell him he doesn't know anything, but I just lean against the bar and direct my eyes back to the stage.

"They're so good, right?" Willa asks. I nod and smile a little, but I know it doesn't reach my eyes.

"You okay?" Willa says next. And I consider lying, but then I just . . . don't. I shake my head and look at her spiky black hair instead of her steady, dark eyes.

"Not really. My dad's an ass," I say. Willa tosses an arm over my shoulder.

"Ah," she says. "Mine too. He likes to think he's the reason I'm gay. And I mean, I get it. He's really full of himself and total trash, but it's like he doesn't understand that I exist outside and in spite of his idiocy. You know? I would have been me no matter what."

Charm starts to sing "At Last," and Willa says, "God, I love this song. It's like, devastatingly romantic." She looks over at me then and squeezes my shoulder. "I'm so glad you're hanging out with us, dude! It's like you were the missing piece to our puzzle." I smile, feeling so grateful for both of them—for Sydney's sincerity and Willa's unmerited affection. For the beginnings of our tenuous but gentle friendship. It won't be a snow globe. It won't be perfect because nothing real ever is. But it will be ours.

Right before we head back to our seats, I stop Willa with a hand on her forearm. I think about Sydney, the hurt in her eyes every time Willa was a little too nice to another girl. It may not be my truth to tell, but I can't tiptoe through the rest of my life—the rest of my relationships—hoping not to do or say the wrong thing. Part of real friendship is not keeping secrets, and I don't want there to be anything between me, Willa, and Sydney when we're all still so new at this. I say, "You should talk to Sydney. I'll stay here."

"What?" Willa asks. She looks from me to our table and back again.

"Just talk to her," I say again. "Let the devastatingly romantic song give you strength."

She still looks a little confused, but she makes her way back over to our friend. She sits down beside her and starts talking. Sydney looks at me with daggers in her eyes, but I'd rather she be mad at me now than hurt by Willa later. They keep talking and Charm's smooth voice fills the air and I watch them. Sydney shakes her head and looks down, and Willa places her hand under Sydney's chin. Then it looks like Sydney wipes her eyes. And Willa's go wide. I see her lips make the shape of "Really?" and Sydney nods. Then they hug, chins tucked over each other's thin shoulders, and when they let go, they look up at the stage. I wait, just to make sure they're done before I head over.

Neither of them says anything about what happened, and I don't ask. I think I'm only realizing now that every friendship is an island. Willa and Sydney's relationship doesn't have anything to do with what's between me and Willa or how much I care about Sydney. We are all important to each other in different but similar ways, and that's all that matters.

At eleven-thirty, I tell them I have to go. They have later

curfews than me, but after I hug Willa goodbye, Sydney walks me to coat check and stands with me while we wait for the woman in the closet to grab my jacket.

"Thanks," Sydney says, and I know she's thanking me for telling Willa to talk to her even though she doesn't say it. She nudges me with her elbow. I squeeze her tight before walking out into the cold.

I'm about a block away from the club when I realize my gloves are missing. "Shit," I say, checking the time. I should still make it home before curfew even if I go back to look for them, but I'll be cutting it close. I retrace my steps quickly, heading back to the club, scanning the sidewalk as I go.

"Are there any gloves on the floor in there?" I ask when I push inside the club and squeeze through the crowd to get to coat check. "They're black and leather with a fuzzy fringe?"

The woman says she'll check, so I look back up at the stage while I wait. My eyes search the crowd for Willa and Sydney too. It takes a minute to find them because Sydney's back is to the door. But when I do, Willa's fingers are all tangled in Sydney's curls, while Sydney's hand is on Willa's cheek. They're *kissing*, I realize all in a rush, and my mouth falls open. I look away quickly, because everything about the kiss feels private and special—like something I wasn't meant to see.

But a few minutes later, as I dig around in my purse for a tip after the woman hands me my gloves, and then for the whole ride home, I can't stop grinning.

—

When I get to my dad's, he's waiting for me. He's sitting on his small sofa and there's a pot of tea on the stove. I kick off my shoes and pour myself a cup. I sit down across from him and tuck my feet underneath me.

"So, Baby Girl," he says, not mincing words. "I won't be able to sleep until we clear the air. At least a little. So do your worst. Where do you want to start?"

Even though it's late, I'm wired from the show, so I ask him to tell me everything, from the very beginning. Did he think Ms. Novak was pretty the very first time he saw her? Did he leave Chisholm because he thought his feelings would go away? Why wasn't he honest with Mom sooner? Or with me at all? Did he realize that they had ruined absolutely everything?

He answers every cruel question I throw in his direction. And he answers honestly. Something about how upset he looks as he speaks lets me know he's finally telling me the whole truth. He was isolated after Gigi died because I was lost in my grief for her, and Mom worked more than she did anything else.

"It isn't an excuse," he says. "But I loved her too, you know. She was your grandmother, and she was Naomi's mother, but she was important to me too. I felt like I couldn't be sad because your sadnesses were bigger." He stands up and pours more tea for both of us. "I was lonely," he says simply. "Mia made me less so." He watches me sip with forlorn eyes, and I watch him right back, trying to see past the person I thought he was and straight through to who he really is.

Just before I head to bed, I realize I have one more question for him. "Are you going to pursue a relationship with her?" I ask, thinking more of how this might affect Mom the most. I'm thinking about parent-teacher conferences and school fundraisers. I'm thinking about how Mom would have to bear witness to the painful truth of them being together.

Daddy looks at his feet. He clasps his hands, and then he looks back up at me. "To be honest," he says, "I'm not really sure. She wants to, but I don't know what a relationship with her would look like. Especially while you're still a student at Chisholm." He puts the tips of his fingers on the table between us, but then he lets his hand fall away. "I don't want to do anything else that causes you or your mother more pain."

For the first time, it occurs to me that Daddy might be the biggest loser in all of this. He gave up most of his life—a job, a family, a home—all for a love he may not even get to experience. But the heart is strange and life is even stranger. Sometimes love can devastate.

I tell him about the Cover Girls. It's a small kindness I feel I owe him for being so honest with me about everything. I tell him about Charm's gorgeous voice and how tiny the club was and that Willa and Sydney are new friends I hope I can hold on to. He listens and laughs and things feel as close to normal as they've felt in days. Then I say the most important thing. I stand up, still cupping my mug in my hands. I imagine this moment as something I'll keep forever: us exactly as we are, encased in glass, glitter fluttering around us like stars.

"I think I forgive you. And Mom. But I'm still upset. And I probably will be for a while."

He nods. "I know, Baby Girl. Sweet dreams."

In my room, it hits me that I've always known that *I* wasn't perfect. I screw things up all the time. So I don't know why I expected Daddy or Mom or Layla to be any better than me. Anything more than human.

I text Dom.

> **You up?**
> Yeah, he sends back instantly.
> **Hi.**
> Hi.
> **I talked to my dad.**
> How'd it go?

I send a shrugging emoji.

> **You know that line from A Midsummer Night's Dream:**
> **"Love looks not with the eyes, but with the mind"?**

> It's late, he sends after a long minute. I don't know if I can stay with you and your Shakespeare quotes right now but I'll try.

I laugh a little.

> **I guess what I don't get is how you're supposed to start seeing things more clearly.**
> **No one tells you that, and I don't want to be blindsided again like I was with Layla. Like I was with my dad.**
> **I want to love the people I love with my eyes wide open.**

I can tell Dom doesn't know what to say, and I guess there's no easy answer to this. And I wish I could kiss him. I wish I could touch the smooth skin on the back of his hand and along the straight line of his collarbone.

I wish I could kiss you right now, he sends. And then, Tell me about the show.

I grin again, and I tell him everything.

EPILOGUE

Everything feels like a memory in the snow, but in the sun, everything feels new.

The day of Dolly's Open Mic Night is unseasonably sunny and warm, and it feels like a sign, a good one, when I wake up to the day's brightness.

In the end, Daddy probably helped spread the word about Open Mic Night more than anyone else. I asked him to hang up flyers, and he plastered the whole library with them, invited all the librarians, and told them to bring friends. Mom helped too, inviting some of her friends and even a few clients. I know my dad is going so above and beyond because he's trying to redeem himself, and I won't pretend that I'm not taking full advantage of his desire to make things right. Still, a part of me knows he can't help how he feels about Ms. Novak, the same way I can't help how I feel about Dom.

Willa tells the softball team, and Jase and Mase rope in most of the soccer kids. I tell choice people in my classes, and I put up flyers in the library, and even one right on the door of my locker.

So when Willa, Sydney, and I head to Dolly's around six to

see if there are any last-minute things we need to do, the dining room is packed, and there's a line out the door. People are ordering small plates, and Dom is getting nervous they won't have enough food to last the night since the program doesn't even officially start for another hour.

"This is . . . unexpected," I say.

"It's so awesome, though," Sydney squeals, flipping her soft curls to one side of her face.

"Can we do anything to help?" I ask Pop when I find him.

"If you wouldn't mind hostessing—" he says, and Sydney cuts him off.

"Cleo will hostess, I'll help take orders. Willa will handle the door. We should have charged a cover!" Sydney says. Pop just grins, but I can tell he's relieved.

"I told you it would be great," I whisper as I head to the hostess stand.

By the time seven hits, the diner is standing room only. I have a list of about ten people waiting to get tables and order food. Willa started taking names of people who actually want to perform, and she has a list that's almost a page long.

I ask Sydney to take over hostessing for me while I walk up to the mic to do a short introduction.

"Thanks so much for coming out, everyone. Dolly's is such an important pillar of this community that we wanted to reintroduce this place to some of our newest neighbors. We hope you enjoy the performances, and if this is an event everyone likes, we'll bring it back next month."

Everyone applauds.

"Without further ado, I'd like to welcome our first guest."

Mason comes on stage and I hand over the mic. "I'm Mase. And I'm going to try some jokes out on you guys, if that's cool."

My eyes widen, and when I rejoin Sydney at the hostess stand, she covers her mouth. "Did you know he was going to do that?" I whisper to her.

She shakes her head. "No. But I bet Jase did."

I watch Mason for the first few jokes. The first one falls a little flat, but by the third one, he seems to have found his rhythm. The room is warming up and so is he. By the fifth one almost everyone laughs.

Dom hasn't left the kitchen, so I sneak back to check on him.

"You okay in here?" I ask, and he nods, but he's sweaty, and the line cooks are too. I can tell they're working hard, and I might just be bothering him.

"When do you take a break?" I ask.

"In like twenty minutes," he hollers over the roar of clanging pots and pans, the heat of moving bodies and fire.

"Come find me," I say, and just before I turn away he looks up at me and grins.

"I will."

When I step back into the dining room, I head in Sydney and Willa's direction. But before I reach them, I see that Willa and Sydney are holding hands. They haven't exactly told me what their deal is yet, and I don't want to force them into anything before they're ready.

I stand off to the side by myself to give Sydney and Willa a moment, and as I scan the rest of the room, I'm surprised to see a few seniors standing in a corner near the makeshift stage. Valeria is with them, and when our eyes meet, she smiles.

"Hey, so a bunch of us signed up. Sorry in advance if there's a lot of singing in a row," Valeria says. The crowd starts clapping. They don't mind. She steps up to the mic and says, "My name is Valeria, and I'm going to sing one of my favorite songs for you."

Her voice is like butter—melty and warm and kind of guiltily decadent. It sounds like something you'd want to eat in the middle of the night. I close my eyes and sink into the sound and I understand in an instant the difference between high school talent and the kind of singing that can make it big. If she wants to, Valeria could be famous.

I spot Ms. Novak just as Valeria heads offstage. I asked her to come, but I wasn't sure she'd show up. The crowd is clapping and whistling, and I see Novak whisper something to a guy standing beside her. It's my dad. Mom isn't here, which I'm grateful for, but seeing them together still rubs me the wrong way. To everyone else, even kids from school, they're just two friends. But knowing that there's more simmering below their surfaces makes something inside me turn red hot.

Before I can get too upset, though, Dom comes up behind me and whispers into my ear. "How's it going out here?" he asks.

"Pretty good, but look," I say, tipping my head in the direction of Ms. Novak and my dad. "That's pissing me off," I tell him.

"Cleo," he says. He steps in front of me and turns my head to face him so I'll stop looking at my dad and Ms. Novak. "They're adults. You can't stop them from talking. You can't really stop them from doing anything, and the only one you're hurting right now is yourself."

He throws an arm across my shoulders. "Take it from me. Parents never do exactly what you want them to. You might as well get over that now. Plus, didn't you tell Novak to come to hear your monologue?"

I nod, and pout for a few more minutes. But then Jase comes over and starts cracking stupid jokes, and Mason hangs out too. I congratulate him on his comedy set and he blushes. Sydney and Willa walk over, cheeks blushy and hands still clasped, and I let myself be swept up in the music and the company. I let myself be grateful everything is going so well.

I hadn't told anyone but Dom, but the monologue I wrote is so intensely personal that I'm starting to get cold feet. The second there's a bit of a lull in the steady stream of performers, Dom looks at me.

"You can do this," he says. "Remember, you're doing it for yourself. And I guess also for Ms. Novak, so she doesn't fail you."

I laugh and roll my eyes.

"But seriously," he says. "Don't worry about anyone else."

I swallow hard and nod. I head up to the front, and Sydney applauds and howls like I've already performed something.

"Hey again," I say into the mic. There are so many people here, and I'm suddenly embarrassed and nervous. For a moment, I have more respect for the girls in chorus, and for Layla, than I ever have before.

"I just have a little story I want to tell you guys."

I look at Novak, so she knows that this is my monologue, and my stomach feels like it's in my throat. My eyes find Dom next, and he's looking at me expectantly, just like everyone else in the diner. I worry that I've made a huge mistake.

Just then, Layla walks through the door. She's alone. I didn't think she would come. But here she is.

I take a deep breath. I step up to the mic.

"The same song was playing the second I met my ex–best friend and the moment I realized I'd lost her," I hear myself say. I look at Dom and he nods encouragingly. I look at my dad, and I have his rapt attention too. I don't look at Layla again.

"I met my best friend at a neighborhood cookout the year we would both turn twelve. It was one of those hot Brooklyn afternoons that always made me feel like I'd stepped out of my life and onto a movie set because the hydrants were open, splashing water all over the hot asphalt. There wasn't a cloud in the flawless blue sky. And pretty black and brown people were everywhere.

"I was crying. 'What a Wonderful World' was playing through a speaker someone had brought with them to the park, and it reminded me too much of my Granny Georgina. I was cupping the last snow globe she'd ever given me in my small, sweaty hands and despite the heat, I couldn't help imagining myself inside the tiny, perfect, snow-filled world. I was telling myself a story about what it might be like to live in London, a place that was unimaginably far away and sitting in the palm of my hand all at once. But it wasn't working. When Gigi had told me stories, they'd felt like miracles. But she was gone and I didn't know if I'd ever be okay again.

"I heard a small voice behind me, asking if I was okay. I had noticed a girl watching me, but it took her a long time to come over, and even longer to say anything. She asked the question quietly."

I take a deep breath before I say the next thing, because I know this could give it all away. That lots of people will know that this story I'm telling isn't some monologue I found online from an off-Broadway play, or a story I made up on my own. After I say the next thing, everyone will know I'm talking about the very real me. And Layla.

"I had never met anyone who . . . spoke the way that she did, and I thought that her speech might have been why she waited so long to speak to me. While I expected her to say 'What's wrong?'—a question I didn't want to have to answer—she asked 'What are you doing?' instead, and I was glad.

"I was kind of a weird kid, so when I answered, I said 'Spinning stories,' calling it what Gigi had always called it when I got lost in my own head, but my voice cracked on the phrase and another tear slipped down my cheek. To this day I don't know why I picked that moment to be so honest. Usually when kids I didn't know came up to me, I clamped my mouth shut like the heavy cover of an old book falling closed. Because time had taught me that kids weren't kind to girls like me: Girls who were dreamy and moony-eyed and a little too nice. Girls who wore rose-tinted glasses. And actual, really thick glasses." A few people laugh. "Girls who . . . thought the world was beautiful, and who read too many books, and who never saw cruelty coming. But something about this girl felt safe. Something about the way she was smiling as she stuttered out the question helped me know I needn't bother with being shy, because she was being so brave. I thought that maybe kids weren't nice to girls like her either."

I chance a glance at Layla then. She's looking right at me for the first time in what feels like forever. I keep talking.

"The cookout was crowded, and none of the other kids were talking to me because, like I said, I was the neighborhood weirdo. I carried around snow globes because I was in love with every place I'd never been. I often recited Shakespeare from memory because of my dad, who is a librarian. I lost myself in books because they were friends who never let me down, and I didn't hide enough of myself the way everyone else did, so people didn't 'get' me. I was lonely a lot. Unless I was with my Gigi.

"The girl, she asked me if it was making me feel better, spinning the stories. And I shook my head. Before I could say what I was thinking—a line from *Hamlet* about sorrow coming in battalions that would have surely killed any potential I had of making friends with her"—the audience laughed again—"the girl tossed her wavy black hair over one shoulder and grinned. She closed her eyes and said, 'Music helps me. And I love this song.'"

I know Layla's remembering that day now too.

"When she started singing, her voice was so unexpected—so bright and clear—that I stopped crying and stared at her. She told me her name and hooked her arm through mine like we'd known each other forever, and when the next song started, she pulled me up and we spun in a slow circle together until we were both dizzy and giggling.

"Some people would say that this was a coincidence, that I met this girl so soon after I'd lost Gigi while our favorite song was playing, and that her voice made me feel like everything would be all right before I even knew her name. But I'm a believer in signs."

I blink a few times, bringing myself back to the present. To this moment in Dolly's Diner instead of that barbecue, years ago. This is my farewell to what we were to each other. I'm finally okay with saying goodbye to her, and this is the best way I know how.

"I was right. She and I, we were friends for a long time. But things happen, and people change, and everything is different now. Still, I hope that girl knows that I'll cherish the friendship we had forever. Even after everything."

Everyone applauds as I walk away from the mic and rejoin Sydney, Dom, and Willa standing along the wall.

"I didn't know you were going to do that!" Sydney says, shaking me by the shoulders. "It was amazing."

"That was kind of fucking beautiful," Willa agrees. Her eyes are glassy, like she's about to cry.

"Thanks," I say, "and yeah. Sorry I didn't tell you. I didn't know if I'd lose my nerve or not, to be honest. But there's clearly something you guys haven't told me. . . ." I look at them, pointing from Sydney to Willa and back again.

"Oh, yeah." Sydney blushes so darkly that her cheeks match her pink earrings. "We're kissing now, but not putting a label on it just yet."

"To be clear, Syd is the one who doesn't want a label yet. But you know, whatever." Willa pulls Sydney to her by the belt loop and kisses her hard on the neck. I clap and grab their shoulders and say, "Yay, yay, yay!"

A few other people, not kids from school, go up onstage next. And I'm feeling really good about everything. There's a juggler, and another person who tells a personal story like I did. There's someone who does a really bad slam poem, but I try not to be too judgmental. A guy even asks Miss Dolly about one of the paintings on the walls, the one of Ella Fitzgerald. They haggle a bit, and he ends up buying it. Dom disappears into the kitchen again to cook, and Sydney, Willa, and I grab a table when one finally opens up.

About thirty minutes before close, Layla steps up to the mic, and I watch her dark eyes as they scan the crowded dining room. I wonder if she's nervous being in front of so many strangers, but she'll have to get used to it before she gets to London. Willa and Sydney are kissing again, but when Layla's eyes land on me I poke them, and at the sight of Layla, they look over at me. "You good?" Willa asks, and Sydney says, "If she does anything even remotely bitchy I'll murder her."

"How long's that murder list now?" Willa asks jokingly, and Sydney glares at her.

"Guys, shhhh," I say.

When the music starts, my heart swells at the familiar melody. And while I know that Layla is lost to me, maybe this is her goodbye to our friendship the same way my story was mine.

She sings the first line of my favorite song—the song that was playing the day we met—beautifully.

She watches me and no one else.

ACKNOWLEDGMENTS

So. This book was a hard one to write. All books are hard to write, I guess, but this one was an exceptional pain in the ass. Maybe because it was my second book, and second books are notoriously difficult. Maybe it was because 2018 was an all-around god-awful year. But mostly, I think it was because I've lost close friends several times over the course of my life in incredibly painful ways, and as much as I wanted to write this book, mentally, emotionally, and sometimes even physically, my body did not want to cooperate.

That said, it's FINISHED! And I couldn't have done it without the kindness, patience, and sometimes tough love of so many generous and beautiful souls.

To my forever-love, Cassidy Chin: Thanks for holding me down, boo.

Parentals: You held my hand and wiped my tears after almost every friend-fight I've ever had. You listened when my feelings were hurt but never hesitated to tell me when I was wrong (especially you, Momma). I wouldn't have made it down the rocky road of female friendship and epic heartbreak without knowing you'd catch me every time I fell. I'll love you for always.

Beth! Sorry I email you so much. But thanks for sticking with me even when I'm freaking out and even when I write awful first drafts that are complete and utter garbage. I can't express to you how happy I am that I got so lucky. Ain't no agent like the one I got.♥

Kate Sullivan, editor of my heart: You just get me, girl. You sometimes know what I want a story to do before I've even figured it out (CAN WE TALK ABOUT THAT PLOT CHART/ TIME LINE THINGIE???). I'm almost certain my work, words, and wounds won't be afforded the same level of compassion and kindness they received while in your capable hands, and not gonna lie, I'm low-key mad you're gone. But I still love you. Thanks for everything.

Alex Hightower, you're a rising star. I hope this industry recognizes your passion, your drive, your smarts, and your undeniable editor's eagle eye. Thanks not only for always believing in Cleo and Dom's love story, but for recognizing the importance of Cleo and Layla's too. I was honestly a lot less freaked out about Kate moving on knowing this book had an Alex-shaped safety net. Stay cute.

And to the rest of the Random House team: Beverly Horowitz, Emily Bamford, Colleen Fellingham, Angela Carlino, and Tracy Heydweiller: Your work, from copy edits to pitches to making the cover gorgeous, is so, *so* important to me. I see you and I love you for it.

To everyone at Macmillan, especially Kathryn Little (the bestest boss in the whole wide world), thanks for allowing me the space to do this writing thing right. I wouldn't want to spend every day with any other group of book nerds but you guys.

I've got the biggest hugs for Melissa Yoon, Melissa Brice, Jess Elliott, and Kell Wilson. Thanks for reading all my stuff with the endurance of long-distance runners and for being the best besties. Love you like a fat kid loves cake.

Shout out to my beta readers: Shveta Thakrar, Mark Oshiro, Greg Andree, Olivia Cole, Eric Smith, Naureen Nashid, and Bidisha Bhattacharya! Thank you for the long emails, text messages, late night gchats, emoji storms, and patience. This story is better in every way because of you.

To the retreat baes—Tiffany Jackson, Dhonielle Clayton, Jalissa Corrie, Justin Reynolds, Saraciea Fennel, Kwame Mbalia, and Patrice Caldwell—bonding with each of you over words written and read, snacks and tea (literal and otherwise), home-cooked meals, inside jokes, and secrets has been an essential and irreplaceable part of this whole journey. You all feel like home.

And to Nic: Thank you for your forgiveness, for your unrelenting friendship, and for telling me to be brave.

ABOUT THE AUTHOR

Ashley Woodfolk has loved reading and writing for as long as she can remember. She graduated from Rutgers University with a bachelor of arts in English and works in children's book publishing. She wrote her first book, *The Beauty That Remains*, from a sunny Brooklyn apartment where she lives with her cute husband, her cuter dog, and the cutest baby in the world: her son, Niko. *When You Were Everything* is her second novel.

🐦 @AshWrites